A NOVEL

# SPRING

## Leila Rafei

**BLACK
STONE**
PUBLISHING

Printed in the United States of America

First edition: 2020
ISBN 978-1-982672-57-7
Fiction / General

1 3 5 7 9 10 8 6 4 2

CIP data for this book is available
from the Library of Congress

Blackstone Publishing
31 Mistletoe Rd.
Ashland, OR 97520

www.BlackstonePublishing.com

*For Baba Nasser*

# 1

There was no good reason to live in Ramses. It was a bad part of town by the train tracks, where more people squatted on rooftops than lived inside its decaying buildings. Sami knew that. Rose knew that. It was the source of many arguments before signing the lease. But for Sami, the one selling point was that the apartment building—dubbed the Diesel on account of a defunct mechanic's sign hanging over its entrance, which conveniently matched the smell in the air—lacked a doorman.

Sami was well aware that was an unpopular take on what was supposed to be an amenity. In Cairo, nearly every residential building came with its own little watchman, usually an Upper Egyptian dressed in a bell-shaped galabia, who lived in the entryway and policed comings and goings far better than any uniformed guard. But that was the thing—doormen knew *too* much. They knew all about each tenant including their guests and lovers, which was a problem for Sami, who lived with a girlfriend nobody was supposed to know about. That Rose was a foreigner made it even worse. In a place like Ramses, she stuck out like a fluorescent beacon of denim and bare hair. No amount of lying or window climbing would help them hide, and not even a late-night order of *koshari* would pass the threshold uninspected and unjudged.

Who cares, Rose would say. What's he going to do, arrest us?

Come to think of it, Sami would rather get tossed into a police truck and hauled off to some dungeon in Tora Prison, never to be seen again, than have word get back to his mother. He could practically hear her gasp, slap her hands against her face in horror. Sami with a girlfriend, a foreigner at that. Living together just the same as they would in say, Paris. What do you think this is, *Ba-rees*? She always said that whenever he did anything she might call decadent or on the verge of (God forbid) gay. She was right though. This wasn't Paris. This was Cairo. And if he wasn't going to live accordingly, then he should at least fake it.

Tonight Sami came ready.

It was the middle of the night on a Tuesday, at the foot of the Diesel. He stood under its namesake sign with half its letters burnt out, looking for Abu Ali, who ran the 24-hour pharmacy next door. But the man wasn't there for perhaps the first time ever. Go figure. The one time Sami needed him.

They hadn't realized when they moved in that the lack of a doorman didn't preclude watchful eyes—specifically those of Abu Ali, who was *always* there, sipping tea from a stool on the curb between customers. Watching. Like every pair of headlights on the street. Sami was certain Abu Ali knew about him and Rose and yet nevertheless, he would never fess up to being there on her behalf, searching for medicine to soothe the nausea that bent her over the toilet every hour or so. Rose? Who's that? As if the man *hadn't* seen Sami enter the building with her each night only to reappear the next morning. Instead Sami would divert the pharmacist's attention with a curveball—he would say his mother was in town, that she'd fallen ill on account of say, the smog, and just hope that Abu Ali wouldn't ask to meet her, perhaps to get a taste of her famous lemon-mint juice, of which Sami had regretfully spoken on many occasions, drumming up conversation in the excruciating window between payment and change. He had it all figured out until he ran smack into its shut door.

When Sami gave up knocking, he peered through the dirty window to confirm the pharmacy's nonsensical closure. The lights remained off, no flicker of fluorescence reengaging. Abu Ali's wooden chair sat upside down on the counter, his prayer rug folded beside it. On the latter, two indentations marked the imprint of his knees. They stared back at Sami through the window like his ghost, a taunting jinn standing between him and the medicine he needed, which was painfully plentiful on the shelves overhead. Even through the muck and darkness he could make out boxes and bottles of unpronounceable elixirs, all organized by ailment. Cold and flu. Nausea and diarrhea. Fever and parasites. Bacterial infection. Pediatrics. His eyes darted back to the counter, where at last, he found the anti-nausea tablets he was after, and stared longingly from the other side of the glass.

Abu Ali's absence wasn't the only oddity that night. As Sami turned to leave, he froze. He'd been in such a rush to get to the pharmacy and get it over with that he hadn't even realized the whole boulevard was utterly empty—and that there was a police truck parked across the intersection, the latter cordoned off with a rope.

What was happening?

All he could think of was that it was National Police Day, though it was a pretty meaningless holiday that usually came and went without notice, and certainly didn't warrant closure of a major thoroughfare like Ramses. He stepped forth slowly, as if some explanation might leap from the curb at the last moment. But nothing did. He was sure Abu Ali would have known, if only he were there tonight.

Sighing, Sami looked back at the pharmacy's door again. It was still closed. The police truck remained parked in the street, listless, and any officers inside were surely asleep as he should be too. He yawned and made his way back to the Diesel, following that half-burnt sign like a decrepit north star home.

\*\*\*\*\*

Empty-handed, Sami returned to apartment 702 to find Rose on the couch with her legs draped over the arm, the TV blaring before her. The news was on, talking about some man who'd set himself on fire on the steps of parliament today, the latest in a string of copycat suicides. Only this one had survived. Now he lay in a full body cast in Qasr El Aini hospital, where MisrTV was broadcasting live from room 251B.

"Come watch," said Rose from the couch, as if Sami had any choice.

He took off his shoes and set them by the door, beside Rose's beat-up boots and the maid's paper-thin slippers, then joined her. Up close he noticed the gray cast to her skin, her eyes glowing like venom against it. He'd say she was beautiful but it seemed callous given her state, not to mention the sad display on TV. Like kissing at a gravesite. Distasteful.

"Know why he did it?"

"Another protest?" Sami reached for a cigarette, then stopped himself as he looked back at the TV. Self-immolation had become a sort of trend nowadays, so common it was no longer shocking and in fact, seemed a more reasonable method of protest with each day, each nameless nobody that became a martyr because of it. He assumed that was the intention. "And to become a martyr."

"Well, duh. But you'll never guess what he was protesting."

"Parking ticket? Electric bill? Rotten fruit? Same old?"

"Nope, nope, nope," she said, trying to maintain her pep despite the increasing pallor of her face. "Bread. The guy couldn't afford it. Not even fino, the cheap kind with bits of sand baked in."

"Crunchy."

"Anyway, the news is saying that his local bakery in Imbaba jacked up the price unfairly. But they're skirting around the real issue, the elephant in the room."

"There's an elephant in the room?"

"I mean they're ignoring the fact that fino is *government* bread. Bakers can resell it for whatever they want, but when there's a subsidy cut like there was this year, the price inevitably goes up. *That's* why the guy couldn't afford bread."

"So he'll go on a diet, cut carbs."

She rolled her eyes. "Not funny."

Sami didn't get it. He was just trying to make her laugh at a story that was almost comical in its absurdity. He looked at his petrochemistry text-book on the coffee table, regretting choosing a field of study that taught him nothing of how to understand Rose. It wasn't the first time she confused him. She never had any desire to live in nicer parts of town like Zamalek, for instance, where foreigners like her were supposed to live in grand villas rented cheap with American dollars. There, buildings were named for flowers and French dignitaries rather than say, gasoline. But Rose didn't care that Ramses was the industrial armpit of downtown. To her that's what made it *real*. Just a brush of a shoulder from so-called *real Egyptians*, the sort who might set themselves on fire over bread.

"I've been researching this stuff all day," she said, reading from her phone. "In the 1960s, self-immolation was a practice among Buddhist monks—do you know what those are?"

Yes, he nodded. Obviously.

"OK, well, Buddhist monks self-immolated to protest persecution by the Diem regime in South Vietnam. The most famous was Thich Quang Duc, who burned himself in the middle of an intersection in Saigon. A bunch of other monks followed, and then eventually the regime fell." She set down the phone and looked back at him. A hint of amusement counteracted the nausea for a moment. "Isn't that neat?"

*Neat* probably wasn't the way he'd describe it.

"And get this. The only part of that first monk—Mr. Duck or whatever—that didn't burn was his *heart*. Even after they tried to cremate him for the funeral, his heart just wouldn't burn."

"Yeah right." He reached for her phone to read for himself. Indeed, the heart remained unburned, and now lived in a glass case in a shrine in Ho Chi Minh City.

Rose gave him an I-told-you-so look as she snatched her phone back. "Now the monk is what they call a bodhisattva. That's a kind of martyr. The Buddhist Bouazizi, if you will."

Sami sank into the couch. Its cushions swallowed him like the jaws of some brocade beast. The man in the body cast, like the other self-immolators as of late, had copied a Tunisian fruit vendor named Mohamed Bouazizi, who last month had instigated the fall of the Ben Ali regime with his own immolation. But today's burning was interrupted when tanks rolled in and put out the fire with a water cannon, just in time to save the would-be martyr. Now he was about to meet the president on live TV.

In silence, they watched the president walk into room 251B in his trademark black suit. Rose turned up the volume. Sami leaned forward, mouth slack. The president was stiff and deep-voiced, solemn to match the scene. Sami couldn't tell whether it was all an affect out of respect for the man in the body cast, perhaps a nod to the funeral that should have been. The guy might as well be dead, anyway. His only sign of life was a straw dangling from the hole for his mouth, and it was unclear whether he was even aware of the camera crew beside him, let alone the president, who proceeded to take his great, white plaster mitt in both hands and kiss it.

Cameras flashed. Sami flinched. Rose leapt from the couch and ran into the bathroom. Not again.

He got up and found her heaving into the toilet bowl, as expected. She'd been getting sick often lately, due to that—that terrible *thing* inside her—but he still didn't quite know how to help. What could *possibly* help? When he got sick as a kid, his mother would squeeze a lemon wedge into a cup of hot water to cleanse the stomach. But their kitchen was empty—no lemons, no medicine, thanks to the closure of Abu Ali's pharmacy as well as the whole street. All he had were dumb jokes to make her feel better, and to distract from the real reason she was sick.

"Have you been eating *tirmis* again?"

He always teased her for loving the salted beans, which she bought eagerly off toothless vendors in the street, despite his warnings. You'll get sick. You don't know where his hand's been. The only people who eat that stuff are, you know, the poor. She never cared. Nor did she care now, as she remained face-first in porcelain, ignoring the half-assed attempt for a laugh.

"Ah. So it must be good old tap water."

Again, no response.

"Well, you know what they say. Once you drink from the Nile, you're destined to return."

He thought the line—an old cliché beaten to death by every song, book, and film any lovestruck traveler ever made about Egypt—would elicit at least a half smile, a wink between heaves. But her face was buried so deep inside the toilet bowl that it was impossible to tell.

Finally Rose lifted her head and asked for water. Sami twisted off the cap of a fresh bottle and handed it to her, watching her down the entire contents in a single gulp. She looked terrible, skin a slick gray like the belly of a fish, hair stuck to her face, making involuntary sounds so guttural it was hard to believe they'd come from a human.

"Don't make me take you to Qasr El Aini. You're in no shape to meet the president."

At this she rolled her eyes. There was life. Feeling somehow satisfied, he helped her up and walked her to the bedroom, where he lay her down to sleep.

*****

Before bed Sami checked his phone to see a flurry of missed calls from his mother, even though they'd already talked earlier in the day. Shit. Tomorrow was the anniversary of his grandfather's death, which meant she would be calling at five a.m. sharp to wake him for prayer.

He tried in vain to scrounge a few hours of sleep before that call, but in the dark, he couldn't get burning men out of his head. The monks in Asia. The fruit-vendor of Sidi Bouzid. All the flames and flesh that had brought about revolution. And today's self-immolator, the would-be martyr, who had fallen short.

Apparently he was only a few years older than Sami, also an only son, who supported his family on wages cobbled together from odd jobs laying bricks and washing cars. Sami felt he understood him. As an only son he, too, was his mother's pride. The honey to her phyllo. The cream skimming the surface of a glass of milk. He, too, had to care for his family. Sami was sure that was why the man had failed to properly off himself. Only sons weren't allowed to die.

He googled the other self-immolators, those who'd succeeded in becoming martyrs rather than half-dead potatoes encased in plaster. But he didn't need to do that to know that each one of them had a brother, perhaps several. He shut off his phone and turned to face the wall.

Coincidentally it was when Giddo died, two years ago tomorrow, that Sami learned what a burden he bore. As the only boy in the family, it was his duty to wash the corpse before burial. He remembered it clearly, despite all his efforts to forget, and despite his will to fall asleep tonight instead of watching it play out on the ceiling above him. The shape of Giddo's bones. The look of his dead body, gray and shriveled. The black bile that spilled out of his mouth when he pressed on his bloated stomach. It was some-thing out of a horror movie, the sick moment before changing channels. He felt guilty for his disgust just as he felt guilty for well, everything else. Smoking hash. Sneaking beer into the dorms. Talking to girls. Her.

He turned to face Rose.

Now her breaths were on the verge of snoring. She never looked so alive, doing nothing at all but breathing, and so dead at the same time, lying beneath a white sheet like Giddo's funeral shroud. It was fitting, he guessed. There was both life and death inside her. He peeled back the sheet to see her clutching a pillow tightly to her chest. He imagined her womb swelling slowly, growing bigger until it ripped through her shirt, and the pillow turning into a nuzzled child. *Stop!*

At first he thought she was joking about being pregnant. A sick prank. But as time set in, and Rose's body started proving it with these nightly toilet bowl episodes, he realized it was true and even worse, there was no escaping it. He would have preferred dying, perhaps even setting himself on fire, but he couldn't. He was stuck there. Living with it. An only son, fated for this since the day he was born.

Ironically, his mother would agree with that part. Suad spoke often of his birth – much to his sister Ayah's annoyance—with a wistful joy in her tired eyes and not a speck of shame for blatantly mythologizing the event. She said the Nile reached the tops of cattails on the day he was born—ignoring the fact that, by all scientific accounts, that stretch of the river hadn't flooded in five decades. Never mind that. As the story went, it was an uncharacteristically cold day in Mahalla, the ground soaked with a winter's worth of rain, and she knew, from the moment Hagga Warda pulled him out of her unmentionables, that he'd be her only son.

There was no escape.

# 2

Each year, Suad made lentil stew on the anniversary of Giddo's death, in remembrance of his dying meal. Her husband always found it morbid but he just didn't get it. Typical of Mahmoud to go on with life blithely. Of course it stung to revisit old memories, but that was the point. Tragedies should be remembered, no matter how painful. It was what she'd want of her children too, when she one day passed.

This year was no different, spent cooking and thinking of the day she and her sisters spoon-fed Giddo his last batch. Men of weaker moral fiber might want something decadent for their final meal, like pigeon or lamb, but Giddo had asked simply for lentil stew, the same dish he grew up on in the village that became Abu Radhi. Some thought it was because of his lack of teeth, but Suad knew better. He wanted to relive the past, to go home and be the boy he once was and eat the same stew his mother made in great vats that lasted through the week, every week, the mainstay of their house of sugar farmers. But in the end it made no difference. Giddo died with a barely touched bowl of lentils beside his bed.

She couldn't remember what they did with that final bowl. They probably just threw it out. It seemed like a sacrilege. If she could do it all over again, she would have taken his spoon and ingested every left-over lentil as if to absorb his last living moment. All she had now was a simmering pot of broth before her, and the memories it induced. That, and the Quran he'd left her after his death, which she kept at her bedside and read nightly.

While the stew cooked, Suad retreated to her bedroom and reached for the Quran. By now she'd reread the whole book, cover to cover, approximately forty times. Yes, in the thirteen years since Mahmoud left, she read it no less than thrice per year—once during the month of Ramadan, when she would race furiously to finish by Eid, and then another couple of times throughout the rest of the year, when she read at least one surah per night. And if you quoted a line to her, not only would she cite the correct surah from which it came, but she would be able to guess the exact page on which it appeared. She was usually within range of five or so pages, which wasn't so miraculous if you took into account the fact that she'd been reading from that very book since she was a child. She'd watched her little-girl hands grow into womanhood around it as the book seemed to shrink. What was once a supernaturally massive behemoth, too heavy to lift with one hand, had now lightened from the wear of its frayed and over-flipped pages. What once seemed like a universe of words, of stories, of meanings she didn't understand, was now as familiar as an old friend. Even more than a friend—the father she had lost. Nobody knew it better. Nobody knew *her* better.

Suad sighed, running her hand across its worn cover. She had tried to transfer this habit to her children and even Mahmoud, but it didn't quite catch on. On his rare visits home from the Gulf, the whole family would read together on the living room rug, gathered in a circle, while she kept one eye on her husband, who hated every second but wouldn't admit it. And nightly, she would read the Quran to her children until they fell asleep, which in the heat of Mahalla, took as little time as saying *bismillah al-rahman al-rahim. In the name of God, the Beneficent, the Merciful.* She would tell them that she was never happy until she became a true believer, and that there were awful things in her past about which she shared no more than a shake of her head. The Quran fixed everything.

Her kids would never believe it, but in old photo albums deep in the boxes and shelves of their house, she bared her thick legs and curly hair in faded Polaroids, and she'd even had a sip of champagne on her honeymoon to the north coast. All of that changed after Mahmoud went away, when she started reading the Quran to pass the hours spent alone. She was at it quite a bit nowadays. There was plenty to fix.

*****

In the afternoon it was time for lemons. The stew had reached a thick consistency, the smell smoky. Suad followed her grandmother's recipe perfectly, adding a splash of citron and a touch of turmeric that gave the stew a golden hue and tartness unmatched by any other bowl in the Delta. She tasted a bit at the tip of her spoon. Just a bit more lemon, and dinner would be served.

But it was difficult to work with her mind elsewhere. As she peeled off a rind over the kitchen sink, she wondered what her son was doing when he wasn't answering his phone. The last time she saw him, he stood in the hallway brushing his teeth in preparation for his trip back to Cairo, looking uncomfortably similar to Mahmoud with his broad shoulders and slightly too-big teeth. Sami bared the latter often, with a wide smile shown generously to any stranger on the street. She couldn't say the same of her husband, whose smile she hadn't seen much of lately.

Suad was so accustomed to not having Mahmoud around that she no longer missed him or looked forward to his visits. Each time he returned to Mahalla, she greeted him with a stiff neutrality, and the joy with which the children met him only emphasized her coldness. She would stand apart, watching, waiting for him to approach her, to present her with a new bauble bought from some exotic merchant in bazaars that he said were even better than Khan El Khalili. *Really*, she'd ask, wide-eyed, and he'd wave away her provincial ignorance while trying to buy her favor. *These bracelets are from India, darling, come see.* And she would hold out her wrist, jangle them around on the end of her sleeve, and slip them off with a terse *thanks*. With pursed lips she'd wait for him to acknowledge her displeasure, but he never did. Mahmoud moved on quickly, if he ever even noticed, and within minutes he would turn his attention to some new topic or gadget or yes, some new woman.

*Ooof,* she yelped, catching a nick. She knew better than to ruminate with a knife in her hand. She watched blood speckle the white pulp of fallen rinds as she held her finger under the faucet. When the bleeding stopped, she tossed a lemon wedge into her mouth and bit her tongue just to feel the acid burn.

She'd long known there was another woman. Piece by piece, all the minute clues had come together—the rushed phone calls, the incongruous laughter, the seemingly spontaneous, independent happiness that arose like a slap of cold water to the face. Just thinking about it sent hot blood rushing to her temples. Whenever they spoke, Mahmoud sounded as if he were smiling into the receiver, quite happy to lie to his wife, the woman who'd never known another man—technically—and didn't mind the lack of reciprocity. He would mention friends who'd taken second wives, quoting scripture in his own defense. How dare he.

It was no surprise when Mahmoud's phone calls and visits began to dwindle, along with the wire transfers and envelopes stuffed with riyals. Now she relied more and more on Sami, who sent half his scholarship stipend to Mahalla each month, poor boy. In time his place in her heart had grown so big and so singular and strong that she sometimes felt as if all her insides would swell and spill out, no room to contain it all. She hated that he, too, was far away—off in Cairo, the big city where the streets stank of beer and hashish, and foreigners ran around half-naked with hair flapping in the wind, legs wide open to every tea boy and taxi driver in sight. She tried convincing him to stay home but could not. There was no future for him in Mahalla, no jobs unless he wanted to pick fruit or spin cotton. All she could do was pray for the day he would come back and bring a good wife into their home. One that she picked, one like his mother.

She opened the kitchen window to let in the breeze, which smelled of citron as did winter, the season of harvest. Before her, lemon trees spanned out from the windowsill to the edge of the yard. She liked to call them her children, planted and raised them from seedlings to full-fledged trees. That's what they were, weren't they? Children by another father. The only role Mahmoud played was in providing the land, perhaps tossing an order every now and then from the doorstep. *Wash your feet before you come inside. Make sure you get the dirt out of your nails. I swear to God, if I eat one more lemon …*

But she shouldn't complain. It was a sin, after all. Best to leave sinning to sinners. Besides, if there was one good thing about marrying Mahmoud, it was that plot of land. He'd inherited it from his father, who purchased it for mere piasters a half-century ago. The plot used to be part of a vast field of sugarcane until the 1950s, when President Nasser divided and redistributed the land among all the workers who'd made it bloom, their family included. To this day, sprigs of sugarcane sprouted occasionally from the corners of fence posts and in between bushes of cotton. It was a reminder of the history of the land and where they came from—as was their family name, Sukkary, which a great-grandfather had taken around the same time.

The plot had been neglected for years by the time Suad married Mahmoud and moved into his family home. It was overgrown and muddy, and the only beings that dared tread its tangled vegetation were stray donkeys and cattle that wandered over from nearby farms. For a long time the family considered selling it, but Suad put a stop to that idea. Farming was far preferable to housework—if it came down to mopping floors or tending to the grove, the latter won easily. Anything to get out of the house, where her mother-in-law Abla watched soap opera reruns from dawn to dusk.

But Suad could never quite escape Abla. Even out in the grove, she always had a half-mind fixed on the dramas unfolding behind her bedroom window, and soon she learned all the characters and plots and subplots despite all her best efforts to weed, water, and till to oblivion. There was Mustafa, the playboy prince, his jealous wife Farida, and all the young mistresses that cried for his affection. All day long, she would hear their wails and heavy breathing, and in time she learned the slight tonal differences between the bad-news music and the good-news music. It was the same formula each episode. She knew something big was about to happen when Abla started screaming out directions to the actors. *Don't marry the officer's son, you silly, stupid girl!* The increasing hoarseness of her voice signaled the end of each episode and the end of another day's work in the garden.

Every once in a while Abla would holler from her bed, *ya Suad!* She hated the way she said her name, stretching each syllable to its limit as if she was scolding her. *Su-AD. Look here, girl.* And Suad would wipe off her hands and come to her window to ask what the old madam wanted. Often it was another cup of tea. But she would have to clean herself first, she specified. So Suad would wash her hands and feet, make a fresh batch of tea, and bring it to Abla on a tray with sugar cubes and a square of *basbusa* drenched in honey. And then without a word of complaint she would return to the field, hoping it would be at least a few more hours of uninterrupted work before Abla called upon her again.

The girl couldn't help it. She was obsessed with the earth; obsessed with the idea that she could revive it and mold it to her liking; obsessed with the power she had over the little buds, wielding water and light. At first she was overwhelmed with all the possibility and couldn't decide what she wanted to grow. She might grow some cash crop like sugar or cotton, and perhaps sell it in small batches to the factories of Mahalla. She could grow greens like *molokhiya* and mint, which would be easy to care for, or fruits and vegetables, fodder for new recipes each day of the week. Back then, Suad dreamed of nothing but red peppers and eggplants, strawberries and melons budding fresh from the green earth.

Row by row, she planted an array of different crops for her first harvest. There were herbs and fruits and vegetables; bitter, sweet, and sour; those that could be eaten right off the vine and those that would need a sprinkle of sugar or salt. The lemon trees were the dividing line between the fruits and vegetables, and they flourished. The lemons grew so well, and were so pungent and pretty, that one row became two, and two became three and four, and finally the entire plot of land was rowed with trees of lemon.

Abla protested from her bedroom window, perching on its sill to ask what on earth the girl would do with all those lemons. *Su-AD!* But neither she nor Mahmoud wanted to deal with the garden themselves, so they relented. It became Suad's. Soon all of her cooking was tinged with the taste of lemon, squeezed over tomato stews and legs of chicken. And in the summers, she would make batches of lemon-mint juice to last the whole season, drank up quickly by her children who smacked their lips in delight. Only Abla refused the lemon-mint juice, preferring her tea and *basbusa* instead.

*****

By dusk the scent of citron gave way to the cacophony of shouting of neighbors. Suad went to shut the window but stopped herself, holding her bandaged finger up in the air as if to say, *wait a minute*. The noise wasn't coming from Dalal next door, who was the usual culprit with her big mouth. In fact, Dalal was nowhere to be found, her porch empty but for an idle cotton wheel. She bent out the window and strained her ear to pick out the voices of Mona and Umm Said, Elgazar the butcher and Abu Felfel with his peg leg. She hardly ever heard from the latter but today he spoke loudest, his old voice crackling, unused to itself.

"The kids have taken the city."

"You've lost your mind, old man."

"They're storming the police station."

"Who?"

"The *kids*, you donkey."

Suad tensed up. Whoever these kids were, whatever it was they were doing, they better not be *her* kids. She looked back at Ayah, who sat staring into her phone, scrolling through Myface or Spacebook or something or another. She never thought she'd be so pleased with the sight. As for Sami, well—she could only hope.

With a prayer she shut the window, snuffing out all the rude voices that dared interrupt her day of mourning, and joined Ayah on the couch where they sat silently, ladling soup over mounds of rice to quell its bite. It had turned out too salty, as if all her pent-up tears had materialized and dripped into the pot as she cooked. She awaited Ayah's complaints, looking forward to the chance to say—with one drawn -out, well-placed sigh—*well, it was seasoned with tears, what do you expect.* But all Ayah did was stare into the hypnotic abyss of her phone, doling out a nod from time to time, or at best a one-word answer.

"What are you doing?"

Nod.

"Who are you talking to?"

Nod.

"Any news from Cairo?"

Nod, nod, all day, nod. Nothing but the click of her keypad. It drove Suad crazy—*click, click, click*—a sound as small and yet obtrusive as the buzz of a fly. She looked over her shoulder at Ayah's phone. The one button shined like onyx from the repeated touch of her thumb, like the mummy cases she saw on a trip to Cairo years ago, which had been fondled by too many visitors with curious hands. Her daughter's hands were similarly mischievous, fingernails jagged with chipped green polish that seemed to chirp with each click.

Wide-eyed, Suad watched the screen light up with strange words strung together in inconceivable ways, echoing those of the neighbors. *Street closures in Cairo. Police station on fire. Three dead in Suez.* She could make no sense of the words but they filled her with rage at Ayah, who gave one last nod before Suad reached for the phone, grabbed it like some kind of monstrous weed, and threw it at the wall, knocking down the framed photo of the president she kept by the door.

Ayah yelped and ran to the phone's side. She scooped it into her arms like a cranky baby, tucking in its red and green and blue wires like spilled lamb guts.

"What's gotten into you, mama!"

What's gotten into mama? Well, nothing, not anytime recently. As Suad set the president's portrait back on its hook on the wall, she watched Ayah put the pieces of her phone back together, sealing the compartments closed with yet another damned *click*. She had to admit she was relieved. Now everything was as it should be, the picture hanging, the phone intact, no sign of her outburst for Mahmoud to one day discover and hold over her head. Funny, the foresight that came to her at times like this. Almost like it took that crash to set her head straight.

"Do you even miss your grandfather?"

Ayah just buried her face in the bowl before her.

*Good*, thought Suad as she watched the steam cloud up her glasses. Better silence than a lie.

After Ayah ate every last bit of stew—Suad made sure of it—she shooed her away to the kitchen, where a dozen lemons awaited peeling. She popped a stray rind in her mouth and returned to the TV, which she hoped would provide some answers. But there were only reruns of *Face of the Moon*, the same soap opera Abla used to watch years ago. There was no word of what these kids that the neighbors were shouting about were doing. In any case she assumed, God willing, that the police would get everything under control by nightfall.

With the rind clenched between her teeth, she pulled out her phone to dial Sami again. It was already past sunset and he hadn't called once, even though he knew just as well as she did that it was the anniversary of Giddo's death. She had planned on waiting it out to see how long it took for him to remember, but she caved around noon and since then, there had been nothing but fruitless outgoing calls, unanswered and unreturned. The boy had become so remote ever since he moved to Cairo. It was only a two-hour train ride away and yet it seemed as though he'd moved continents and changed time zones like her husband, God forbid. Good thing Ayah had stayed home for university unlike some of her friends, whose foolish parents cared nothing for their daughters' reputations and shipped them off like lamb's meat. But Suad cared. She cared for Sami's reputation too. Other mothers might let their sons run free to partake in whatever filth they saw fit, but Suad monitored Sami closely for any sign of sin. Floozies. Hashish. Satanic rap music. So far it seemed he'd been good, mostly, although at times like these—when he wouldn't answer his phone—she had her doubts.

One more try, Suad lied to herself, as she reached for the phone again. The phone must have rung about a hundred times until finally, it stopped. By that point the rind had become a mangled sliver on her tongue. She took it out to say hello. To her joy, there was an answer—and to her horror, it was a woman.

# 3

The pimpled American couldn't mask his shock as Jamila removed her veil and draped it over her chair. His mouth hung open, as if he were about to say something—*Miss, you forgot your ... ahem ... Miss, despite the zits, I'm actually a full-grown man, a strange man—and a white man at that—and perhaps you'd feel more comfortable putting that thing back on.* Perhaps *he* would feel more comfortable, she thought, reading in his face the shy softness of sudden, unexpected attraction. It was surprising, she supposed, for a girl who'd been through all she'd been through to have retained a shred of beauty—despite her tiredness, despite the sallow tone of her skin, despite the pregnant belly just beginning to show under the folds of her abaya.

The chair creaked as she sat down, and the table was sticky beneath her hands. But that didn't matter, just as the veil didn't matter, because this was the moment she'd awaited for months, counting the days like a prisoner chiseling lines into the wall. It was her resettlement interview, and no protests, traffic, or tear gas would get in her way, though they tried. She'd arrived at St. Fatima's two hours beforehand and had sat in the fly-ridden courtyard flitting through her paperwork five, ten, fifteen times. There was her refugee ID card, and that of her husband Yusuf; her diploma from Al-Safwa primary school; an assortment of ticket stubs and receipts proving time and location; and a book detailing all her internationally ordained rights as a refugee. Whatever that meant.

"Please, make yourself comfortable," said the boy, wiping sweat off his brow. He introduced her to the interpreter, an older Sudanese woman from Khartoum, and the two women nodded across the table as he turned on his laptop. "This piece of junk can take a while to start up."

Jamila braced herself for the questions that would inevitably follow, ranging from horrific to mundane. At her first appointment at St. Fatima's, just weeks after she arrived in Cairo, she somehow had to recall the most minute details of her life—the orientation of streets Omdurman, the way to the tomb of the Mahdi, the shape of the river where it parted in two to form an island named Tuti. That was the easy part. Then she had to describe the precise time and date of everything that ever happened, from each of her siblings' births to the hour of day when she last saw her mother. At the end of the session the case worker had told her to call back in two months' time. So for two months she waited until finally, she was granted asylum. She went again to the little office off Talaat Harb to pick up her identification card and an envelope of one hundred dollars cash—quite a thick stack in Egyptian bills—which she'd carried back to her apartment with downcast eyes, hands gripping her purse straps.

This appointment, which would determine her eligibility for resettlement, would be more challenging. She couldn't believe it when she first learned that St. Fatima's would help a select few refugees—a *very* select few—to settle permanently in a third country. Most went to places like Canada, Australia, the USA—places that filled her head with daydreams of dancing under falling snow, dressing in denim and maybe even high heels like Fifi Shafik, strolling with her baby-to-be through tree-lined streets.

But on that Thursday afternoon, it was anything but high heels and snowflakes. She should have known better. All around her, she heard stories that couldn't be obscured by the flimsy cardboard dividers between each intake desk in that narrow room, nor by the buzz of mismatched fans and the hard slap of hands on rustling paperwork, like flies. She heard it all. They came from Juba, they came from the Nuba mountains, they came from Darfur. Some came from Eritrea and wore crosses around their necks. It was the dead of winter, but they swatted flies from their arms and lips as they recounted the various atrocities that had landed them in that office. Jamila's heart was racing and the meeting hadn't even started yet. She knew the American boy wouldn't be asking about her dreams and wishes, what kind of neighborhood she would like to live in and what kind of work she would do. He would be asking about the worst.

"Alright, this is the hard part."

The boy picked at a red cyst on his forehead as he scanned her paper-work. Did he even realize he was doing that? She grew angry at his lack of manners, or at the very least his lack of basic awareness. This was the moment she'd been awaiting for months, the moment that could change the whole course of her life, and here was this boy popping a pimple in her face.

"Would you like something to drink?" He asked, as if to atone for his rudeness.

She looked at the interpreter, who sat with only her hands folded before her, no drink. Jamila shouldn't drink either. She feared it would somehow reflect poorly upon her and God forbid, thwart her case. After all, if she succeeded in this resettlement business, then she would be in eternal debt to St. Fatima's—and this zit-faced boy. She shouldn't ask for too much. As she shook her head, her foot tapped against the floor like a clock ticking, screaming to get it all over with, until finally, they began.

"Now, I know you've already gone over some of this stuff in your last intake. But we'll need to revisit a few questions to set a clear, you know, backdrop to your present situation."

She nodded.

"Can you describe what *exactly* the rebels did when they came to Omdurman?"

She knew very well what the rebels did. In fact, she was trying to forget it. The interpreter shot her a look, as if daring her to tell the truth, but she couldn't.

"I don't remember."

The boy stopped typing and looked her in the eyes. "You don't remem-ber what they did to you?"

"It's right there," she said, pointing to her file on the table. She sensed he wanted more—specifically about the things she didn't want to talk about. It hadn't occurred to her until right then, as she sat before the boy with the oily face, that there was no way she could tell him the whole story, no matter how badly she wanted this. There were simply some things a woman had to keep to herself. Especially when there were men around.

"What about your parents, your brothers and sisters?

"No."

"What about the sheep and the cattle?"

Not even that.

Even though he could barely understand her, the boy paid close attention to each word and gap of silence, frequently looking back at the interpreter to make sure she hadn't left something out. When he confirmed that she hadn't, and that Jamila just had nothing to say, he ran a hand through his lank orange hair and continued.

"Look, I want you to think about your old home in Sudan—the mountains, the river. It was a long time ago, but I need you to tell me exactly what happened. Did the rebels hurt you?"

Her gaze fell to the desk, nodding, but she wouldn't say more. Telling him what happened would leave her feeling as violated as that day the rebels came. She wouldn't even tell her father what happened if she had the chance. How could she tell this stranger, this boy popping pimples right in front of her face? Somehow it was even worse that the interpreter was there and that she was Sudanese too, which made Jamila even more ashamed to tell the truth. What would she think? Who would she tell?

It didn't take long for the boy to give up. "We'll be in touch," he said, shutting his laptop with a thud. There were a dozen others in line behind her that day, hundreds more this week. Jamila was wasting her time just as much as his. She was relieved to be done with it, but that relief faded to worry as she watched him carry her files away and close the door. Was that really it? She stood and put on her veil slowly, as if waiting for the boy to return with something, *anything*, to assure her that this uncomfortable experience wasn't for nothing. But he didn't come back. On her way out, the interpreter stopped her.

"You're not helping your case by not talking."

The interpreter's look was stern, verging on angry, but she held Jamila's arm softly.

"But I don't remember."

"Of course you do."

Jamila couldn't help but notice the pale blue of her hijab—the same color her mother wore, the color of the metal latticework on the windows of her long-gone home. That closeness that had terrified her just moments before now put her at ease, and she felt her arm cave into the interpreter's grip, her resistance melting away. Perhaps because she was all out of options.

"If you stay tonight, we can redo your intake with someone else. A woman, if you prefer."

And before Jamila had the chance to answer, the interpreter took her by the arm to the office, where they cut a serpentine line to make another appointment at the front desk. This time with another American, a woman named Dolores.

Jamila could never remember anybody's name from St. Fatima's. They were all simply caseworker number 1, caseworker number 2. The American, the German, the one of indeterminate origin like the soap opera stars on TV. Even the interpreter with her sky-blue hijab melded into the mass of sweat and stress and red eyes that overcame her whenever she stepped into that narrow intake room. But she would remember the name of Dolores—the unfamiliar, languid loll of its sound, how it matched the lazy rasp of her voice and the way she blew cigarette smoke slowly into the whirring fan.

Dolores was even older than the interpreter, tiny and shriveled, with wrinkled skin and spindly limbs. The smell of cigarette smoke clung to every pilling on her clothes, to each gray hair on her head. Her kindness was shown not by laying a hand on Jamila's shoulder and telling her it was all going to be alright—such warmth wouldn't befit her—but by staying late to give her all the time she needed. And about an hour after evening prayer, well after the room had emptied, Jamila's memory came back like pinpricks, piece by piece.

She started by recounting her basic information. Name. Date of birth. Place of birth. Phone number—scratch that, *new* phone number. The questions were so routine that Jamila could recite all the answers in her sleep. Until one.

"Marital status," said Dolores, waving away a cloud of smoke. "Married."

Jamila fixed her eyes on the tangle of veins covering the woman's hand. Yes, she was married, but her husband had disappeared was now reported to be dead. Was she still married, then? Was he even really dead if there was no proof? She supposed she could begin with what she knew. She knew it was months ago when the police came around looking for men of a certain description. Poor, black, Sudanese. Between the ages of fifteen and fifty. She knew Yusuf had done nothing wrong and yet they hauled him off as she cried, bare-headed and alone in their cinder-block room. She received a call shortly after. They said Yusuf had died in custody. *Died?* How could one just ... *die* in a prison cell? Lots of ways, they assured her. But when she went to Tora prison to retrieve the body, she knew it wasn't his. The skin was gray and mottled, the eyes stuck open in the black, vacant manner of a dead fish. Dead, it was. But it wasn't him. She knew it.

"Dead bodies can look very different from the living." Dolores looked straight into her eyes with a strange intensity, as if speaking from experience.

"I know it wasn't him," she repeated. The nose was all wrong, straight while Yusuf's was curved, and there was no crooked front tooth like his, though much of the latter here had been knocked out.

"That could all be an effect of, you know, what happened to him."

Jamila returned her gaze to the veins on Dolores' hands, fanning out from her wisp of a wrist to each knobby finger tipped with a gray nail. She was sure they themselves reeked of cigarette smoke. The things she thought about at a moment like this. She looked at the interpreter, who again scolded her with her glare. What did they want her to say? Yes, the body was his? Would that make it better?

As a matter of fact, it did.

"We'll just say he's dead for now," said Dolores. "It'll help your case as a *woman at risk*—the UN's words, not mine. It's a category for women who are particularly susceptible to sexual violence. And you, my dear—a pretty girl all alone—certainly fit the description. Nobody's told you a thing about how this goes, have they? The worse shit you tell me, the better your case. I'm tempted to say it shouldn't be that way but really, it's only fair. You should be rewarded for all the shit you've been through. So please, go ahead and tell me about any harassment or assault you've experienced. With details, please."

Jamila took her time, counting the rings on the table left by a thousand cups prior. One, two, three. Big mug, small glass. One from last year, one from this morning. All that was left of terrible moments like this.

"Look, we've all been harassed—even me, believe it or not." Dolores let out a hoarse laugh, unleashing a brief coughing fit, then took another drag to clear her throat. The stench of nicotine wafted forth as she leaned close. "It's those piece-of-shit harassers who should be ashamed. Not you."

Jamila looked at the door to make sure it was still shut. It was. She breathed in the smoke, as if taking a puff herself, and began. Each memory unfurled from her tongue in a chain reaction. If she said this, then she might as well say that, and if she said that, then why not spill every ugly detail from the recesses of her mind, where she'd shoved them all this time, onto the sticky table to join the residue of tea and tears and dead flies. Yes, she had been harassed by employers and neighbors and strangers on the street, and it was why she veiled her face in public— not out of piety but of a will for anonymity. It was the harassment that caused her to change phone numbers, too, thanks to man who stalked her in her neighborhood, Kilo 4.5, a slum named for its position on the highway to Suez. And then, the hardest part—she told her everything that had happened in Omdurman, all the events that led her to flee in the back of a pickup truck heading north to Khartoum and then across the border. She remembered it was a Friday afternoon, and that her family was drinking coffee with ginger and cinnamon when the rebels came. She remembered how their approach was announced by the galloping hooves of their horses. She remembered the journey to Cairo and the way the smuggler extracted his payment, and everything that had happened since. With time she spoke louder, her fear dripping away with each memory finally acknowledged out loud.

Dolores ended the interview by stubbing out her cigarette and shaking her hand. It was tiny and frail, but warm against Jamila's bloodless fingers. She led her back to the office, where she printed a stack of papers too thick to staple. "This is your testimony. It's a record of everything you told me, everything that we'll submit in your case to the UN. Oh and Jamila." She stopped her with one foot out the door. "Any little bit helps. If you could get your hands on even a phone record—just a statement showing you changed numbers because of the harassment—that would support your case too."

On the bus ride home, Jamila clutched her testimony like a newborn child. Amazing how everything could be condensed into this one stack, and that it didn't offend her but rather felt like relief. She leaned her head against the window and sighed, making the exasperated sound of someone with the world to tell, for once, and nobody to tell it to. If only she could call Yusuf right then and share everything that had happened—the first meeting that went nowhere, the interpreter who stopped her at the gate, the woman named Dolores who smelled of cigarettes. She dialed his number just to hear the Nilofone recording that had replaced his voice on the other line. It was a sort of nervous tick she'd developed ever since he disappeared, as if to pretend his phone was only out of battery. A way to ease the pain of not being able to tell him all that had happened.

Before Yusuf disappeared, he'd known the resettlement appointment was approaching. He could see it in the jittering edge to her movements, the way her eyes darted across their little cinderblock room as if she was checking off every last detail. He said she was getting her hopes up for nothing, and perhaps owing to his cautious nature, he warned her not to bother. *You're wasting your time.* Getting resettled was about as likely as finding a diamond in the sea. He reminded her of Mustafa Mahmoud Square, where five years ago two thousand Sudanese had protested the eternal limbo of their resettlement cases. *Two thousand open cases.* The police started shooting. *And then what happened?* They died. They went to jail. They died and went to jail and not one of them got resettled.

But nothing could stop Jamila. What was the point, after all she'd been through, after coming all this way? As long as there was the tiniest fraction of a chance, she would keep searching for her diamond in the sea.

*You are the diamond and this*, said Yusuf, pointing to Cairo all around them, *is the sea.*

*****

Upon receiving her asylum status, St. Fatima's had set Jamila up with jobs cleaning houses in three very different corners of the city. Zamalek, Dokki, and Ramses. A dancer, a dissident, and a foreigner for bosses. Tonight she was at the home of the latter, Rose, a young teacher living with her Egyptian boyfriend. Jamila wasn't comfortable with the situation but she couldn't complain. Both Rose and Sami treated her kindly, and at least tried to maintain a facade of decency—pretending, for example, that he was only a friend. A friend who was always there. A friend who spent the night in a place with only one bed.

She was winded by the time she reached apartment 702. As she caught her breath, she noticed that a trash bag by the door had been torn open by stray cats, who'd found the contents unsatisfactory and left them strewn across the hall. The trash collectors must not have come by today, she thought, invoking God's name under her breath. It seemed she was the only one still working in this city. She bent to the floor to clean up all the usual water bottles and cigarette cartons that made up the bulk of the garbage. But one item stood out from the rest. It was some kind of tool, white and plastic, like a thermometer or even—could it be? With her shoe she jostled the bag to see more of it. Yes, it was a pregnancy test. She recognized the shape from the one St. Fatima's had given her weeks ago, yet another bit of proof to build her case as a woman at risk. But this one—did it belong to Rose? She looked at the light beaming out from under the door, the soft sound of chatter behind it. It had to be hers. Nobody else lived there.

At that moment Jamila would have rather run away than face Rose and pretend she had seen no such thing. But of course she couldn't do that. Not to Rose. For all her faults, this unmarried woman with a pregnancy test had always been good to her and in fact, held a little piece of her fate in her hands. Jamila had told Rose about Yusuf even before St.

Fatima's, and Rose had promised to help find him—or at least, his body—using every ounce of her white, American power to do so. It was help more valuable than guineas, than any discomfort she'd feel tonight. And so with a sigh Jamila tied the garbage bag closed and disposed of it before knocking. She pushed open the door with her hip, too distracted to wait for an answer.

Tonight the couple sat on the couch—Rose with a pile of papers, Sami with his carton of cigarettes, which he drummed against the table. Just the two of them. Owners of that haram thing in the trash. Without a word, Jamila lifted the veil over her head and felt the cool air on her cheeks, unzipped her abaya down to the ground, and stepped out of the swathes belly-first. She gathered her garments in a neat bundle and hung them on the hook by the door, which was always empty and awaiting her many layers, like an obliging hand extended from the wall. The lady of the house wore no scarves or jackets—she was always warm, always at home.

"Hello," said Jamila as she entered the room, eyes on the floor. She never talked much, but that evening she was particularly curt, afraid that any word uttered would expose what she'd just found. Rose, as usual, wouldn't let her be.

"How's the baby?"

"The what?"

"The baby." Rose pointed to her belly.

*Oh*, thought Jamila, *mine*. For once Rose's habit of drawing shapes with her hands while speaking to her, loud and slow, had proven useful. Little did they know, Jamila understood much more than detergent and Dettol, and any slowness on her part was on account of knowing *too* much—knowing that she needed to be careful with her words. But tonight she would play along. She placed a hand on her belly and said, "almost ready," as if she were an oven carrying a loaf of baking bread. Oh, how she wished there was nothing but bread between them.

Sami gave her a look with his big, dark eyes, as if he had something to say. *Please don't*, she thought, eyes flitting down to the crisscrossing planks of wood on the floor. If he kept looking at her like that, she might confess to everything—that she knew he slept with Rose and that they were not married, that she found the proof in the trash, and perhaps worst of all, that she'd answered his phone when his mother called last night. She knew she wasn't supposed to answer it, but what could she do? The woman had called and called, her name lighting up its screen every hour from its lone spot on the bedside table. A flash of worry—*what if it's an emergency*—had made her pick up. Jamila wanted to assure her that all was well and that Sami was safe, but all she heard on the other line was a gasp, and then the woman hung up. Did she know too? Surely she didn't if Sami was sitting right there tonight, alive and shameless, without a shoeprint on his face.

"The internet is down again," he said finally.

Jamila exhaled. With a dishrag, she wiped a day's worth of dust off the windowsill.

"It's so weird," said Rose. "I know I didn't miss a bill."

As she fiddled with the router, Jamila tidied the table, hoping she wouldn't extend this conversation because she really didn't need to hear it. She believed Rose. Despite the boyfriend and the haram thing in the trash, Rose was always true to her word, especially when it came to money. She never paid her late and sometimes even paid early just in case she forgot. But she never forgot. Jamila was sure it was the same with the internet bill. She wanted to tell Rose that it wasn't the bill—that whatever was wrong with their internet had also struck Zamalek, where her other employer, Miss Fifi Shafik, had been so idle and aimless without her usual social media gadgets that Jamila feared she might start tearing down the wallpaper again, like she did during the power cuts last summer, doling out hours of extra, unpaid work. Just the memory was exhausting. At least Rose would never do that—there wasn't even any wallpaper to begin with. What she might do instead was use the time to pester Jamila with conversations she didn't want to have. And that she did.

"Jamila," Rose said, a singsong lilt to her voice. "Will you come have a cup of coffee with us?"

She would have declined but the coffee was already in front of her, giving off rich steam in Rose's hand. It was the good kind, thick and tinged with cardamom. She knew the coffee was just excuse to talk to her. There was a desperate brightness in Rose's eyes, as if she were doing her best to make this night a good one, if only to please Sami with his wide, worried eyes, and Jamila with her own downcast, a particular soberness hanging about her like nicotine in Dolores' hair.

Out of something like pity, Jamila relented and took the cup. She followed the couple to the balcony. It was one of those narrow ones, more decorative than made for actual use, but they tried their best, squeezing a trio of tin chairs onto it and sitting facing the street as if there were a pleasant view before them, perhaps of the Nile instead of soot and concrete. As she sipped from the cup she looked out at the endless city, all its bricks and satellites and minarets, wondering if it was mere coincidence that the two houses she cleaned had the same internet problem, on the same day and on opposite sides of the river. Something about the odd quiet of the street told her it was no coincidence. Not at all.

"See those guys," said Sami, pointing to two police trucks beneath the overpass. "They're hiding."

She had to squint to see them. Hiding indeed. Their headlights glinted like the eyes of jackals in the dark.

"At least they aren't blocking the intersection like they did the other night."

"I still don't believe that," said Rose.

"Well, you were asleep." Sami's face flushed as the words left his mouth, as if he'd just confessed to sharing a bed with Rose, as if Jamila didn't know. Of course she knew.

The balcony fell silent. The three of them darted eyes across the balcony, unsure of when and whether to break it. Both Sami and Rose ended up looking at Jamila, as if it were her responsibility to save them from this uncomfortable moment—the moment they themselves had created. She exhaled, preparing to talk about herself once more. By now they knew that her husband was missing and that she lived in Kilo 4.5, a place they hadn't heard of before because it didn't exist or rather, wasn't *supposed* to exist beyond a measure of length. And they knew she came from a city nestled on the crystalline Nile, the same river that ran gray in Cairo. What else could they possibly want to know?

Rose leaned toward Jamila with her cup again, this time empty, but with the same desperate glow in her eyes. "Read my fortune?"

How could she forget. They knew she could read coffee cup fortunes too. Apparently it was noted in employment forms from St. Fatima's, which listed under *job history* a former gig reading coffee cups for tourists in Khan El Khalili. Rose had probably hired her for that reason alone—she'd asked Jamila about it on her very first day of work. Jamila, though put off, had obliged. Tonight was no different.

She reached for the cup, looping her finger through its tiny handle, and remembered how she'd learned the art from her mother, who'd learned from *her* mother, and so on. It was a main attraction of any gathering of Abdesalam women, from birthdays to weddings to regular Friday afternoons when they baked corn flour bread to dip in milk and honey. Most wanted to know where they would travel, what they would do for a living, whether they would live well into old age or should watch out for the evil eye from this or that side of the family, or from some stranger they hadn't yet met. But all were interested in one thing in particular—love. Kids wanted to know about it. Mothers, widows, eternal spinsters. Even little boys, whose fortunes they would read for fun, came with questions about what kind of girl they would marry—whether a voluptuous beauty like the late singer Aisha Musa Ahmad, or a scraggly runt like such-and-such classmate—and they'd stick out their tongues at their fate for the latter. But it was no joke. The search for love was universal and constant. Perhaps it was the part of life one could least control. You could choose to buy a ticket somewhere, pick one profession over another. Even death could be avoided, somewhat—or brought upon oneself with a single jump off a bridge. But love? There was no controlling who, if anyone, would find you, or when they would.

It was no surprise, then, to find love written in Rose's eyes when she held out her cup, emptied after the requisite three or four sips but for a thick coating of sludge stuck to the bottom. Jamila flipped it over, letting the remaining grains seep down its porcelain insides, then turned the cup by its handle, once, twice, three times around, as a crack on its lip made a light, hypnotic squeak on the saucer. As she peered inside she could think of nothing but Yusuf, who'd long ago appeared in her own coffee cups, foretold with a horse and a bushel of wheat.

Sami and Rose must have thought she was just taking her time.

Perhaps there was simply a lot to decipher inside. There was. Jamila strained to focus on the task at hand. Finally, a pigeon's coo broke the silence, followed by Sami.

"*Yalla*, let's see what you've got." Sami leaned back on the leg of his stool and blew smoke over the balcony railing, keeping his eyes on the all-knowing cup. Funny, how nonchalant he tried to come off, when she could see very well the fear in his eyes. Fear of the fortune. Fear of that thing in the trash. Fear of his mother, whose calls he couldn't ignore forever. Sami was in such a mess of a situation that the fortune should be the *least* of his concerns, though it might at least determine his mood going to bed that night. The same bed he shared with Rose and didn't think Jamila knew.

She sat for a while, concentrating with a hard face, thinking of what to say. One shape in particular stood out: a rounded depression in the grains, almost circular, but with two interior spots like eye sockets. Together they formed the rough shape of a skull, the symbol of death, but of course she couldn't tell them that. Though it was universally dreaded, the death fortune wasn't always literal, and often meant simply the end of a job, a marriage, a lease. Nothing final, by any means. One could always find another job or home, after all, and even dead relationships lived on in those late-night, early-morning, half-woke dreams bound to be forgotten by dawn. But it was because of that ambiguity, as her mother always said, that it was as important to see the person as it was the grains. The shapes would emerge in the cups, yes, but it was in the subject's eyes that they were defined—whether skulls for death, rings for marriage, mountains for great successes or great struggles ahead. She never really understood it until right then, as she looked at Rose. She was chewing on the inside of her lip as she waited, growing anxious as Sami puffed smoke to fill the silence. Yes, there was death. But she would have to put it differently.

"I see a circle, the circle of life. You'll be reborn again." This was her diplomatic way of translating death. Birth was death's flipside, after all.

"Hmmm, circles," said Rose, looking deflated. "Sounds about right."

Though Rose was far from home, Jamila was reluctant to tell her she'd one day return. She sensed, somehow, that she didn't want to. She looked straight at the woman, from her verdant eyes and down to her ink-stained hands. They must be around the same age. She couldn't understand why this foreign woman who should be married by now had moved to Cairo with nothing but a rolling suitcase. And when she opened her mouth, she ended up asking what she'd been thinking all along.

"Why did you come here?"

A smile crept up the corners of Rose's mouth. It seemed she'd answered this question many times, but judging by what followed, she had yet to find a satisfactory answer.

"It's hard to explain. Life is so much better here."

"Better?" Jamila thought of her resettlement case, the entirety of which was built on the argument that there was no place worse. If Cairo was better than a place like Rose's home, then what was she fighting for?

"Well, let's start with the weather. It's what, January? Right now, it's raining all the time, the sky's permanently gray. And don't even get me started on the people. Everyone is sad, mad, pissed off. Sure, there's a short period of time in the summer when people will air out their toes in flip flops and sit on their porches and talk to strangers. But it's like that all the time here. In Cairo, it's always summer."

There was a dreamy, pleased look on Rose's face as she looked off in the distance, as if a glittering city lay before her rather than a ghostlike, run-down Ramses. How unfathomable she was. Jamila tried to mask her confusion. Eternal summer sounded like hell, and the things Rose loathed about her home were hard to envision—the angry people, the stingy sun. Jamila thought of Rose's eyes when she invited her for coffee—love written in every tine of her iris—and decided to change the subject. Cairo wasn't the only love she was thinking of.

"Well you're in the right place, and with the right ... one."

Sami held his cigarette in this right, light hand as he exhaled over the balcony railing, out of respect for the pregnant women before him—well, at least one—as if each singular breath made a difference against the smog. Jamila couldn't help but pity him despite what he'd done. There were countless others who'd done far worse and went on without a word about it—she'd heard it herself in the corridors of St. Fatima's. And Jamila, as if she had the power to dictate fate, put the cup down, leaned in, and repaid them for their relative kindness, or at least, that cup of good coffee.

"Love is a rare bird. Like a black-footed ibis."

Sami coughed, choking on smoke. Perhaps he didn't get it. She should rephrase it.

"Or rather, like a diamond in the sea. The only thing harder than finding it is keeping it. So be careful."

"That's beautiful," said Rose. "A diamond?"

"A diamond in the sea."

# 4

Something about the buzz of the fan made Sami remember, as he awoke Friday morning, that he'd forgotten the anniversary of Giddo's death.

He grabbed his phone off the floor to find it oddly devoid of any missed calls. Suad must be furious, too angry to even talk. He began dialing, then stopped. Should he? Yes, he should. But when he punched in the numbers, his fingers moving in autopilot, he heard not the sound of her fury but that of the line cutting.

Had she hung up on him?

No, that was impossible.

He realized what had happened as he reached for his jeans and watched coins slip out of its pockets. He was simply out of phone credit. What a relief it was only a matter of money—and better yet, that he could use it as an excuse to put off calling her even longer. *See, I didn't forget. I was just out of credit.* For now, he added credit to his list of errands for the day—on top of picking up some textbooks from the dorms, calling Nilofone over the router, and buying a birthday gift for Rose. The latter was just days away and yet he no idea what to get her. Last year had been easy. He bought her a silver necklace with an evil eye—the sort of thing one would get for his sweetheart, not knowing what a mess she'd cause later.

He grabbed a black T-shirt, as if in Giddo's honor, then paused before putting it on. Sami never wore black. It reminded him of his mother on the day of the funeral, the first of forty straight days in which she wore nothing but the color. Odd that he'd forgotten the anniversary, when he could forget nothing else about Giddo's death. When Sami closed his eyes, he saw Giddo the way he'd left him—skinny and semi-lucid in bed, skin the color of ash, mouth hanging agape as if shock had rendered him speechless. Sami could still smell the phlegm and cold sweat of the dark room where Giddo died. Any brush of skin reminded Sami of the papery touch of his hand, and his fear of grasping too hard, as if he were holding together a pile of ashes. In his textbooks he saw cataract-clouded eyes in the spaces between each word, each ugly equation; and could think of nothing else each time he took the train home and watched the bricks of Cairo turn to shoulder-high grass—the grass that had grown over his grave.

Most of all, Sami would never forget what he did that night. It was a stupid decision, made in a split second. He hadn't seen his friends in years—they'd lost touch since he moved to Cairo—so when they called, having heard he was home in Mahalla, he didn't hesitate to meet up just to smoke and stand in the street like the old days. It seemed far more preferable than returning to Giddo's death chamber, where his mother and sister were spending the night. Besides, he was sure Giddo would soon recover, eat a full bowl of stew in no time, get back into his pressed suits and sharpen his moustache to a waxy point like an Ottoman pasha. It seemed safe to leave his side. Sami realized he was wrong when he woke up the next morning, the house empty, not a sound but the deafening whirr of the neighbor's cotton wheel. Giddo was dead.

Sami looked at Rose lying in bed. He was somewhat resentful of her ability to sleep through his distress. She didn't even know what happened two years ago. He hadn't told her—partly because he hated talking about it, but also out of fear she'd judge him, as she tended to do, or even worse use it to draw a conclusion about *every* Egyptian. Not just Sami but each taxi driver, kiosk vendor, and self-immolator—hell, even the president himself. They were all the same. He could hear her already, *Egyptian men are shit at taking responsibility*, the thesis of some anthropological study. Sami never acted on his own—he bore the whole country on his back—so he was careful around foreigners like Rose, who could never understand the faint distinction between culture (expectation) and his own failings (what actually happened). It was one of the many things he hadn't thought about when he first met her, more than one year ago, when all he could see was the blazing light in her eyes, the thrust of her pale hand reaching for his, shameless. How could he have known? She was the first girlfriend he ever had, his first everything. A single step that brought the whole floor down. Before her, life was so simple. Pray. Study. Call his mother. Follow the rules until it was time to come home and find a wife. A wife that could not be Rose.

They were never meant to be, despite Jamila's fortune. It would never work out, even if they got married and she moved to Mahalla and started covering her hair and reading from the Quran. They'd found each other by accident, the way one might stumble upon a fresh pack of cigarettes in a pile of trash—just a coincidence as good as it was bad for you. Certainly not a diamond in the sea. He could have laughed it was so tragic. Kind of like Giddo's death. Ha-ha-ha.

He patted his pockets in search of a brick of hash to make it go away. Sami always preferred breakfasts of THC to Vitamin C, but today it was justified, even though the hash didn't do much lately. Maybe his tolerance had increased like it had with alcohol. Just one beer used to turn him to a smiling buffoon with limbs of jelly. Now it took a whole case, and then some. Or maybe it was the … situation. He looked back at Rose, still lying face down on her pillow, mouth agape like Giddo on his deathbed. Yes, that's why his mind was mired in iron that not even hallucinogenic drugs could permeate.

Of course, he was all out of rolling papers, so he went looking for scraps to do the job instead. On the coffee table he found a stack of textbooks, the majority his. *Advanced Petrochemicals. Introduction to Crude. Chromatography for Beginners.* He hated the sight of them just like he hated his major, petrochemical engineering, which he chose after years of brainwash from a father who'd gone into the same trade. Baba believed there were three courses in life: doctor, engineer, or *khara* (shit). Sami was too squeamish and soft to be a doctor. He could never cut somebody open or look at a human body like the biological slab of matter it really was.

And as for shit, well, he already felt like shit much of the time, so he didn't need to *be* shit, too. Shit in the eyes of his father who, even far away in the desert, still judged his every move.

The textbooks had better use as kindling, but something stopped him before he ripped out a page wholesale. The book didn't even belong to him. As part of his scholarship, the university had loaned it to him just as they'd loaned him a dorm room, which he had pretty much abandoned to live instead with Rose. That was bad enough. If they ever found out he was tearing up textbooks too, they'd kick him out and ship him back to the sugar fields of Mahalla. A waste of a good scholarship.

With a sigh, he set down the textbook and reached for a stack of papers that Jamila had swept neatly into the corner. Much of it was Rose's classwork—drawings and half-filled worksheets from her third graders. He stopped on a blank math quiz, which she'd used to take notes on Sunday, January 23, when she evidently had run out of notebook paper. On the margins she'd penciled a silvery border. For a moment all Rose's faults dripped away as Sami imagined her doodling in class, clicking her teeth against her tongue as she scribbled unintelligibly onto any paper in sight. He had to squint to read what she'd written, which was so small it seemed purposeful. It seemed to be a shopping list. *Toilet paper. Kleenex. Q-tips.* When he reached the edge of the page, he flipped to find the list continued on the back. *Milk. Sugar. Tea. Bread,* then *breadcrumbs,* with *crumbs* underlined with a deep lead gash. Underneath, *crumbs* and *crumbs* and *crumbs* again, in successively larger, stronger print, as if stuttering. By the end of the page, the letters were almost black, scraped so hard into the paper that the pencil had almost gone straight through.

What had gotten into her?

At first, he thought it was the hash. Maybe it was a good strain, one laced with chemicals seeping into his bloodstream from the palm of his hand. He ran his finger over the words, feeling the grooves in the paper to ensure its existence, that it wasn't some ghost that would disappear when he turned to face the light. But it was there—paper. Like the touch of Giddo's hand. It slipped out of his grip and he dove to catch it. Maybe it wasn't such a good idea to use Rose's notes for rolling paper.

In the end he was left with one option—yesterday's edition of *Egypt Today*. But a headline caught his eye before he got the chance to tear off a sheath and get on his way.

## PRESIDENT ORDERS ARREST OF BAKER IN BURNING OF IMBABA MAN

**January 28, 2011**

In response to the burning of Ahmed El Masry, 27, the president has ordered the arrest of baker Zeid Marzouk, 31, son of the infamous Islamist drug lord "Pinky" Marzouk, who was responsible for holding patrons of the Kit Kat kebab house hostage during the terrorist insurrection of 1992. Marzouk is accused of illegally marking up the price of government bread from ten piasters to an unaffordable fifteen in an effort to fund the undercover drug ring he inherited from his father. He is also charged with funneling arms from radicals in Gaza and dispensing them on the streets of Cairo. It is believed that Marzouk provided the weapons used in the recent murder of Madame Ingy Girgis, 82, of Garden City.

At a press conference this morning in Qasr El Aini hospital, El Masry thanked the president for keeping the country safe from crooked bakers like Marzouk, who would like nothing more than to bleed the regime's generosity in order to sow chaos and radicalism.

If you or anyone you know has been victimized by a baker like Marzouk, please refrain from attempting to martyr yourself in the manner of El Masry, and instead, call the municipal police.

Sami set down the paper, confused. He imagined the man in the body cast speaking to the press through that hole for his mouth. *Thank you, Mr. President.* The news was trash. Now it was clear why they usually stuck to football scores and hotel openings—any story verging on the political came off like a joke.

There certainly was no mention of the demonstrations rumored to begin at noon that day. Apparently the events in Tunisia had fired up a bunch of Egyptian youth who wanted a revolution of their own. Sami thought immediately of Ayah, who was far more political than himself. She'd die to take part somehow, if only to post news clips from her phone. He understood the instinct but never had the urge to get involved himself. What was the point? No protest ever amounted to much. The only one he'd ever seen was about a year or so ago, when mobs stormed the street incensed by the outcome of a football game, 1-0, Egypt knocked out of the World Cup by its African rival, Algeria. It ended just as fast as it began, when trucks and tanks rolled in to hush the whole city to a pall. Whatever was due to happen at noon today couldn't be any worse than that. This was no football game.

With a huff, he tore the article down the middle and got on his way.

\*\*\*\*\*

In Khan El Khalili, Sami braced himself for a morning spent shoving his way through ambling crowds, tripping over stray cats and oriental gadgets, dodging overeager shopkeepers perched on stools waiting to reel in customers. What he found, though, wasn't quite the case. Almost all of the bazaar was boarded up, unrecognizable without the usual adornment of scarves and lanterns casting flecks of light up and down the alleys. He would have thought it was the hash again if it weren't for an elderly couple blocking his path. They wore the usual tourist gear—safari vests and cameras around their necks—and held a map outstretched between them, looking as confused as he was to find the bazaar's state a reality. A reality he needed to reconcile with a long list of tasks to accomplish before noon prayer. He needed to find a gift quickly. He bounded up and down the alleys until at last he found one open store, a hole in the wall full of antiques. The place dripped Rose.

Inside, a bald man sat behind a desk fixing a watch with a tiny screw. He looked up from his handiwork as Sami walked in, eyebrow raised in suspicion.

Sami didn't give him much thought, distracted by piles of centuries-old

junk all around him, dumped haphazardly like the contents of a treasure chest. There were mounds and mounds of leather, brassware, and
unpolished metal, all covered with dust and yet still luxuriant; pins bearing portraits of dead dictators and the insignias of long-defunct empires;
clocks and pots and coffee jugs strewn about; glasses and gadgets that left
him goggle-eyed. Yet somehow—as if each dim, dusty bulb in the shop hit
every brass cranny just enough to shine a spotlight in his path—a nonde-
script little camera caught his eye. He reached for it and wiped off the
dust, uncovering its logo. *Meikorlens. Made in Japan.* A retro model from
the 1950s, square and classic. It was much older than the cameras looped
around those elderly tourists' necks, though it befit them. It befit Sami too.

"200 pounds," said the shopkeeper.

Sami turned to find the man still at work with the watch, not even
looking. He stayed silent, feigning uncertainty even though he'd already
decided to buy it. He liked that the camera came from Japan—somewhere
as far away as possible, where he and all his mistakes were unknown,
unpronounceable. It seemed a suitable receptacle for whatever pictures
he'd take nowadays—pictures of Rose, of Ramses, of their upcoming trip
to the beach. He was so captivated that he forgot to play the haggling
game and said, in a quick breath, he'd take it.

The shopkeeper flipped open his cash box, pleasantly surprised. Deal.

"Wait. I need something else. A gift for … a friend," said Sami, obscur-
ing the gender of this *friend* with a deft misuse of grammar. That the gift
was for his girlfriend wasn't any of the man's business, but since when did
that matter?

The shopkeeper seemed to see through it. He took a bracelet out of the
jewelry case and set it in Sami's palm. It was heavy, composed of silver coins
that jangled like the ankles of belly dancers. Honestly, Rose would love an
old bracelet like that, an impractically oriental trinket left behind by some
Victorian tourist, like herself in a past life. But he wasn't about to prove the
shopkeeper right.

"It's for my brother."

"Well, what does your brother like," said the shopkeeper, returning
the bracelet to the case.

Sami said the first thing that came to mind. "He likes to write, I guess." It was true—Rose was always scribbling notes on scraps of paper, in bed and cafés and taxi cabs. Notes like *crumbs*.

The man walked to a shelf packed with old books and magazines, comics and newspapers from days when people actually read. He slipped out a leather-bound journal, "from the era of King Farouk," and opened it to prove that it was wholly unused. As Sami watched the blank, yellowed pages flit between the man's wrinkled hands, he imagined them filled with Rose's notes, the scribbles and the crumbs. Yes, this was the one. Useful, unisex. Again, he didn't even bother bargaining. There was no time anyway.

***** 

After leaving the bazaar, Sami stopped by a grocery store and picked up some items from Rose's shopping list—milk and sugar and toilet paper, even breadcrumbs, as if to insist there was nothing strange about it, nor the harsh stutter with which it was written. Crumbs and crumbs and crumbs. Maybe she was baking a cake again, like that one disastrous attempt she'd made months ago, which left the house stinking of burnt metal for a week. He supposed he would find out later. He put the Meikorlens and journal in his backpack and walked to Salah Salem Street, where he stood on the curb with his arm in the air, trying to find a taxi to take him back downtown. It was more difficult than he thought. Every now and then a cab would totter past, roll down its window hesitantly, and then scoff at his proposed destination. *Ramses? No way.* As if he'd asked to be driven off a cliff.

The bags grew heavy and the streets more desolate as Sami waited. He thought of calling Rose to tell her he'd be late, but he'd forgotten to buy phone credit and the only kiosk in sight was closed, like Hashem's. Was *everybody* praying? His only company was a beggar woman sitting on the curb, selling fish from a bucket at her feet.

"Very good fish," she said as their eyes met. "Nile fish."

Sami grew uncomfortably conscious of his two full grocery bags, as if he were flaunting them in her face. Food for him and not for her. Trinkets bought elsewhere. He set down the bags to make them less conspicuous, but she'd already seen them. Even as she beckoned him, there was a certain scorn in her glare, as if she knew all about Sami and how he'd forgotten his grandfather's death like an item on a grocery list. Tissues, maybe. Something insignificant like breadcrumbs. Only he didn't forget those.

Despite the disciplinary look to her face, Sami couldn't help but feel bad for the beggar woman. He wondered if she had any kids whose lives she was currently ruining. She looked about Suad's age, mid-forties, with wide hips under her galabia and thus, many kids and many ruined lives. He smiled to himself, looking like a fool with his hand in the air, flagging taxis that would never come. It felt good to commiserate with the imagined children of this woman who sat in the street with a bucket of fish. He rejoiced in his insignificance. He was one of many young men in Cairo, a place with no shortage of young men, a place where young men were so numerous they melded into one coagulated mass of denim and hair gel and skinny limbs. They were the *shabab*, a singular, collective force. He was only one measly molecule among all the indistinguishable youth who, on normal days, would gather around microbuses to go to sweat or study or loiter downtown. And for a moment all his problems seemed utterly moronic. He reminded himself, *God does not burden a soul beyond that it can bear.*

And with that, Sami crossed the street toward the beggar woman. He expected this to surprise her, but she looked undaunted, as if she'd known all along that he'd make his way over sooner or later. *Mothers always know*, as Suad would say.

"Only one guinea, *one guinea*, my boy. I'm telling you, there isn't a better deal in town."

He held his nose and peered into the bucket, where a single gray catfish bobbed in murky water. Of course, he wanted nothing to do with that fish, but he felt he had no choice. He opened his wallet and dug around for a guinea. There was his government ID; an assortment of creased business cards from odd doctors and engineers he'd encountered from Mahalla to Cairo; a folded post-it scrawled with *I love you* in Rose's perfect, studied Arabic hand. But there was nothing in the money fold but a fifty-pound note. Not the petty coin he was after. He could have run back to the antique shop to get change, but as he looked down at the woman's sleepy, worn eyes, which reminded him of his mother's, the thought of breaking the bill felt impolite, as if it might elicit a slap. So he reached for the fifty and handed it to her. The woman's eyes widened in caution as she made out the numbers, as if it were a trick.

"Take it."

She pointed to the sad, limp fish at her feet. It seemed like she *wanted* to give him the fish—whether by some motherly urge or an aversion to being made a charity case.

At first he shook his head. In the end he accepted with a listless, "alright."

The woman took the bill, folded it, and slipped it under her sandal. She pulled the fish out of the bucket and slapped it against her arm to dry it, spraying Sami with lukewarm droplets. He didn't budge, eyes stuck to the ground where the money he thought would dazzle her now sat wedged between her foot and the asphalt. Her feet were tiny but hung over the edge of her plastic flip-flops, which were covered in pink Minnie Mouse print. He would have thought he was looking at a child's feet if it wasn't for her one overgrown toenail, which curved downward like a witch's claw.

"Where are you going, my boy?"

His eyes jolted up to find her bearing an off-putting smile, teeth caked in brown grime like grout between tiles. Now she was getting too friendly. This was why he should have minded his own business and got on his way.

"Ramses."

"You better get there before the protests."

"Protests?"

There was something different about hearing the word aloud, as if it were now real. The emptiness of the street was no longer a novelty—it gave him a chill. He needed to get back to Rose. He asked the woman if she had a phone he could borrow, which felt dumb but he was all out of options.

"Bah," she laughed, tossing a cheap phone out from beneath her skirt. "It won't do you any good. They cut the phones. *All* the phones. Yours and mine. They cut off the whole city."

"They?"

"You know who."

She wrapped the fish in newspaper, tied it up with twine, and gave it to Sami. It hit him, with the stinking fish in hand, that no amount of credit or phones or service would let him reach Rose or Suad or Ayah—not any of the women in his life, nor the twenty-four-hour pharmacy, nor even the police. He felt precariously weightless, like a balloon set loose in a violent wind. The beggar woman could be the last person he spoke to today, or tomorrow, or however long this phone business lasted. It gave him an odd reluctance to leave her—this woman with the bucket and the rotten smile—but he had no choice.

Sami started toward Ramses by foot, giving up on catching a taxi, on picking up his textbooks, on chasing down this router problem which he assumed had something to do with the phones. How could it be? His mind spun in such confusion that he found himself all the way at the 6 October bridge with the foul fish still in his hand. He'd forgotten to toss it as planned. He was about to chuck it onto the curb when he saw the Al Fath mosque at the end of the street, with its one massive minaret looming like Suad's glare. Haram. What a waste, she would say. He decided to leave the fish outside the mosque instead, where the needy could find it alongside government tomatoes and bread.

Behind the mosque Sami could see the sign to the Diesel building, and the seventh-floor window hiding Rose, who was no doubt ambling around with coffee, half-awake. Home seemed within reach. Not only home, but Rose—but all remaining connectivity in this disconnected city. He tightened his grip on the plastic bags, which were stretched to their last fiber, and the stinking fish that would soon be delivered as charity—only to be stopped with the blunt punch of a whistle.

"No crossing! The street is closed for prayer!"

A police officer blocked him from walking any further, whistle in mouth, arms outstretched to mimic the barricade that stretched across the street behind him. Despite his bluster he was only a boy, no older than twenty. Narrow as a stalk of sugarcane from shoulder to shoulder. There was a glint of fear in his puppy-like eyes, as though Sami were the one with the gun on his hip. Sami stepped back, took a breath, and explained calmly that he was only trying to get home.

"I live over there, boy—I mean, sir."

The officer blew his whistle again, this time letting out an arid, listless squeak. "Step away from the line! I said, step away from the line! Not even the president himself could pass," he lied, "so please, step away from the line!"

Sami stifled the urge to puff up his chest at the boy, shut him up along with that stupid whistle. Behind him sat a police truck with a dozen other officers packed like beans inside. Though their guns were most likely empty—loaded at worst with rubber bullets—Sami backed away in hesitation, as if he might summon those bullets just by just thinking of them. Better to be safe. Besides, it was Friday prayer. Fighting wasn't a good look, even for a screw-up like him, and it wouldn't get him any closer to the Diesel. He figured he would wait it out. Prayer wouldn't last long, and then he'd make his way home.

He sat on the steps of the Banque Misr, where he watched stragglers rush to wash their hands and feet. It didn't take long to realize this was no normal Friday prayer. The first sign was the sheikh himself, who delivered his sermon outside rather than remaining at the minbar. In his hand was a bullhorn instead of a modest microphone. Prayer rugs spilled out onto the street, no room for them all inside. And the police had now assembled across the intersection of Ramses and El Taawon, their shields raised.

"God is great," said the sheikh.

In response, there was nothing but the sound of foreheads touching mats.

Sami never felt comfortable watching prayer and not taking part, but this time he had company—up above, neighbors gathered on rooftops to do the same, hands on their hips instead of kneeling. He thought of his family back in Mahalla and how they must be praying at that same moment, Ayah in her jeans and Minnie Mouse socks, Suad draped in the floral sheath she used at home. If he were there, he'd be praying too, nudged gently by Suad, perhaps more so today for forgetting the anniversary of Giddo's death. But this was one day he wouldn't complain. There was something hypnotic about the way the men bent in unison across Ramses Street, not a cough or sneeze or twitch among them, their backs forming a blanket of rainbow patchwork. It was beautiful in the literal sense and none of that spiritual gibberish. But if he closed his eyes and listened to each rhythmic thump and whoosh, he was sure he'd eventually feel that too.

When at last it was time for the final prostration, he picked up his bags, preparing to beat the crowd to the Diesel's door. But something knocked him down. He heard it first—like a wave rising to a crest before breaking—then saw it.

At once, the men sprang up from their mats and turned away from the mosque to storm the police. There seemed to be thousands of them, thousands more than before. They poured out of the mosque and from the alleys as smoke filled the air. They were chanting, but Sami couldn't make out the words. Their voices battled one another for predominance until they found a rhythm, and then the words came out like bullets in the breeze:

"The people!"

"Demand!"

"The fall of the regime!"

It sounded melodic. Musical, even. Like the hook of an Umm Kalthoum song. Sami caught himself mouthing the words, then promptly stopped. The police were *right there*, and he was sure at least one of them was from Mahalla, too, and would recognize that unmistakable Sukkary gleam that said he was supposed to be shoulder deep in a field of sugarcane and not there, fighting them in the street. They would haul him off to Tora prison in the back of a truck, like an Eid sheep, and then deliver some nameless corpse to his mother like they did with Jamila's husband. Only Suad, unlike Jamila, would hear only one thing – that Sami broke the law. That's what they were doing, wasn't it? The people weren't allowed to say things like *the people demand the fall of the regime*. The people weren't allowed to flood the streets like this, let alone raise their fists to the police. To Sami, the thought of getting arrested—and worse yet, Suad finding out—was enough to plant him in place for the entire week, if need be. But the people on the street didn't seem to be afraid. The chant rang out again and again.

*The people demand the fall of the regime.*

Sami gripped the railing of the staircase, as if he might blow away. He fixed his eyes on the Diesel's front door. It wasn't so far. It would take only a few minutes to reach it if he could somehow forge a path through the crowd. As the masses swirled around him, threatening to suck him in like the tide, he decided he had no choice but to try. He looped the bags around each wrist, took a deep breath as if about to dive underwater, and stepped down into the throngs. It felt like the sea.

*The people demand the fall of the regime.*

He didn't realize he was moving against the flow of the crowd until he was in the thick of it, bumping into shoulders, running into fists. By then it was too late to turn back. He was in it. And when the police fired back at the protesters, they were aiming for him too. And they got him.

At first he didn't know what was happening. His eyes began to water, and then his nostrils tingled, and then his whole face burned. If it wasn't for the crowd shouting *tear gas*, *tear gas*, he would have thought his skin was peeling itself off. He scratched at his face but it only worsened the sting. He coughed, but the poisoned air blazed down his throat with each desperate gasp that followed.

Then there was a bang.

It came again, *bang bang*, like the blunt hit of a baton.

He cracked his eyes open a sliver and saw the silhouettes of kitchen tools punching through the smoke. Had the smoke gotten to him? Had the gas seeped up his nose and into his brain? It seemed absurd and yet, the longer he strained to keep his eyes open, the more apparent it became that it was true—that the protesters had armed themselves with saucepans and spatulas and whatever they could find, and were hitting the iron railings of the street as they came at the police.

*The people demand the fall of the regime.*

A crowbar flew out of the smoke toward Sami, and to his shock, he caught it. He was tempted to say something came over him, but nothing did. It was just that—nothing, an involuntary movement occurring in the absence of any forethought. He took the crowbar and hit the railings too, and before he knew it, he was walking with the crowd and not against it, and when they reached that intersection where just moments before, a boy soldier had told him not even the president could pass, he saw that the barricade had fallen and the police were gone, and people were indeed passing, jumping over discarded shields as they ran southward to Tahrir Square.

This time, Sami stayed back.

When he turned around the street was empty, left ravaged from curb to curb. Storefronts bashed. Cars overturned. Asphalt littered with broken glass and pots and pans. In the distance, burning cars turned the sky a deep purple. The tear gas had dissipated, leaving just a faint hint in the air that gave him a tolerable tingle. He hadn't realized he'd lost his grocery bags until he saw their contents splattered on the sidewalk. The carton of breadcrumbs had burst open, its insides scattered like ash on the ground. The catfish lay at his feet, unwrapped, staring at him with its vacant, unblinking eyes. With a jolt he grabbed at his backpack behind him. It was still there, the journal and the Meikorlens tucked safely inside.

He dropped the crowbar, letting it make one final clink. For some reason he took out the camera and proceeded to aim and click. It was an odd first picture but he felt like it was a moment to keep—all of it—the fish and the breadcrumbs and the charcoal sky. Who would believe him when he explained what happened? Not even Rose would believe that he'd brought groceries to her doorstep only to have them ripped apart by sudden, spontaneous war. Now he'd have a picture to prove it, and at the very least, she'd know he tried.

And Sami realized, just then, that he he'd forgotten all about her in the middle of the march. There was no Rose and certainly no baby inside her. There was no Giddo and no death to relive. There were no bills, no schoolwork, no phone calls to return. He felt something like joy but deeper, seeping down into the marrow of his bones. And for the first time in his twenty-three years, Sami thanked God and meant it.

# 5

Jamila hadn't always covered her face in the street. It was only months ago that she got the idea to tear panels of fabric from an old dress, rip out the threads, and reuse them to sew the folds into an envelope for her eyes. When she first saw her reflection, reduced to a sliver of eyelid and brow, she felt powerful in her anonymity—like she could shove people out of her way without recourse, like she could wear one of Fifi Shafik's glittering negligees underneath, feel sequins dig into her overflowing breasts, and all the while look publicly like a wife of the Prophet, too holy to touch.

The decision to veil was not one of piety or even modesty. It was a decision borne of fear—and not any kind of fear she had experienced before. It wasn't like the fear of thunder, nor wild dogs. It wasn't the fear that came with the rebels, that of crunching gravel and swinging machetes. Those fears were loud and common. Those fears had company. *This* fear was silent and unseen, yet it was always there. It clung to the air. It followed her into bathrooms where she bathed with a bucket as fast as she could, just to go back to watching the lock on the door. It followed her to bus stops and into the backseats of microbuses, rearing its head each time a stranger's thigh brushed against her own. It hung from clotheslines crisscrossing through alleyways, casting shadows to conjure up flashes of grabbing hands, fingers curled like claws.

This was a fear unlike any other—it was the fear of a particular man.

She didn't even know his name. She knew only that he was a neighbor in her nameless slum, and that he spent his days eating sunflower seeds on the street, pestering passersby with his hyena-like smile, his missing front tooth. He quickly took a liking to Jamila, and naturally, started making her life a living hell. Especially after Yusuf disappeared.

At first it was only the sunflower seeds. She could have sworn there were none anywhere when she first moved into that windowless apartment, which was nothing more than a black hole as gaping as the space in between his teeth. Then the first seeds appeared at her doorstep. With each day there were more and more, lying in the corridor and in the stairwell, from the ground floor and up to the top of the roof. Soon they were everywhere, in the dark corners and under the bright light, in the trash heaps and strewn across the tiles, some blackened and some an underripe white, some with naked kernels and some with hulls intact, having missed the jagged edges of the sunflower man's remaining teeth.

Jamila reminded herself that they were only seeds. So tiny she could crack them under her bare heels. They grew on cheerful flowers stuffed into decorative vases. They were gobbled up by little birds and by millions of normal people who had nothing to do with her stalker.

They were seeds, just seeds, and yet she was terrified.

She tried convincing herself that she was exaggerating, that it was nothing but litter. Could she be imagining this all, seeing double and triple? But when she blinked her eyes to correct her vision, the sunflower seeds remained. They were real and they were insane, more frightening than even the touch of his grubby hand.

In the beginning, she did what anybody else would do and simply discarded any seeds that fell close to her door. But they kept coming back, multiplied, and the more they grew in number, the more afraid she became to even touch them. And so she let them pile up outside the door until the cats got to them. They pawed and nibbled and fought over the remaining seeds until finally they started to dwindle. Now that she ignored them, the sunflower man had gotten bored—either that or it just wasn't the season. Eventually there was only one seed in the hall, a lone reminder that he hadn't gone anywhere.

Then came the knocking. The man would call for her at all hours of the night, *Jamila, Jamila,* through the crack in the door. Somehow he'd found out her name, which had likely been passed around on the smoky breath of all the idle men in the street. She became such a fixation that she couldn't imagine what on earth they talked about before she moved in. But none were as keen as the sunflower man. He waited for her in the stairwell each morning, and when she passed he would lunge toward her, tug at her headscarf and shout sweet nothings, tossing in a few obscenities for good measure. *Hey honey, my darling, give me a kiss. Come here you bitch! Hey slave. You're black!* One day he came for her on the back of a motorcycle, black seed stuck in the gap of his teeth, laughing and blowing kisses. *Habibti!*

But for all the knocking, the taunting, the hallway-stalking, she thought she was safe as long as she was inside the apartment with the door bolted shut. Her flatmates knew not to answer when the sunflower man came calling, and one, Sayyid Hassan from Sennar, threatened to beat him up if he saw him. Of course, that didn't work, because the sunflower man was no refugee, but a native. He belonged there and they did not. It was an unwritten law that everybody understood—cross the line as a Sudani and get tossed out like yesterday's trash. Or worse.

It all ended one day when Jamila answered her phone to hear his voice. Enough was enough. Within a matter of hours, she changed her number, covered her face with a veil, and moved into another apartment on the far side of the Ring Road—all so he wouldn't find her.

\*\*\*\*\*

Jamila awoke Saturday morning to the sound of pellets hitting the ground, like rain, like sunflower seeds. She leapt out from under her blanket, hitting her head on the low ceiling above her. But as she rubbed her eyes open, there were no shells on the floor, and when she opened the door a crack, there were none in the halls, nor in the alleys of that sandy shantytown. It was only a dream. Sleep was the only place the sunflower man still stalked her.

She never expected those seeds to end up helping her in any way, but they turned out to be key to her resettlement case. She wouldn't have brought up the story at all—thinking it seemed silly—if it weren't for Dolores pressing her. *It's those piece-of-shit harassers who should be ashamed.* She said the sunflower seeds built Jamila's case as a *woman at risk*, and that there was no real asylum in Egypt, where her situation was untenable. All Jamila needed to do was track down some proof. It never occurred to her that the proof could be something as mundane as a telephone record.

That's why Jamila was on a mission to track down those records today. It had only been hours since yesterday's street battles, and now she was out on those same streets, tripping over the remains of Molotov cocktails, burnt-out cars, tin tear gas cannisters, bullet casings that rolled like marbles under her feet. Not even the citywide service blackout could stop her. She imagined a line of twenty million people stretching out the telephone company's door. She would try anyway.

The neighbors had warned Jamila to avoid Tahrir and take a detour through Boulaq, and she did as they said, veering off the main avenue and into the sleepy side-streets that would take her to the corniche with less chance of catching a bullet. She probably should have been afraid, but for some reason she wasn't. Why would a veiled woman like her draw any attention, anyway? She wasn't the army. She wasn't the police. She wasn't one of the iron-fisted youth screaming for the downfall of the regime. She wasn't anyone of consequence in this city—she was just a woman with a belly swelling through swathes of abaya, all alone.

When Jamila reached Boulaq, she found that the neighbors were right. It was free of demonstrators, so ghostly it caught her off guard. Walking its streets felt like trespassing, like she should tiptoe to prevent being caught. The only sign of life was in overhead windows, where she caught the round little faces of children locked up by their mothers, dying to get outside. It filled Jamila with sadness. She thought of the kids she and Yusuf could have if he was only there—and the one that existed, no doubt unwanted, in Rose's still-flat belly.

An odd sound tore through the breeze, guttural, like the call of an ibis.

"J-junk, junk, junk. Old junk, new junk, rich junk, poor junk, my junk, your junk. J-junk, junk, junk."

Jamila turned to see not a bird, but a junk collector, at work with his donkey cart as if it was a regular day and not one of revolt and barren streets. It gave her hope that at Nilofone, somebody else might be working too.

The man must have sensed the change in her mood. He nodded in her direction and said *salam* as he passed.

"Need a ride, sister?"

Jamila looked at the junk collector. He was old, harmless with his frail hands. The bed of his cart was empty but for a tire and a pair of mismatched shoes. She thought of the long way to Nilofone and the unlikelihood of finding a microbus when all of the city seemed to be in Tahrir. Hesitantly, she asked how much a ride would cost.

"For you, madam—nothing."

He couldn't see it, but she was smiling under her veil as she gathered her skirt and stepped onto the cart. He pulled a peeled guava out of his pocket and offered it to her before they set off.

"Please," he said.

She shook her head. "Take me to the Nilofone shop in Munira."

His eyes widened into caves under his eyebrows, overgrown like gray hoods. "Nilofone? Why would you go to a place like that? A phone is about as useful as a three-legged donkey nowadays—or rather, a car with no gas. No service, no phone. I wouldn't even take one if it fell in my path. And I'm a *junk collector*. I'd toss that thing into the river, *plop*. It's how they control you, you know."

"Who?"

"The government, sweetie! That's why I can't imagine why you'd want to go to Nilofone of all places. Today of all days."

Jamila had a million reasons—one for every sunflower seed. But he didn't need to know that. She reiterated her need to get the phone shop—before noon, please—and sank into her spare tire for a seat as the junk man crowed on.

"You sound like my kids. All this technological stuff can do no wrong."

The main streets were blocked to all vehicles, even a rickety donkey cart, so they had to take a detour past the El Wekala fabric market, which had never looked so sparse and colorless. As they rolled onward, a deep voice bellowed from the radio at the junk man's side: *The armed forces will not resort to the use of force against our great people.* Jamila hadn't felt a shred of caution until now—she was too determined to get to Nilofone to be afraid—but the airwaves gave her a pang with each word. Who said anything about the army? Why the declaration of peace? If you could even call it that. She leaned forward, veil billowing in the wind kicked up by the donkey's feet, and shouted so he could hear.

"What's happening in Tahrir?"

"What's happening? More like what *isn't* happening." He looked back at her, and as they locked eyes through the slit of her veil, he guessed, "You don't get out much, do you, sister?"

She nodded, not wanting to explain that yes, she got out—every day, in fact, from morning until night and to each end of the city—but she had other things to worry about. A missing husband. A resettlement case. Phone records to determine her fate. *You try keeping up with the news.*

"Tell me, uncle."

The old man was happy to oblige. "Listen, sister. There are one hundred thousand in Tahrir right now. I would join them if it wasn't such a good day in the junk business. You should have seen what I found the other day. A pair of leather boots. A policeman's cap. A computer that someone threw out the window, probably because of the internet," he laughed, wheezing. "Even a gold tooth." He held out his hand, where there lay a composite of yellowed enamel and precious metal, traces of blood at the root. She shuddered, thinking of the gap-toothed smile of the sunflower man.

"Yes, I can imagine it is a good day for junk," she said, looking away. "But what do the protesters want?"

"What do we want? I'll tell you what we want." He slowed the donkey and turned to face her, counting with his fingers: "One, the pharaoh is no fun. Overthrow the president. Two, by the sole of my shoe. No emergency law. Three, like sugar for tea. Dissolve the People's Assembly and the Shura Council. Four, there's room for more. Form a transitional government. Five, no honey in the beehive. Six, enough tricks. A new parliament and a new constitution. Seven, for those in heaven. Justice for the martyrs.

And finally …" He took a deep breath, as if it were his last. "Eight, it's never too late. All those who stole from this nation—each and every one—should get a speedy trial and a nice long prison sentence. God-willing." He clutched his belly, wheezing from laughter. "Oh, I almost forgot. There's three more."

She wished he'd get on with it.

"We want bread, freedom, and social justice—*aha*!" He spat a hunk of guava to the asphalt, then pointed to the spotted pulp remaining in his hand. "You see this? Worms in my guava, even in the dead of winter. This is the regime's doing. They take all the good fruit for themselves and leave this *shit* for people like us. Anyway, I was going to tell you about the curfew."

"What curfew?"

"Exactly. Nobody cares about the regime's damned curfew. They say that anyone out on the streets past three p.m. will be arrested, fined, shot." He held up bare wrist as if to check the time. "Tick tock, soon it will be three o'clock. Will you go home? No? Neither will I. Haven't you heard?"

"Heard what?"

"We're not going, *he's* going!"

Jamila recognized the chant, which was one of many booming through the streets nowadays. But here in deserted Boulaq, where the only sound was that of the donkey's hooves, the cart rolling, it gave her a chill. The words came out of the old man's mouth like *hello* or *goodbye* or *yalla, donkey, yalla*. Stronger in their matter-of-factness. We're not going, he's going. It seemed a good thing, this *going* on the part of the president, but what would happen next? Would the city crumble? Would Jamila have to flee again? Would St. Fatima's close down, send her papers fluttering out the window, sink all her dreams of refuge in the waters of the Nile? It was already getting harder each day to find food and get to work and do all the things she needed to do to survive until tomorrow, and now the thought of *tomorrow* was so nebulous she felt the ground caving in beneath her. Of course, she couldn't explain all of this to the junk man, so she sat silently as the cart rolled onward, and from his quick glance she could tell he was waiting for a response that would never come.

When a song came on the radio, the junk man turned up the volume and hummed along. *My beautiful country, my beautiful country.* It was a decades-old classic that still pulsed through radios, even back in Sudan. Jamila couldn't help mouthing the words under her veil, thinking of Omdurman and its women swathed in bright yellows and reds, carrying baskets on their heads, and the curve of the Nile where it branched into the Blue and White. The song blurred to static as they rounded the corner by the journalists' syndicate, then stopped abruptly with the screeching wheels of the cart.

A group of men were blocking the road, clubs and bats in hand. One had a gun strapped to his hip. The junk collector lowered the radio. The only sound was that of wheels crunching over debris on the asphalt. Broken bottles, burst-open cans of tear gas. Jamila eyed them nervously, feeling guilty—of *something*—just for being in the same vicinity of all these tools of disobedience. The donkey was scared, too. The animal tossed his head in protest as the junk collector urged him onward, step by step, until the armed men motioned with their hands to stop.

The man with the gun approached first. Jamila held her breath.

"Identification cards," he said, hand on his gun.

"I don't have one," said the junk collector.

He huffed and looked at Jamila in the back. "And you?"

She didn't hesitate to dig out her paperwork from St. Fatima's—the only ID she had. As he flipped through, not knowing he held her whole life in his hands, there was something in his pained expression that made it seem he didn't register any of the pages before him – a deep crease between the eyes that indicated far too much thought for an ID check. He stopped at a blurry Xerox of her bare face. That was what he was looking for—a photo. He couldn't read, could he? It seemed to be to her benefit because he handed back her papers readily. He looked skeptically from the junk man to Jamila and back, and asked where they were going, where they lived, what were their names and their father's names, and in the junk man's case, even his father's father's name.

"I'm only a junk collector," said the old man, holding his hands up in surrender.

The other men looked on from the intersection, their own weapons in hand. A baseball bat, a crowbar, a rope ready to tie them up and hang them if need be. They looked Egyptian but seemed somehow foreign in this context—nothing like Sami with his sad, sweet eyes or even her other employer Mr. Salem, who could break a sweat reaching for the TV remote. With their street clothes and mismatched weapons slung over their backs, they looked like the rebels back home. And as the man with the gun examined her, eyes to belly, she tried not to betray what she was thinking—that he could kill her and that nobody would ever know. Not Yusuf, if he was even alive. Not Rose and not Sami, who'd think she just quit. Not even St. Fatima's, which would lose her file and forget her among the sea of identical cases.

"On the ground," he said, pointing with his gun.

They stepped off the cart and watched the armed men search it. She noticed how tiny the junk collector was, standing beside her. He came up to her shoulder. If he was scared, he didn't show it, arms crossed in defiance, chin in the air as if to say *I told you so* to this ragtag army before them. He turned out to be right—there was nothing in the cart. Nothing of significance, anyway. The man finished his search and threw the tire and boots back onto the cart. For a second he looked unsure, as if this small act of consideration might compromise his power. To take it back, he reached for his holster. Jamila held her breath. And then with the other hand, he waved them through.

Once the armed men were out of sight, the junk man looked back at her. "Don't be afraid," he said. "I know they don't look like it, but they're the good guys. They're just protecting their neighborhoods from all the criminals on the loose."

"Criminals on the loose?"

"Yes, haven't you heard?" He looked back at her with a smirk. "Of course not. Well, let me inform you, sister. There were clashes at the prisons last night, some burned down, some prisoners escaped."

"Which prisons," she yelped. She thought of Tora, where Yusuf had been taken.

The junk man shrugged. "Abu Zabaal, mostly. Full of a bunch of bearded types. And some people are saying that two of the escapees were the police officers who killed Khaled Said."

She froze. Her throat was too dry to give her the gulp this moment required. She knew about Khaled Said, a young man beaten to death by the police last year. Now he was a martyr, a cause for revolution, both alive and dead in Tahrir. Jamila trembled thinking of his infamous autopsy photo, showing a face so disfigured with violence you couldn't even tell it was his. The police had bashed out any hint of an identifying feature. There was no mouth to match the modest smile in his government ID. There were no brown eyes glinting with a shade of sadness—as if he somehow knew the fate awaiting him on the other end of a baton. She realized, with terror, that if the police had done that to a middle-class Egyptian boy like Khaled, then her husband was a goner. The difference was that the world knew Khaled was dead. He had become a martyr. Yusuf, on the other hand, seemed to have never existed at all.

"It's the price of revolution," said the junk collector. A smile spread over his face as he pulled up to Nilofone. "God be with you."

As Jamila stepped off the cart, it was hard to believe God was with her. It certainly didn't seem like the case. God wasn't with Nilofone, either—that much was apparent by its shattered storefront and ransacked shelves. She would have to start over.

Next, she tried the Nilofone shop in the Arkadia mall. She hoped this one was safe thanks to the massive building enclosing it—no storefront to break open—only to find it in even worse shape, the whole thing burnt and ransacked. She hadn't realized that the mall itself was a hotbed of loot: cash registers, clothing racks, designer bags and DVD players. Looters had even stolen a faux Christmas tree from the window display of a Swiss fondue restaurant on the ground floor, its lights still blinking like an emergency beacon.

Who on earth would steal a Christmas tree? Who on earth were these looters in the first place? She tried figuring it out by listening to passersby, but it only made her more confused. Some said the looters were protesters from Tahrir. To others they were just criminals on the loose. They were CIA operatives, jihadists from Afghanistan, maybe even the police. She thought of Khaled Said, the burned prisons, the men in plainclothes doing the job of police who'd all but disappeared since the riots began. What at first seemed crazy became more plausible with each step.

# 6

aving even more trouble sleeping than usual. Who could blame

time she closed her eyes she saw fire and chaos, scenes from the

her son lived, unreachable. Not even the quiet of night could

et rest. In fact, it made it worse. When night fell—after Ayah

d, the TV shut off, and the cotton wheel next door stood still—

d the voice of the woman who had answered Sami's phone,

again.

it be ... her?

hs ago, when Sami came home for a blip of a visit, Ayah had

assport in his backpack. Suad didn't know why her daughter had

r brother's backpack to begin with but didn't complain—in fact,

oud of Ayah for caring so much for her brother to take things into

ands. And that she did. The girl ran to her bedside with the pass-

ing it around like a prize. *Look, mom!* Suad remembered it clearly,

he pushed her glasses up her nose and said *what's this*, the way she

t the sight of first, a woman, and even worse, a *foreign* woman.

ort was blue, with a bird embossed on the front. From the United

ah said. The woman in the photo stared back solemnly. She had

a holograph, dull and flat from one angle, and full of far-away

from another. Likewise, she looked both young and old depend-

e feature. Bareheaded and fair-haired, like a young girl. The tired,

She walked home exhausted, the da
was the price of revolution, as the jun
cost, she wouldn't let it stop her—not a
lations) seventy-eight other Nilofone s
keep searching.

Suad was
her? Each
city wher
help her
went to b
Suad hea
again and
Coul
Mon
found a
been in h
she was
her own
port, wa
the way
cringed
The pass
States, A
eyes lik
thought
ing on t

seen-it-all look of an older woman. Who was she? Suad needed to know, and yet dreaded the answer. She envied days of the past, when she blissfully believed Sami was studying when he didn't answer her calls. Now she couldn't help but see that woman's face each time she listened to the phone *ring, ring, ring,* and then get snuffed out by his voicemail. *You've reached Sami Sukkary. Sorry I could not answer your call . . .*

But someone had answered her call the other day. That was the problem. Suad was tempted to think it was that woman—only a foreigner would be so brazen—but in her gut she felt it wasn't. She could have sworn she detected the faintest hint of Nile water on the breath used to utter that sole *hello.* It sounded too crisp, too easy, to have come from a foreigner. Did that mean there was another? Oh, Sami. He seemed to be taking after his father more and more each dreaded day. She tried to convince herself that all would be well—that he was a good boy, that she was a dutiful mother—but that woman's voice had followed her like the buzz of a fruit fly ever since.

Sami didn't know it, but Suad had been working in stealth to correct him for many months. It all started with the passport episode. She never brought it up directly, of course—just uttering the words would make her faint—but she hoped he'd get the message with a few hints and nudges. It helped that it was Ramadan. She reminded him that it was a month of reflection and good behavior. Smokers quit smoking. The stingy donated to charity. Fornicators kept their pants on. The wayward caught up with their prayers. Even Nagwa kept her wild stories to herself, vowing to quit gossip each Holy Month. Girlfriends clearly had no place in Ramadan, and she didn't need to spell it out for him.

To test Sami, Suad decided to surprise him with a visit. She baked his favorite lemon sponge cake for the occasion. Cake in hand, she took the train down to Cairo and carried it all the way to his dormitory. He wasn't there, but the concierge let her into his room with the master key. Sami was her son, after all. Normally she would have taken the opportunity to go through his things, but something stopped her this time. Perhaps it was fear. God only knew what she might find. So instead she just made his bed and sat there, waiting, until finally she heard the key in the door. By then

the night had come and passed. Sami said he'd slept at campus after studying all day. She didn't believe him but she didn't press further. He took her
hand and led her to the corniche, where he showed her his favorite spot
on the river. The benches were crowded with teenage couples sitting too
close, fingers ringless, and the air smelled strange, probably from hashish.
The view wasn't so bad, though. The water was murkier than in the Delta,
but the river was wide and the skyscrapers cast reflections onto its rippling
surface. Later Sami dropped her off at the train station with the spare key
she requested, and with a kiss on the cheek they parted. She couldn't help
being disappointed that she hadn't caught a trace of that woman.

The next plan of action consisted of spitting girls' names at him at
rapid fire. Ilham and Doaa and Mariam and Malak. Naima and Nashwa
and Lulu. Lulu's older sister Halima—no, that one was married, but her
husband also had good girls in his family. Any female ever born to any
relative, neighbor, or friend was fair game, whether or not Suad had even
known of the girl's existence prior. It became quite ridiculous, she had to
admit. She had no idea whether any of these girls were indeed suitable,
whether they looked like their pictures or prayed regularly or had reputations that checked out. It was only necessary that she be connected to
Suad somehow, and—most importantly—that she got to pick her.

She spent many a daydream designing the type of girl she wanted
for her son. Someone young, with many childbearing years ahead of her.
Someone modest and loyal, uninterested in silly internet rubbish like
Ayah. If the girl had any gardening experience, that was a plus. A major
plus. She thought she had found his girl when she met Yosra. Simple,
young, uninterested in the world beyond lip gloss and silly cartoons.
Problem was, Sami wouldn't agree to meet her. So Suad brought her to
him instead.

She invited Yosra's family down from Damietta, coincidentally the
same time Sami was home for a visit. When they met, she scanned her son
eagerly for any sign of attraction. How could he *not* be attracted? The girl
was a genetic anomaly, with skin like fresh cream, eyes a straight azure. A
bit plump by modern standards, but back in Suad's day, no man wanted a
woman who couldn't fill two bus seats with her rear-end, and certainly not

a skinny foreigner who, even from that one-by-one-inch passport photo, appeared to have the figure of a dried-up chicken bone. But to her dismay, Sami was alarmingly loyal to the chicken-boned lady. He greeted Yosra no different than he would a great aunt who had come to pinch his cheeks. They talked only of schoolwork and universities and, at the most excruciating moments, the weather up in Damietta. It was particularly hot that year, yes, hot enough to bake bread on the sidewalks. Suad was ready to pry their lips together with her own hands, if she had to.

After the house emptied, she phoned Sami. She could hear his train departing as he brushed off questions about Yosra. Later, it came out that chubby little Yosra was quite taken with the older boy and had told all her friends about him. Suad told her to give it time. And since then, that was all they had. Time.

*****

Playing matchmaker reminded Suad of her own engagement so many years ago. She was the eldest girl in her family and as such, her parents had a particular anxiety over her that dissipated by the time it reached the fifth daughter. Back then, she was just a girl. One day she turned around and had an enormous rack, the bane of her existence and the subject of all the local boys' whispers and giggles. She hated them all, except for one: Gamal the gas man.

Gamal came to their apartment every month to fill up the gas canister in the kitchen. Unlike all the boys at school, he was tall and didn't have one of those awful pre-pubescent mustaches. He had a smooth face and a dimple on his chin, perfect teeth and a flop of slick hair like Abdel Halim Hafez. He would smile to her from the street each time he came around, and Suad would wait for him in those days. She knew his schedule exactly: the first Monday of the month. Abu Radhi was the last neighborhood on his route, and he'd reach it right after making the rounds in El Nasser and El Sadaat. It would be afternoon by then, the unbearable, humid hours. After finishing her schoolwork she'd wait by the window until she saw him coming—keychain dangling from his finger, sweat casting a sheen on his light brown skin—and she'd perch on the sill and wave, making sure that her breasts were pushed up as high as possible under her dress. It was shameful, but it was only for Gamal. She was sure that nobody else would notice until the day their conversation got personal up in the dark, hot apartment.

It was the first time she baked date cookies all by herself, and she invited Gamal to take some home. He declined politely. A hot flush spread from her temples all the way down to her toes as she imagined that he must be married. She looked at the powdered crumbles in her hands and asked if his wife made them too. He said he didn't have a wife. And the words made her so happy that she broke into a smile, the kind of smile that's pulled so hard across the face that it hurts, the kind of smile that gave her away. In the other room, Teta was listening and knew exactly what was happening. She saw the smile. She heard the singsong voice. She noticed the tight dress Suad happened to be wearing that day and come to think of it, *every* day that Gamal the gas man came around. Later, she cornered Suad.

*All the boys in the neighborhood are calling your name.*

*Oh?*

*They see what you do with Gamal and they think they can do the same.*

*Wallahi, I don't do anything with Gamal.*

*It doesn't matter. They think you do. And soon they'll be lining up at the door calling, ya Suad, ya Suad!*

Not long after, Suad found herself sitting in her living room beside her second cousin, Mahmoud. She'd only met him at weddings and funerals, the kind of events her parents had to drag her to. This time he came with a ring and a dish of baklava just for her. He was no Gamal but he seemed OK, so she took the ring on her finger, the pastry into her parched mouth. It wouldn't go down. She had to spit it out into a napkin when he wasn't looking. Her mother scolded her with an eye from across the room. She wanted to scream. The time had come for her to marry, apparently, and nobody cared what she thought about it. They didn't even ask. She went on to wed Mahmoud and moved into the big house on the edge of town. It was outside of Gamal's gas route. She never saw him again, but his image remained as sharp and vivid in her mind as that day in the kitchen, when she stood close enough to feel his breath.

From time to time Suad wrote Gamal letters, the kind not meant for sending but for hiding away in bedside drawers. Her first letter was sparse—she didn't know what to say other than *I miss you*—but by the time her husband left for the Gulf, she had a flurry of news. She wrote of her lemon grove, her children, her regrets over marrying Mahmoud. *I should have said no*, she wrote on page after page, all covered with broken-hearted scribbles that Gamal would never see.

Later she realized that she didn't get married as a regular course of action, according to schedule. She got married because Teta thought she was a slut. She figured it out with each successive sister. Nobody pushed plain, big-footed, studious Sara to get married at that age. There was nothing to worry about with her. It was the same with Salma, who wore glasses under a too-tight hijab. Then there was Sabah, who cared only for baking sweets and going to bed as soon as the sun went down. But when Sanaa turned seventeen and started holding hands with a boy in class, she was married off right away. Marriage was for the sluts.

\*\*\*\*\*

Suad spent the whole morning on her knees, ripping weeds out of the dirt between trees. She kept her phone in her pocket in hopes that at last, Sami would call.

Each time it rang, she'd wipe off her hands with two firm thigh pats and hold her breath, yet each time, it was everybody else: Sana, yelling over a crying baby; Hagg Ali, whose delivery boy wouldn't come that day; nosy Nagwa, whose presence never ceased; Ayah, putting off her schoolwork; Amo Ahmed, breathless from memories of the riots in 1952. Even Mahmoud called, and they shared a few lines of small talk over the course of a whole minute as she knelt on muddy knees in the weeds.

When Suad hung up, she looked at her forlorn phone and figured she might as well try Sami once more. Her thumb hovered over the speed-dial for the duration of the pre-recorded message that she would inevitably hear.

*The number you have dialed is not in service. Please hang up and try again.*

*The boy you have dialed is busy sinning. Please let go and look away.*

*The city you have dialed is now revolting. Please shut up and let the kids have their way.*

Suad heard that miserable recording so many times that it began to taunt her as the dial log reached triple digits. By that point, there was a faint callus at the tip of her cramped thumb, and it stung from the acid of lemons where the skin parted. She paid it no mind as she continued her work, even more vigorously than before.

Weeding was a regular task, especially after a good rain, but there had never been so many. The nasty little things were the jinn of her garden. They appeared abruptly—one moment, she would be saying goodnight to unblemished, freshly raked soil, and in the next all her lemon trees would be choked by green monsters covering the ground like rabid spiders. They tended to appear when her spirits were low, which was quite often as of late.

Since dawn that day, the weeds had either multiplied or Suad was seeing things. She could have sworn there were only a dozen to begin with, but after hours of weeding there were a dozen more. These demons were relentless. She moved quickly to catch them all, scanning the ground, up and down, until a fresh one caught her eye. And with both annoyance and pleasure, she got down in the dirt and ripped it out of the soil, careful to make sure she got every last one of its damned, dirty roots. *I got you, demon.* Soon she filled a whole sack with weeds ranging in size from a rosebud to a head of lettuce.

It was Giddo who'd taught her how to weed properly, to grip the plant at its base and shake every tentacle loose. Somehow, he'd learned the ways of the land despite spending his life in factories. He said it was in his blood. Just the memory made her feel like bursting to tears right there in the grove. What a loss. Deep down in the unmentionable recesses of her mind, Suad sometimes grew tired of relying on God. There were so many prayers that had gone unanswered. Gamal never reappeared again. Sami had become

even less religious. And not once did Mahmoud suffer divine payback for scorning her. In fact, things seemed swell on his end. She was tired of wishing and waiting for all these men who'd disappointed her, and ironically, it was only another man—the first man, Giddo—who could console her. There were times, like this, when what she needed wasn't faith but flesh to hold close, words to cool her worries. Worries made worse by the sound of a door swinging open.

*Tut, tut, tut, screeeeech.*

On a balcony overhead, the neighbor woman Nagwa sat squat on her stool and hitched up her skirt to make room for the spinning wheel between her legs. She reached into a basket of freshly picked cotton puffs and fed each to the wheel, one by one, which spun them into thread with much groaning.

Suad's heartbeat quickened with the ticking wheel. From the ground she waved to Nagwa, who nodded but didn't stop spinning. What nerve, to come out and destroy the peace of the grove and not even say hello. Suad often thought of hurling a lemon straight at that contraption of hers—and she wouldn't feel bad about it, not one bit, because everybody else seemed to indulge Nagwa, starting with her family. They had a farm in Kafr El Sheikh and sent her a bushel of cotton each month to sate her useless obsession. Now spools of thread lay stacked at the edge of her balcony to gather dust, untouched.

What was her family thinking? Did they not find it odd she spent all that time spinning and neither sewed nor sold what she produced? They didn't seem to realize that for Nagwa, spinning cotton was more than a wasteful vice—it was a way to feign preoccupation while she sat on the balcony all day, scanning the neighborhood for gossip. That's what she was really after: stories to spread from one end of Mahalla to the next, as far as all those spools of thread would take her.

\*\*\*\*\*

Night fell, but neither woman would relent. Suad tried to block out the sound of the wheel as she moved furiously through the grove with a

flashlight. At the edge of the plot, she found a monstrous growth choking her best tree, one with ten lemons for every branch. It was over her dead body that she'd let this demon have its way with that tree.

Suad sucked on her wounded thumb as if to prepare it for battle. Then she started digging around the weed, feeling the wet earth under her nails. She grabbed its base and pulled and pulled until sweat formed at her temples, but its roots clung to the earth as if its life depended on it. But its life *did* depend on it, she smiled. She would take a break and come for it again in the morning, when she would have more strength and the sun by her side. Perhaps by then Sami will have called.

"Suad," called a woman's voice through the trees.

She stood to see Nagwa wading barefoot through the mud, slippers in hand. Suad had been so into the weeds that she hadn't realized the wheel had stopped, and that this time it didn't mean Nagwa was minding her own business. How could she be so silly? It had been hours since they last traded words and naturally, she was bursting with some new story to tell her.

"Any news from Cairo?"

"I've tried calling everyone." She shook her head with a flourish, like some kind of soap star. "*Everyone.* In-laws, cousins, classmates, people I had forgotten all about until now, like the girl from the bodega on Ayyad Street who married and moved away—you know, the one with the *bazaz*." With her hands she made two massive mounds over her breasts, snickering, but Suad wouldn't have it.

"Noha. How is she?"

"Not so good. Not one child yet. Ironic, isn't it? A girl like that could feed a whole orphanage with those *bazaz*." The stench of cigarettes wafted from Nagwa's clothes as she leaned toward Suad and whispered, as if the trees had ears. "They say her husband goes with men."

That's it. Suad chucked her sack to the ground and looked straight at the woman, eyebrow cocked, the way she looked at her children when they brought rubbish to her ears. By instinct, her eyes flitted to her feet where, in different circumstances, she'd reach for a slipper to brandish. But there was no slipper, and Nagwa was not her child, and—for God's sake—there was a horror afflicting the nation, if she hadn't heard.

"Anyway, enough about Noha, poor girl. What do you think caused this business with the phones in Cairo? I *still* can't reach my boy. I swear, if I get that dial tone one more time, I'm going to march all the way down to Cairo *myself* and request an appointment with the president at once."

"And say what?"

"I would say, 'Mr. President, I wish to speak for all mothers in Egypt.'"

"Ambassador Suad from Mahalla."

"I would say, 'Our nation is the mother of the world, and mothers are the backbone of our nation, and mothers are the—well, mothers—of our sons. And for the sake of all mothers and the terrible stress we are under, please fix these phones right now, Mr. President. Have mercy on the mothers of this nation. It's in the Quran."

"The phones?"

"No, silly." She shot Nagwa a cross look. It was hard to know whether she was being wicked or just dimwitted. "The Quran says: *We have enjoined on man kindness to his parents; in pain did his mother bear him, and in pain did she give him birth.* And right now, I could use some kindness."

"Well, wait till you hear this. Kholoud says they bombed the phone tower. That's why the phones are down."

Suad's eyes widened, but she reminded herself that this was Nagwa, a lady who embellished stories like the tufts of a wedding gown. If the news had come from anyone else, then the horror would have struck her dead right in the middle of the lemon grove—which granted, wouldn't have been a bad way to go, so long as she managed to remove every weed first. Sighing, Suad returned her attention to her tree. Nagwa was fiddling with a leaf, twisting its stem as she made things up. The leaf wasn't the best specimen, with yellowing edges—first sign of a coming death—but Suad had to bite her lip to keep from scolding her. There were more important issues at hand and, real or not, she should play along with Nagwa's story if only not to look careless.

"You're kidding. Who bombed the phone tower?"

"The Israelis."

"Of course."

"And Iran."

"*Ya salam.* You don't say."

Suad could tell there was a question at the tip of Nagwa's tongue as she continued fingering the leaf, this time even more vigorously, almost tearing the stem off wholesale. She braced herself.

"I noticed that your husband didn't come home this winter. Is everything alright?"

Suad reached for the yellowing leaf between Nagwa's fingers and ripped it off the branch. That was her answer. Nagwa had probably heard her yelp Mahmoud's name when he called earlier, setting the engines of her silly little mind reeling like that damned wheel of hers. Tales of bombs and war were pretty good, but they were nothing compared to the old-fashioned troubles of a marriage—especially *this* marriage, which had begun and unraveled and vanished through the tines of her cotton wheel. Obviously, it was the real reason she had come over.

Nagwa must have gotten the hint for once, because she didn't press further.

"Well, there's a lot of oil to pump out there in Dammam. *So* much oil. Really, way too much oil. I'm sure he's just busy, busy, busy."

"Yes," said Suad, "he is."

When Suad returned inside, she found a hypnotized Ayah hunched over the computer, back curved as a crescent moon. She looked like a thirsty palm bent over the river. About as mindless too, mouth hanging open without her knowledge, phone hanging limp in her hand, notebook draped carelessly over the keyboard, as if using all devices at once. An empty cup of lemon-mint juice sat before her, the drink so long-gone that the pulp had dried stuck to the glass. The girl hadn't even bothered to take off her hijab after class, nor her ratty old sneakers, which Suad hated—a pair to match her brother's, straight from some stall in El Muski strewn with bootlegged cassettes and neon lingerie.

"Girl," called Suad as she washed the dirt off her feet. "Aren't there better ways to spend your day? Don't you have studying to do, prayers to catch up on?"

Ayah didn't answer.

Suad walked toward her and slapped the phone out of her hand. "Sit up straight. What are you, a camel? Keep up like that and you'll end up hunchbacked like Hagga Warda. And no one will marry you."

"Egyptian in-*soor*-jens."

"What?"

"Egyptian in-*soor*-jen-t-s."

Crazy girl. Suad looked over Ayah's shoulder at her notebook, where in place of homework she'd scribbled unpronounceable English words. *Anarchy. Riot. Excessive force.*

"*In-sur-gent.* One who rises in opposition against lawful authority."

"Ayah," Suad clapped. "Did you hear what I said?"

The girl finally listened, but not without a childish groan. As she sat up, her back cracked from joints moving for the first time in hours, no doubt. Suad's eyes never left her as she leapt back into that notebook. She'd never seen Ayah so engrossed, other than say, the season finale of *Arab Idol.* What kind of nonsense was she reading about now? The girl's regular studies were silly enough—digital communication, whatever that was. Her test scores had been too low to enroll in medicine or engineering like her brother, but it didn't matter anyway. Upon graduation she'd marry and move into her husband's home just as Suad had. She tensed, as if she just then realized there were only a few more years until she'd be alone completely. All the more reason to rein in that ridiculous girl while she had the chance. And that meant none of this in-*soor*-jens business.

Suad pointed to the nonsense in her notebook. "Homework, girl. Where is it?"

"I told you a thousand times. I finished my homework. I'm all caught up with prayers, too."

Ayah looked up at Suad, eyes red and glossy behind cloudy lenses. It was time for new glasses. The poor girl had inherited her father's vision. Romantically, it didn't seem to hold *him* back, but Suad worried about her daughter. Glasses tucked into a headscarf was not a good look. Though she feared the day Ayah would leave her too, she was anxious to find her a suitor—if she missed the brief window between ripeness and rot, she might never find anybody, and the prolonged companionship Suad would get in return would in no way make up for the shame of having an

unmarriageable daughter. For now, the best she could do was to arm her
with charms of duty.

"Go fix your mother a cup of tea."

Suad sat down as Ayah scurried off to the kitchen. She returned with
an overflowing cup, tea sloshing onto the saucer, and handed it over with a
sigh, as if she'd exerted herself. The girl was hopeless. Suad held her tongue
as she watched Ayah return to the computer to watch some vile new video
from Tahrir Square. This time there was a bald man with a bullhorn. The
crowds gathered around him, cheering. He looked strangely dignified
despite the setting—almost handsome in his round glasses. Men were so
lucky, she thought, picking a lemon slice out of her tea. They could go bald
and wear unsightly glasses and still greet masses with arms outstretched.
She checked his finger for a ring but couldn't see through the chaos.

"Who's that?"

"Shhhh."

She slapped Ayah's fingernails out of her mouth. *Shhh?* The girl had
nerve.

Suad settled into the couch as the bespectacled man began to speak.
Suddenly, he didn't look so dignified. To her, at least. *You are the owners
of this revolution.* Revolution? Somebody ought to shoot her dead right
then. These hooligans in Tahrir couldn't be trusted to tuck in their shirts,
let alone lead a … a …

"In-sur-rection," said Ayah, proud to use her word of the day.

*What we have begun cannot go back.*

Suad swallowed the lemon rind and felt it sink slowly down her throat,
inch by inch, word by horrific word. Whoever this man was, he needed to
shut his mouth before kids like Sami and Ayah heard. They were foolish,
impressionable. Especially Sami, God protect him. He would follow his
friends off a cliff if they thought there was so much as a Kinder Egg on the
other side. The thought that she couldn't reach him at all while there were
people out there screaming rubbish into microphones in the same streets
he walked in Cairo—well, it was too much to bear. Suad's throat tightened
as breaths struggled to get out. She took a sip of tea thinking it would help,
but all it did was drown her, rushing into her throat like the river tide.

Tea could do nothing to calm Suad now. Nothing could. All those words of solace she'd always told herself—that everything would be fine—had proven to be false, zilch, meaningless. Everything was *not* fine. The realization filled her with a bitterness that no amount of sugar cubes could fix, though she tried, stirring a fourth helping into her tea.

*****

As the night marched onward, Suad heard the *tut-tut* of Nagwa's cotton wheel starting up again. She slammed the window shut, making sure to be as loud as possible. Some things were perfectly normal tonight, and *that* was absurd.

As absurd as Mahmoud calling twice in one day.

She almost choked on her tea when his name appeared yet again on her screaming phone. She had to look twice to make sure she'd read it correctly. No, it wasn't her uncle Ahmed, nor was it Yasser the trash man, who shouldn't have her number, anyway, but she wouldn't be surprised. Her hands shook around the phone, which vibrated to match. There he was, her husband, calling twice in one day. On the last ring, she took a deep breath and answered in a sweet, syrupy voice.

"What's gotten into you, Mahmoud? Do you miss us here in Mahalla?" She stood up with the phone—it was the kind of call that demanded she be on her feet and at attention, ready for whatever bad news her husband had in store for her. Certainly not reclining on the couch.

"What, I can't call my wife when I want to?"

There was violence in the laugh he delivered back to Suad. It enraged her. How dare he laugh. How dare he call her his wife. How dare he reveal that happy, rootless tone that could only mean one thing—he was mocking her in the presence of another woman. Maybe that woman was beside him at that very moment, wearing a silken nightgown, listening in and cracking jokes at his aged wife back in poor old Egypt. She was sure they had a nice, plush bed out there in Dammam, and a stable full of maids and hot water from the taps and cold air from vents in the walls. She asked him if he had her on speaker phone, but he said he did not, though the connection sounded off to her ears.

Mahmoud moved on quickly though, as he always did.

"Have you heard anything from Sami?"

"No."

"No?"

"Why don't you try calling him yourself? I've been calling all day. The phones are still out."

"Look, *ya* Suad. I've been busy out here in Dammam. Barrel prices are through the roof and I'm losing a fortune each second I spend relaxing. I only have a minute to talk tonight and I chose to talk to you. I could have …"

"Could have what?"

"Never mind. Anyway, stay safe out there. Keep Ayah at home. Find Sami, please. I'm going to try to come next week."

"Next week?" Suad was gripping the phone so hard there was sweat between her fingers.

"I need to be in Egypt right now."

"How convenient, all of a sudden you need her and will get her."

Mahmoud grumbled but didn't change his plans. He requested a big plate of *molokhiya* ready for when he came home from the airport. She was also to buy a case of pomegranate soda and fresh tobacco for his pipe. Suad felt nauseated at just the thought of that pipe, and his foul, sullen mood when he smoked.

Feeling hot, she opened the window above the couch. A dog barked in the darkness outside. After hanging up, she returned to the couch and switched on MisrTV, which was much more reliable than whatever donkey dung Ayah had been watching.

Ayah snapped out of her daze. "Baba's coming?"

Suad swatted at her but hit only air. "Shhh, the news."

She fixed her eyes on the television screen, hoping to submerge the sour aftertaste of that phone call in the square jaws and smooth voices of late-night anchors. But all she could hear was Mahmoud, the audacity and violence of his cheerful tone. *I need to be in Egypt now. Bah!* How generous of him to bestow his presence upon them for the first time in what—a year? The one thing she had on him—the *one* thing that gave her a tinge of satisfaction—was that she was in Egypt, where this so-called revolution was taking place without him.

Suad turned up the volume, in search of any word at all from Cairo. But the news made no mention of the protests at all, which only worried her more. It must be *really* bad. "Ayah," she said, uneasy with the sound of her voice as she asked, "have you heard anything from Tahrir?" She took another sip of tea to wash down the word, *Tahrir*—just uttering it made all the hysteria more real.

Ayah beckoned Suad to the computer. Cautious, she inched closer. As Suad watched over her daughter's shoulder, she gasped, blinked, bit the inside of her lip. She tried to find something redeemable in the unrest, something to boast to her husband upon his return. But as expected, in Tahrir there were only hooligans, young men with too much time on their hands and too little money in their pockets. Instead of spending their Friday at the mosque, they chose to set cars on fire and run like wild animals through the streets, screaming in the faces of police officers who defended the city. The protesters almost looked foreign to her, Afghan perhaps, and she asked Ayah if they were indeed Egyptian.

"Can't you hear them? *Hold your head up, you are Egyptian.*"

And the thought that these were locals was somehow even more disturbing. Egyptians, just like her Sami. Oh, if she could only get to Cairo. She felt her pockets for spare change, but she had none. All the banks had been closed for days. The only way to get there was by car. Suad didn't know how to drive and had never particularly wanted to. Until now.

Ayah slid her fingernails into her mouth again, but this time Suad let her. As the girl sat entranced, Suad slipped out of the house in search of the old Peugeot. She could see its shadow in the dark, sitting in its decades-old spot under a pair of Siamese-twin banana trees, one dead and one flourishing. In her haste, she rammed her toe into the tire and set off the alarm. It rang out for a few torturous seconds until, with her good foot, she gave the old tin box a kick and it stopped.

The night settled back into its proper silence. Through the kitchen window, Suad could see Ayah right where she left her, the "revolution" too transfixing, apparently, to hear the alarm. *Mashallah*. If only she could apply that focus to her chores.

Mahmoud had left the car behind as a gesture of so-called goodwill, though if you asked Suad, *she* was the one with the goodwill for taking in his junk. That's what it was, after all. The old thing broke down so often she gave up driving it years ago, and now the only one who ever sat behind its wheel was Ayah, who seemed to have better luck for some reason. She had always refused Ayah's offers for help, thinking it pathetic to need a child's aid to do a thing as silly as that. *To drive? Just put your foot on the pedal and turn the wheel! How hard could it be?* But tonight, as Suad found her way into the front seat, she wished she had accepted the offer just once—if only to know which key would start the car.

Suad ticked off the keys she recognized as she fumbled before the ignition. There was the key to the house, the key to the grove's gate, the key to Sami's dorm room, the key to her parents' house in Abu Radhi. Each dangled from its own trinket, keychains of the Pyramids, the Sphinx, and a calligraphic *Allah*. When she realized the key for the ignition was the same one that had unlocked the door, she let out a satisfied *a-ha*. She turned on the car, spirits soaring, on the road at last. But a loud beep struck her down. There wasn't a drop of gas left in the tank.

Before returning inside she sat for a while in the front seat just to grip the steering wheel a bit longer. It was bigger than she'd imagined, and she had to strain to see over it. She wished more than anything to speed straight down to Cairo, queen of the road, over the river and into Zamalek where she could find her son safe and sound. And alone. *Inshallah*.

# 7

Jamila was elbow deep in dishwashing suds when she heard a phone ringing down the hall. Not again. She waited for the ringing to stop, but of course, it didn't—Sami had stepped out, Rose was napping, and the mother on the other line was disturbingly persistent. When Jamila couldn't take it anymore, she threw down the sponge and went looking for the phone. She shook her head as she picked it up off the bedroom floor.

The regime had finally restored service—calls only—but it seemed Sami didn't care. The phone was never on him, never answered. She was beginning to wonder if it wasn't an accident. One would think the service reconnection would make him cling to his mobile, never let it out of his sight, like she did with hers. One would *think* he wouldn't leave the little thing on the floor like a dirty sock, letting it ring unattended while he was out running errands. Then again, what did thinking have to do with anything nowadays?

On the screen flashed the caller. *Ummi*. As expected, it was his mother again. It still felt like lying to watch the phone ring, over and over, and to not do a thing to answer. It was right in front of her. With just a click, Jamila could say *hello*, explain Sami's whereabouts, and soothe his mother's worries if at least for the time being. But it wasn't any of her business. She set the phone on the dresser facedown, as if it made it less impolite to ignore, and got back to her chores in the kitchen.

Work was plentiful that day anyway. Crusty dishes and junk food wrappers peppered countertops, and black grime coated every nook—particularly by the windows, which Rose and Sami seemed to have left open during the protests, as if trying to let in the smoke. All the mess was the result of a week of canceled classes and nowhere to go. Nowhere but Tahrir, that is. But the only sign of any involvement on their part was a pair of soot-stained jeans in the laundry hamper. They were Sami's. It was confusing. She could sooner picture Fifi Shafik in Tahrir, where at least she might find opportunity for photos, a dramatic new backdrop to tally up likes. But Sami? He looked particularly morose lately. There were more empty cartons of cigarettes in the trash, and the apartment stank even stronger of hashish. He barely seemed to muster enough energy to get off the couch, let alone march in the street.

Jamila almost yelped when Rose walked into the kitchen, behind her.

"I'm all cooped up," she said, yawning. She placed an empty coffee cup in the sink and looked back at Jamila as if awaiting a response. But Jamila couldn't even figure out if it was a complaint. *Cooped up.* To her, staying in was far preferable to getting outside these days, but she had no choice. There were seventy-eight other Nilofone shops to locate, and two other employers with houses in the same disheveled, restless state. There was no time to rest—and certainly not as much as Rose, who seemed to need even more of it the less she had to do. Jamila had *never* slept that much. Not even back home in Omdurman, where she and her siblings stayed up late to enjoy cool nights, and mornings rose early to the crowing of chickens. It must be because of the pregnancy. She stiffened at the memory of the little white stick in the trash as she swept the kitchen, the broom heavy, the floor like thick mud.

"I'm not sure if I told you," said Rose, standing by the door. "On Thursday we're going to the Sinai, so we'll be out of town for a few days."

Jamila stopped sweeping. For days, the woman hadn't ventured outside for so much as a bottle of water and yet, she saw fit to go on vacation. In the middle of all this … this whatever-was-happening. Rose had already seemed detached from reality when she was complaining of rest. Now she seemed as reckless as a Molotov cocktail soaring across Ramses Street— the same street she would brave to travel to the one place more dangerous, Sinai, which had been lawless even before the protests, a deathtrap for many Sudanese who tried to cross the border for asylum, only to be held hostage for whatever petty ransom they could get. The rumors had traveled all the way back to Omdurman, but she never believed them until she got to Cairo, where such stories were commonplace in that narrow little intake room at St. Fatima's.

Granted, Rose was white and not black, an expat and not a refugee. But the Sinai was still dangerous—far more than she understood. It wasn't Jamila's place to speak, but she felt that she must.

"It's unsafe, dear."

"Maybe. But it can't be any worse than here, right?"

Jamila returned her attention to the floor to keep herself from shouting. Rose seemed to notice. From the corner of her eye, she could see Rose's gaze drop to the tiles, following the broom strokes.

"Look, I get it. It's not the smartest move in the world. But we booked this trip months ago. And you know, it's my birthday. The protests are exciting and all, but it's no way to celebrate."

"I understand," said Jamila, though she didn't. There was no stopping Rose. She was a glass bottle heading straight for a concrete wall.

"You're welcome to stay in the apartment while we're gone."

It took a second to process this strange, unwanted invitation. Stay there? As if she lived there? As if it were *her* key that fit the lock? She looked up to the ceiling, where ornate moldings swirled around a crystalline light fixture. The apartment was a palace compared to her cinderblock room in Kilo 4.5, but that wasn't the point. Nobody wanted to sleep in somebody else's bed—no matter how plush and comfortable it was compared to the flattened mat that awaited her tonight.

"Please, Jamila. It's safer for you in this big building. You can chain the entrance shut, bolt the doors. Abu Ali is usually here, so long as the pharmacy is open. And you won't have to travel as far to get to work. The other houses you clean are in Dokki and Zamalek, right? Practically a couple of skips across the river." When Jamila still didn't respond, Rose took a breath and continued. "It's safer for us too. You know, you don't want to leave your house empty with all these looters running around."

Alright, Jamila nodded. Now that Rose had revealed the offer was more of a favor, she felt more appropriate accepting. There would be no debt to repay. Besides, Jamila was used to making herself uncomfortable in order to comfort others—it was part of her job. She watched a grin spread over Rose's face, like daylight. It felt good to please her, to do as she wanted, because she sensed she was the only one doing so as of late.

"We leave the day after tomorrow," Rose said, still smiling. "I'll leave the keys under the doormat for you—and please, make yourself at home. My house is your house."

Jamila thought they were done talking but Rose lingered in the kitchen, making herself a cup of coffee. Nescafe this time, no cardamom—they were out of the good stuff. While the water boiled, she could feel Rose's eyes on her belly, a word screaming to leave the tip of her tongue. At last she spoke.

"Jamila."

"Yes?" She set down the soapy dish in her hand and turned off the faucet, anticipating something serious, judging from Rose's uncharacteristic caution.

"When you read my coffee cup the other night …"

Jamila sighed, reaching for the faucet again.

"Did you see anything about a baby?"

This time she let the water run. "No," she said, shaking her head with a touch too much vigor. No she did not—she'd seen *nothing* of the sort, not in the coffee cup, not in the trash.

"Like, not *ever*?"

"I didn't see anything."

"Oh."

As Rose reached for a mug from the cabinet, her T-shirt shifted to reveal a sliver of flat stomach. No sign of pregnancy yet. Soon it would be unavoidable, the question pointless. Hopefully by then she and Sami would be married, if only for the sake of appearances. Jamila hated the thought of Rose with a big belly and no ring on her finger. She didn't know what came over her when she blurted, without thinking, as if it was any of her business, as if they were the friends Rose so badly wanted them to be, "Do you think you two will get married?"

Rose's eyes fell into her coffee cup as she stirred in powdered creamer. She took a deep breath as if she were about to speak but cut herself off— as if her tongue cramped up in that moment, as if a gust of ashen air had caught her throat in a stranglehold. She looked like she wanted to run off to the bedroom, leaving Jamila in the kitchen unanswered, in equal need to disappear. But Rose would never do that. So she took a sip of coffee, licked the foam off her upper lip, and looked straight at her. "I don't know," she said. Her eyes, though, said otherwise.

*****

Jamila had thought it was foolish to venture out in search of food. She told Sami as such, in the best way she could, when he expressed his revolutionary idea to go grocery shopping after a week of subsisting on little else but canned fava beans. *Now* he thought of that? As if days of fire and carnage had spurred him, finally, to seek basic sustenance. As if somewhere in that ashen city, there existed an open shop, or at least a stray vegetable cart. Jamila certainly hadn't seen one. When she peeked into Alfa Market that morning, there was nothing but a cracked jar of Président cheese rolling on the floor, unwanted by looters who'd wanted everything else: water and soda (fuel for protesters), bread and cookies (for the street children), even laundry detergents and broomsticks (items made irresistible by the free-for-all). So, she wasn't optimistic about what Sami would find, especially with his phone left behind yet again. He had no idea how far he would have to journey to find a single loaf of bread. To her surprise, though, he came back hours later bearing groceries like gifts in his arms.

"You wouldn't believe how deserted this city is," he said, catching his breath. "Well, apart from Tahrir."

Rose leapt to her feet and threw her arms around him, as if he'd come back from war. Jamila looked away as she gave him a kiss and asked, like a child, if he'd seen anything exciting.

There was a shade of disappointment in his black eyes. "Not really. I tried to stay out of all the dangerous areas. El-Galaa, Mohamed Mahmoud. Only hopped on Ramses when I was close enough to make a run for it."

Jamila both smiled and rolled her eyes as she took the grocery bags and set them on the counter. That Sami. Other men would have embellished the danger, some might outright lie. Especially those like Sami, with something to prove. Yet he was too honest for his own good. That was probably why he screened his mother's calls—he might let slip that he was not in the dorms, but in Ramses, with his *girlfriend*, who was *pregnant*. Then everything would come crashing down. That foolish honesty reminded her of one of her brothers, Malik, whose rear end met the sole of a slipper all too often because of it. To Jamila it was both endearing and worrisome, knowing what she knew now.

Sami opened a carton of mango juice and drank straight from it. Jamila dove for a glass. "It took forever," he continued, "but I finally found a man selling looted goods outside a church in Shubra. Everything was two, three times the price, but at that point I didn't care. Would you?"

Jamila shook her head, though she wasn't sure if he was talking to her. She was too distracted thinking of what she'd cook for today as she unloaded the grocery bags. Neither Sami nor Rose could cook, so they usually left meals up to her. They were content with anything she whipped up, so long as it would last for repeated reheating throughout the week, with enough left over for Jamila to take home for herself. What would they eat if it weren't for her? Chips and cookies from the kiosk at the corner, no doubt. Greasy takeout every night of the week. Several times Jamila had offered to teach Rose to cook, but she never was interested.

It turned out there was plenty to work with. Bread, tomatoes, basmati rice, even a bushel of okra. Wouldn't you know it—almost all the ingredients to make *bamiya*, an okra stew that Jamila would rather avoid. Hesitantly, she opened the cabinet looking for an excuse not to make it, only to find just enough salt and cinnamon. She set the spice jars on the counter with a huff. There was no question. Tonight she would make *bamiya*, a dish she at once cherished and loathed, a dish that would bubble in the pot before her, nevertheless. She hummed as she scooped tomato pulp out of a can, a song she couldn't place stuck in her head.

There was a time when she couldn't even stand the smell of it. *Bamiya* stirred too many memories to bear. It was an old favorite, synonymous with her childhood in Omdurman, and thus when she fled she left behind any urge to make it, taste it, smell it, or even hear its name ever again. At one point Miss Fifi had made it for a ladies' lunch (the one time she cooked, it had to be *bamiya*) and Jamila had to hold her nose as she mopped the apartment, over soaping the bucket in hopes the scent of suds would fill the air instead.

The smell of the stew, with its minced garlic and cumin, conjured more than just memories, but ghosts. That of Jamila's mother. The house she grew up in. She could practically hear the metal latticework on its windows creak in the wind. They no longer existed, but *bamiya* would trick her, if only for a second. And in that foolish second it was hard for her to separate then and now, and she swore she could hear her mother calling her name, and the warm little fingers of her youngest brother, Idris, tugging at her leg. Sometimes the feeling was so strong that her skin would turn into the plucked hide of a chicken, covered in goosebumps, hairs standing on end. Then she would remember everything she wanted to forget—that it had been three years since she lost everything and came to Cairo, where she lived in a sunflower-seed-strewn slum with no name instead of her family home, which had been turned by fire into dust along with the bones of everyone she loved. It was too much for Jamila to bear. Not then, not when she was all alone, not after everything that had happened and before anything good came along to strengthen her heart— because surely, good always accompanied the bad, as the Prophet said. For years, she'd waited for that something good with her nose held.

Eventually she confronted the reality of not having options. If there was okra on the table, then it must be eaten. Besides, there was no better way to cook okra than stewed with tomatoes and poured over rice. And she made it and smelled it and ate it and made it again. Now she didn't need to hold her nose anymore, and she looked straight into the bubbling pot and saw nothing but hot stew.

*Bamiya* wasn't just any dish, like sheep's offal or hoof stew. It was more complex, more to it than money for the butcher, and as such it was one of the recipes her mother taught her as Jamila neared the age of marriage. Before then, she only knew how to make foul and eggs for her siblings, simple breakfasts that would keep their bellies full until nighttime. But to be the best bride on the Nile—as her mother wanted—would require a full repertoire of household services. Bread baking, cattle feeding, rising at dawn. It turned out that preparing for marriage was good training for being a maid, as she would later become, unforeseen by anyone.

Looks were not enough, though they all praised God that she had them. Literally. Jamila was often greeted with a *mashallah*. It wasn't always the case. When Jamila was young she was too skinny, with long limbs that could never fill out no matter how much clotted cream her mother rammed down her throat. Her hair would never grow, so she gave up on smothering it with oil each night and instead kept it braided. She was taller than most of the boys in school, and she was always outdoors, letting the sun tint her skin to a rich chocolate. Even now, standing in that kitchen in Ramses, Jamila could feel her mother's iron grip around her wrist, the way she would hold her arm up to the wall and yell this and that about genes and geography and the treacherous sun, and how they all had conspired to doom any chance of her finding a husband. *You can go outside when there's a ring on your finger!* No whitening cream worked—not even the elixir of milk and sandalwood that her mother swore had turned an aunt's skin to honey. Jamila remembered that aunt and the fishlike pallor that had become of her face, and was thankful no such remedy had worked for her.

Cruelest of all was her name, Jamila, which meant *beautiful*. Naturally, it became a joke in the classrooms of Al-Safwa primary school. There couldn't *be* a worse name. She wished her mother had chosen something more serious, like Khadija for the wife of the Prophet, or Iman, simple and true. Anything but *Jamila*, a name that reminded her that she was *not* beautiful, a name that was too comically ironic for any grade-school boy to resist. Until it was not.

One day everything fell into place, as if all that clotted cream had caught up to her overnight to fill out her thighs and hips, turn her from gangly to goddess. Her face matured to match her features, no longer goofy but now something like her mother, who seemed to love her even more because of it. Suddenly her name wasn't so ironic anymore, and she learned to like it, even in the harsh, gummy Egyptian accent.

Her mother acted fast to marry Jamila off, calling up all her friends in search of eligible men. It was only a matter of weeks until she got her first suitor, and in a few months' time, four men asked for her hand. But none succeeded.

The first was Ali, who sold peanuts from a cart in the vegetable market at Al-Masalma. One day he saw her, made seven-feet-tall by the crate of sweet potatoes she carried on her head, and he proposed the same night. It was an instant no. Not from her, but from Baba, who saw no need to rush and accept the first offer, especially from a peanut man from the wrong clan. He sent Ali off with a friendly *I'll think about* it as Jamila watched from behind the door, relieved. Her first suitor had caught her unready.

Then there was Bilal, who would have been a good choice if he were only half a foot taller. He would gaze up at her in admiration, dreams in his eyes—not so much of her in a wedding dress, but of sons who could see over the back of a horse. Then came Hatim, who ruled himself out with his unsightly henna-dyed beard. Baba wasn't impressed either. Next.

The last suitor was the best. To her, anyway. Mohsen was a young doctor, a good match by measures of height and profession and intellect and looks. But there was one problem—her father hated his. Baba warned Jamila not to marry the descendant of a long line of swindlers and usurers—a bloodline which, according to him, would make itself apparent no matter his education or wealth. One day she would awake to find all her jewelry gone, sold for new tires, for instance. He would suck the whole family dry, pawn off every penny.

Just wait, said Baba, and another would come.

But he never got to greet another suitor. Not long after that, the rebels came and destroyed everything. The house, razed. The bones of her family, sunk into the Nile. And Jamila, a missing appendage flailing alone in the wind. She left Omdurman in the trunk of a Toyota, a single woman in her fast-waning prime, wondering what would have happened if she hadn't succumbed to her father's distaste for Mohsen, as if it would have changed the whole family's fate altogether. Maybe her father would have mellowed by age or bearing grandchildren would have softened his grudges. She and Mohsen could have moved away to Khartoum, far away from their families. Perhaps if she'd resisted, if she'd said the right thing, added one more lump of sugar to his tea, awoken on her left side and not her right—then none of this would have happened at all.

Time and time again, she reminded herself there was no hiding from fate. It wasn't easy to swallow but she supposed it made her feel better when she found herself in Egypt, all alone. In Cairo, she was stunned by the crowds, the cars, the sea of unfamiliar faces who stared but didn't see her. It seemed certain that she would never marry. She resigned herself to a life alone, thinking it was better that way considering her situation, until one afternoon in Khan El Khalili.

It was her first job when she arrived in Cairo. She would walk the alleys of the old bazaar and paint henna onto the hands of foreigners for a few guineas.

One area in particular was a hot spot for peddlers—a café called El Fishawy, where tables lined the alleys and were always full of customers puffing from water pipes and sipping tea. To show off her skills, Jamila would paint swirling flowers onto her own hand and walk past with tubes of black and red ink in her palm. She learned quickly to ignore the Egyptians and go for the white people (some of the whitest she'd ever seen), tourists who accepted the first price she gave them and said thank you in funny accents as they parted. One afternoon, she was painting the freckled forearm of a middle-aged Swede when a man tripped over her foot and caught himself just in time. When she looked up, he was trying to balance a crate full of bread on his head. Her face grew hot just looking at him. She could sense the Swede watching her from her chair, but she didn't interrupt, hand held out, wet ink drying in the heat.

After the Swede paid and left, the man came back around and introduced himself as Yusuf. As he came closer she noticed a thick fringe of lashes that lined his eyes like kohl. Later, when Yusuf was hers, she found out those eyes came from a distant ancestor, Ibn-so-and-so, who traveled from the Red Sea on horseback carrying a sword and a satchel full of pearls. He made it all the way down the Nile to a village not far from her own, where he spawned a man she had somehow missed all her life, only to find years later in Egypt, at the mouth of that same river.

# 8

The million-man march had yet to begin, but the bridges and corniche were clogged to a standstill as the brave few who ventured out—Sami included—raced to get where they needed. That morning, what he needed was coffee. They'd run out at home and much of the city was still frozen in a post-apocalyptic state. It was rumored that Café Tasseo was not only open but stocked with enough coffee to fuel the revolution for another month—reason enough to brave the crush of traffic.

Sami sat in the vinyl back seat of a microbus, counting the minutes that passed without movement. Five, ten, fifteen. The bus hadn't moved an inch for the duration of an entire Umm Kalthoum song.

"That's how you measure time here," said Rose, beside him.

"We measure time here?"

"Only with Umm Kalthoum," she smiled, looking more cheerful than she had in days. The sun beamed into the dark little bus and cast a golden glow to her hair, and she'd never looked as pretty as she did right then, framed by soot and disarray. "It takes one listen of 'Enta Omry' to get to Heliopolis on a good day. But if there's an accident, *ooof*," she shook her head, smile remaining. "Then it'll take a whole performance of 'Alf Leila wa Leila'—one of the later recordings from the 70s. You know, when she was a real diva, and nobody minded an hour-long instrumental while she caught her breath."

And if it was a day that promised the biggest demonstration yet, then it took a whole play of 'Fakarouni' just to make it to Tasseo—a trip that should have taken no more time than an 'Aini ya Aini' B-side, on the worst day.

"Let's just walk," said Sami.

They jumped out of the microbus at a defunct falafel shop, which marked the location of a nameless alley that led to the café. As they walked Rose pointed toward the sky. Up above, multicolored cutouts of stars and crescent moons hung from wires zigzagging across the alley. It wasn't anything they'd never seen before, but there was an enchanted look in her eyes.

"Someone didn't bother taking down their Ramadan decorations." He couldn't help taking her down a notch. It was a little disturbing that she could feel that way—gleeful, glowing—despite, well, *everything*.

Sami softened when they reached Tasseo. It was a happy place—one full of good memories, where he first met Rose and where they spent hours studying on more normal weekends. The door stood under a massive acacia tree that had grown against the side of the building, which was twice the size it was when they first met a year ago. Rose claimed she loved Tasseo *first*—before him, before they even met—because it was the only place she could get any work done. Most cafés in this part of town were full of old men, smoking waterpipes and playing backgammon on crowded tin tables. Tasseo was one of the few where you could actually get any work done.

Today was no different. Inside they found the usual crowd—expats and diaspora kids who spoke Arabic with an accent and couldn't roll their r's. They typed maniacally at laptops through clouds of nicotine, taking full advantage of their canceled classes—the third day in a row now. At this point school was out for the foreseeable future. Sami nestled comfortably into a booth by the window, savoring this break from the textbooks he hated, the classes he slept through when he wasn't skipping. The petrochemical morass that would consume him on any other Tuesday. He ordered coffees and toast for the two of them, then turned to Rose.

"Can you believe this place is open?"

"Of course it's open," said a young man in thick-framed glasses from the bar. "Tasseo is where this revolution started." He held out his hand and introduced himself as Ahmed, "a.k.a. RadicalAhmed82."

"Sami … just Sami."

"Nice to meet you Sami, Rose." He nodded in her direction. "Feel free to stay all day and talk, chat, mingle, read the news, whatever. We still don't have internet but Bassem over there is trying to figure out how to set up a VPN."

All around, hipsters yammered in their rolled-up jeans, pencils sticking out of their frizzy mounds of hair. Sami lit a cigarette and held it in the open window, listening as they debated all things Tahrir—the president, the army, the Brotherhood, the martyrs. He perked up at the latter. For all the men who'd set themselves on fire as of late, there was only one martyr people were still talking about. Khaled Said. A twenty-eight-year-old who the police had beaten to death last year in Alexandria. Apparently he was dealing drugs, or loitering at an internet café, or doing nothing at all depending on who you asked. One thing everybody could agree on—at least, everybody in the café—was that he shouldn't be dead.

The sound of cheering threw Sami off as a chiming rang through the café—one, two, three, four, five—a row of repeated dings that indicated SMS service was back. The whole place rejoiced. At first Sami jolted for his pockets, thinking it was Suad—he'd been conditioned by the sound—but the pockets were empty. On Rose's phone, he saw not the name of his mother (thank God) but the Supreme Council of the Armed Forces, better known as the army.

> We implore all loyal Egyptians to confront traitors and criminals.

> Protect our people.

> The nation is forever.

> Watch over her.

> Protect our precious Egypt.

The messages were less interesting than he'd expect, given their absurdity. He'd never gotten a message from the army. Who even thought of a thing like that? The army, texting? Anxiety gripped him as he realized that the restoration of service meant more texts would follow. There had been peace in disconnection, like being suspended in air and watching the world turn in silence down below. It was also the perfect excuse to avoid his mother. In a way he was disappointed that service was back—in many ways. Rose felt differently.

"That reminds me," she said, grabbing back her phone. "I need to call Tora."

"For Jamila?"

She rolled her eyes. "No, for fun."

Sami sighed, stubbing out his cigarette in an ashtray full of burnt filters. "You're wasting your time. Her husband is *dead*."

"So what? We have to try." Rose punched in the numbers, which she now knew by heart, and listened to the phone ring until the line cut.

"There are no police anymore, remember?"

"Shit."

*****

The café grew busier as more kids stopped in on their way to Tahrir for the million-man march. Sami watched a girl with tattooed arms use a broom-stick to turn on the ceiling fan. It was getting muggy in there with the hot breath of patrons who wouldn't shut up about the news. He thought the restoration of service would distract them, draw their attention to their phones, but it only seemed to fuel their chatter. The opposition's latest remarks and those of the vice president, thugs called hatchet men hound-ing the square. Sami spent the morning eavesdropping while Rose was strangely engrossed, scribbling notes on loose-leaf paper.

"What are you writing?"

"Just some observations."

"Observations of what?" He cocked his head to see, but all he caught was the word *Nadim* before she snatched it away.

"Tahrir, Ramses, the whole thing, know what I mean?"

Yes, this was a noteworthy moment, but what did that name have to do with it? He was struck with a flash of jealousy. Who even was this Nadim? It took a while to realize she was referring to a famous oud player they'd seen perform under the 15th of May bridge weeks ago. Nadim Salah. She said she liked the name—so much so that she'd consider it for her child. They had a huge fight after that.

For a second Sami wondered if Jamila had seen the baby in Rose's coffee cup last week. But that was ridiculous. Coffee cup fortunes weren't magic. They were just a way for women to pass the time. What they called fate was only a matter of circumstance—the way the grains settled into peaks and valleys had to do with the way they were brewed, or the temperature outside, or the residue left on the lip of the cup from each prior sip. Even if Jamila had seen a baby, which she didn't, she'd never say so. Instead she said something about diamonds, as if that's what he and Rose were—diamonds and not two idiots who'd made a terrible mistake.

It wasn't that he didn't love Rose. That part was certain. He had tried time and time again to imagine a parallel universe where their relationship could work out. They would do what they could to make it seem legitimate, like get married right now and claim prematurity seven months later. They would live in Cairo, obviously, because Mahalla was no place for a foreign wife and a half-foreign baby, born to an only son who should have done better. Maybe his family would finally accept her and they'd all drink lemon-mint juice together, Rose and Suad and Ayah gathered around the table, feeding rice pudding to little Nadim. Sami smashed the end of his cigarette into the ashtray, burning the tip of his thumb. It was impossible.

His eyes fell on the wall, which was covered in napkin drawings that fluttered under the force of the fan. He knew those drawings. He knew that wall. Leaving Rose to her scribbles, he got up and walked toward it, in search of one napkin in particular. It was a drawing of a bird, an ibis on the Nile. He'd copied it from a postcard Rose had brought back from Aswan last summer. He wanted to show off his dormant artistic skills, which he'd given up years ago when there was no longer any use. That must have been just after primary school, when everything he did started being scrutinized for its bearing on his future, its importance. And art was not important. Petrochemicals were.

Layer after layer, Sami peeled away napkins until he found the ibis. It stared back from its thumbtacked space on the wall, looking happy and rainbow-bright, signed by the two of them, dated too (July 31st, hottest day in a decade). At its feet were the unfortunate words: *Sami and Rose forever*. It still hung beside the same Fairouz lithograph. The thing hadn't moved in a year. And he realized, as if it were some revelation and not the natural conclusion of a feeling that had been festering in the back of his mind all along, that the measly napkin ibis would outlive their relationship. *Sami and Rose forever*, forever on that wall. A love more fleeting than torn paper. He thought about asking the waiters to take it down but couldn't bring himself to do it. His hand hovered at the napkin's edge, ready to rip it off, but he couldn't do that either. It was too final.

*****

Tahrir was so packed they couldn't even enter. They followed hearsay about a side entrance at the museum and snaked through crowds until they found a checkpoint controlling entry, with separate lines for men and women.

"Even the museum's been looted," said Rose, pointing to the enormous building looming above them. "The looters got in through the roof in the night. They smashed a few vases from the Ptolemaic era, ripped the head off a three-thousand-year-old mummy."

"Where did you hear that?"

"The news," she said, holding up her phone.

"Local or foreign?"

"Local. So you know, take it with a grain of salt."

Sami looked up at the museum. Its terra-cotta facade looked tangerine against the sky, which had dulled to a smoky white since the morning. There was no sign of the heist, which seemed surprising compared to the singed remains of the nearby Arkadia Mall. The looters, if the story was true, had been merciful to the museum. Thankfully. He'd only ever been there once, on a trip with his family when he was a boy. After years in Cairo, it was only now that he wanted to return.

"Apparently there are a bunch of criminals on the loose," she said. "I guess that's why there's so much security."

At the checkpoint there were no police officers, but instead citizens in plainclothes who searched the bags and pockets of each and every person trying to get to Tahrir. As Rose walked off for the women's line, Sami watched the tattered hem of her sweatshirt bounce against her backside. For once she'd followed his advice and wore baggy clothing, but some things were just hopeless.

When it was his turn to be searched, a heavyset man pulled him aside and asked him first to empty his pockets. Luckily, he'd packed light, with only the Meikorlens and a kaffiyeh that stank of vinegar—a remedy against tear gas, he'd learned. The man shook out the scarf, making a face as the stench wafted out. "Smart," he said, tying it to his neck. "But keep here to be safe." Then he searched the camera. He flipped open its battery compartment then peered through its lens, taking his time, holding it close to his eye as if he wasn't sure it was real. Sami had to admit was an odd contraption to carry into the square, clearly an antique. But what choice did he have? Bringing his phone would have been like bringing along his mother, shrunk down in his pocket, where she could scream at his every move.

"Identification?"

He slipped out the plastic card. As the man inspected it, Sami looked at the worn sneakers on his feet, affixed with a knock-off Nike logo. Straight from the factories of Mahalla. The place was inescapable. On his ID card, too.

"Sami Mahmoud Sukkary," the man read aloud, mumbling through the bristles of his beard. "From Mahalla. Muslim. Army?"

"No, I'm not in the army."

"Have you served in the army?"

"No, uncle, I'm an only son."

Sami felt the man's eyes scan him from his head and down the length of his body. Young and fit, two arms and legs, an inch or two taller than average. Unlike the pear-shaped man before him, Sami would've made a perfect soldier. *Would've*, but he wasn't. The government waived all only sons from conscription on account of their blessedness and all the responsibility that came with it. Perhaps the man would deny him entry for that same reason.

But the man said OK. He opened the gate and hurried Sami through, onto the next.

*****

Rose was waiting for him on the other side. The women's line had moved quickly. The guards hadn't even touched them.

In the middle of the crowds, though, all eyes were on Rose. People stopped her left and right on the way to Tahrir. Some thought she was a celebrity and asked to take pictures with her. Sami was always the designated picture-taker. He would roll his eyes behind the camera as they posed beside her, standing self-consciously with hands clasped before them, some waving flags in the air, some with clever signs. Some thought she was either a journalist or, just by virtue of being white, someone who should hear their struggles. As if she could do anything about it.

"Please, America," a man shouted at her. "Put a good president for us!"

Occasionally she'd turn the camera around on her subjects, who were happy to pose. One wanted to show off his hat made of bread rolls, and they laughed—a hearty, true laughter that was rare nowadays—until a man in a gray jacket swooped in and snuffed it out.

"No photos," he said, holding his arm out to block the lens. His voice was gruff to match the thick stubble on his face. He spoke as if he were the police, but he wore no badge.

"What do you mean, no photos?" She wrestled her camera over his arm. "Sami," she called out. "How do you say, *get away from me?*"

But before Sami could say anything, the man backed away and disappeared, swallowed whole by the crowd.

"What was that?"

"Who knows. Just stay right next to me."

He grabbed her hand to keep from drifting as they moved toward the epicenter of Tahrir Square. They seemed to move in circles, pushed round and round by the whirlpool force of the masses, which grew stronger by the minute as more and more poured into the square. Eventually the riptide won out, tight as he held her, and he lost her in the dense crowds near the KFC. Sami stood on tiptoes under its brash red banner, the chicken man's face smiling incongruously on, but he couldn't see through the signs and flags and funny hats. A stranger offered him a leg up. He stepped into the man's cradled hands and scanned the crowd. When Sami spotted Rose's dun-colored bun from afar, he leapt to the ground and hurried to catch up, apologizing for each shoulder brushed on the way.

The throngs dragged them deeper into the square as voices grew louder, unafraid.

"He steps down today," said one man.

"We need to be careful," piped in another.

"The Brothers are making a deal."

"A deal with who?"

"The regime!"

"Whatever happens, the president steps down. It's just a matter of time."

"No, no, you're mistaken. The Americans won't allow it."

The words sounded strange out in the open, fuzzy and warped as if he were listening underwater. Sami had never heard such commentary apart from chatty taxi drivers who at best, might complain about the price of tomatoes while stuck in traffic. He could barely recognize the faces around him, and even Tahrir itself looked different gridlocked with crowds and not cars. Though the masses blurred in motion, he tried to pick out threads of the familiar. A man with a prayer bruise on his forehead, like Abu Ali. A sliver of brown skin behind a face veil, like Jamila. There were even a few foreigners like Rose, though they tended to be actual journalists with cameras hanging from their necks. From signs and accents he counted representation from every city: Sohag, Suez, Mahalla, from one end of the Nile to the Delta, from the Sinai to the barren edges of the western desert. There were men and women, toddlers and elders, secularists and Salafists, Saidis from the south and Iskandaranis from the north coast. He even spotted the jerseys of Al-Ahly and Zamalek, two arch-rival national soccer teams whose fans were often in fistfights, but not today. They all shouted one word, *leave*. Some on the sidelines whimpered *the army and the people are one hand.*

In Tahrir, it didn't seem to matter anymore that he came from the farms of the Delta and not the villas of Zamalek, that he lived in the latter off subsidy from the rich, that his mother's love verged on embarrassing obsession, that his father had almost completely disappeared, that his whole existence was one of apostasy, that he'd fallen for the wrong person, Rose, and was awaiting the disastrous result the same way Giddo had awaited death with a dry mouth, open and wordless. He bumped into Salafists marked with beards and prayer bruises, who smiled and never said a word of the white lady on his arm, though he braced himself each time like a dog awaiting a kick. He saw university kids, the rich ones with houses in the suburbs, who greeted him like he was one of their own and not a bumpkin from Mahalla. He came across round women with tight hijabs and the same tired eyes as his mother, who raised their fists to his face and said nothing but *long live Egypt.*

In Tahrir of all places—the vast roundabout that he crossed each day, dodging traffic and tissue peddlers—he belonged.

# 9

Suad hated El Shoun. There, dusty roads crisscrossed to form the sandpit it called a town square, and it stank permanently of hot fuel streaming from cooling towers that watched from above. There was about a twenty-to-one ratio of men to women in the street, and even at her age she could feel gooey eyeballs stuck to her rear end as it shook with each step. It was these moments in El Shoun that reminded her to be grateful for her lemon grove. Imagine, the closest some people would ever get to paradise—which to her, was the feeling of damp earth between her toes—were grains of sand lodged in their sweaty shoes. *Poor souls*, she thought, *and lucky me.*

But for all El Shoun's unpleasantness, it was unavoidable—there were some things you couldn't find in any old bodega. Suad was in search of *molokhiya* and basmati rice, pomegranate soda and that nauseating tobacco for Mahmoud's pipe. The latter sat in a cupboard gathering dust since his last visit ages ago. She made a mental note to clean it when she returned home, just to give him one less reason to complain.

Today the crowds were thicker than usual. She strained to thread together all the disparate voices coming from car windows and market stalls. Camels and Tahrir. Thugs and the Pyramids. There was news and somehow those words were connected to it, and she was so distracted that she walked right past the spice souk and had to turn back. How could she help it? She was going on ten days with no word from Sami, and though he wasn't the type to get caught up in protests, she could never be sure. She calmed herself with the belief that at the very least, God knew. He knew about every leaf in the trees, from its birth to the day it fell.

Much like God knew the fate of each of the dried rosebuds that lay in an open sack before her. In a spice shop in a dark alley, Suad held a bag of saffron and scanned the shopping list in her head. The roses weren't needed tonight, though they always drew pause with their sweetness— buds snipped off at the stem, with un-sprouted petals ready to part and sprinkle over rice pudding. Around them, there were piles of sumac and thyme, hibiscus and dried chili, and a slew of powders of yellow and red and green, all the colors of the earth from brown all the way to the neon purple of indigo. The spices cast a complex musk around her, and she stood picking out individual threads of pepper and tartness, thinking of all the stews she could make with a stock like this—the best in town. Hagg Ali's shop was a secret of hers, operating out of an open garage in an alley that was shaded by clotheslines. He sold Suad the saffron for a special price of twenty guinea, a perk of being the cousin of his brother-in-law.

Suad had just tucked the saffron into her purse when she saw the boy, about six or seven, with gangly limbs and a honey-brown face. There was a dimple in his chin, and his hair lay in soft waves that shone like silk. He chased a ball bouncing from one side of the alley to the other. When he scooped up the ball, he flashed a mischievous grin, and she realized that he must be the son of Gamal, the gas man.

"If you don't stop it right now, I'll rip that ball to shreds with my bare hands."

A woman swooped in like a vulture, swathed in black, and yanked the boy off the ground. He smirked, holding the ball under his arm to protect it from those bare hands of hers. The woman still had the boy's arm in a death grip as she passed Suad, who stared at her with enough intensity to elicit a sideways glance. It had to be Gamal's wife. She hadn't any proof, but her instinct told her it must be true, for Suad never got these feelings for no reason. The fact that the woman had felt her gaze and looked back was evidence enough. It was the intuition of romantic rivals, however many decades apart.

And as she walked home to that house on the edge of town—the house that was outside of Gamal's gas route, where the city began to dissipate into fields of sugar, where she lost him forever—she could think of nothing but the woman's face. She was young, no more than thirty. And come to think of it, her eyes were long and fringed with thick lashes like his. Suad was sure that she was his cousin, this bitch of a wife.

*****

Today was a day for pickling, and to prepare, Suad had amassed three bushels of lemons and still had a surplus left over. She sliced each with a cross and watched their rinds open up to expose pulp like a blossoming lotus, then sprinkled in a mixture of seeds and saffron flowers. One by one, she dropped each lemon into a bubbling pot, and as she stirred, she watched the contents swirl like loose leaves in a cup of tea, turning the water to the color of rust to match its earthen odor. She realized she had been staring into the pot for minutes now, watching each seed sink to the bottom. It felt a bit like looking into the Nile, which ran red during winter floods.

The last time Sami visited, Suad sent a container of pickled lemons back to Cairo with him, against his will. He said they would stink up the train, that the brine would leak into his luggage and destroy his textbooks and he'd never again be able to crack them open in class because of the unforgiveable stench. Suad pushed aside her annoyance—*the stench, really?*—and used her iron grip to seal the jar shut. She covered it in foil and plastic several times over, until finally, he accepted the will of his mother.

"This isn't like him," said Suad. On a cutting board marred with crisscrossing scars, she chopped another lemon into paper-thin slices and threw them into two cups of tea, along with sprigs of fresh mint. She handed a cup to Ayah just in time to catch her rolling her eyes.

"Not answering the phone *is* like him, mama. This is how he is now." She picked out three sugar cubes from the crystal bowl on the counter—a wedding gift from a cousin more generous than Mahmoud—and stirred them into her tea, watching them turn to sludge before disappearing completely. Ayah looked like she was concentrating on the process, but Suad could tell she was thinking of something else. When she spoke, she divulged what Suad suspected.

"Look," said Ayah, pulling up the news from Cairo on her phone.

Suad didn't want to look, but how could she not? She slipped her Quran-reading glasses from where they hung on the collar of her dress and held the phone close as she took in unimaginable scenes. Deranged photos of men and beasts. Crowds so massive they looked like the sea. Flashes of flags alternating with the blades of machetes. "What is this, a serial?"

"Watch, there's more," said Ayah, tapping the tiled countertop. Her fingernails had been chewed to stubs, dulling the sound to a soft drumbeat.

Suad brought the phone right up to her lenses, as if each millimeter would help her make sense of it all. But it seemed that the more she learned, the less she understood. Apparently there had been another day of mass demonstrations in Cairo, led by a gang of troublemakers calling themselves "the Jan 25 Youth." They'd filled Tahrir with so many people that not one square inch of asphalt, not one blade of grass, not one cobblestone could be seen between them. And now—chaos. Bandits were tearing through crowds on camels and horses, slashing and trampling any bodies in the way. Suad's hands shook as the camera zoomed in on a man waving a machete from atop his camel, shouting something so awful it contorted his face. It was a face which, if Suad was being honest, looked like the work of a demon or perhaps drugs.

She wanted to tell Ayah to shut it off at once, but didn't. She couldn't look away, either, and invoked God's name because of it. Each time she thought that was it, enough was enough, heel readied to spin and walk away—there was one more rearing horse, one more cracking whip, one more punch from bleeding knuckles, one more sword swinging low, down to the crowds, as if human heads were sheaths of wheat to be culled by the blade of a scythe. She was tired of this, whatever it was, and it must end at once.

Her only comfort was that the president was trying everything he could. The other night he had calmed the nation with a televised address, in which he'd wisely cautioned the people against this banditry. "There is a thin line between freedom and chaos," said Suad, quoting him. She caught Ayah rolling her eyes again. That girl would never learn. How could she think it was a good thing, this chaos?

Suad was about to spin around and leave when she again noticed the poor shape of Ayah's fingernails. "See," she said, grabbing the girl's hand. "This is from all that typing. *Tac-tac-tac* on your phone, *tac-tac-tac* on the computer. Go to your room, Ayah, and fix your nails. Now." She snatched the phone as she turned to go. That girl.

*****

In the afternoon Hagg Ali sent one of his men to buy the surplus of lemons off Suad. There was much he could do with the spare lemons—the rinds could be preserved or ground into powder, and the pulp could be squeezed into juice to mix with mint or garlic. And so Hagg Ali's man arrived near afternoon prayer with a tuk-tuk and a burlap sack the size of a hot air balloon. When he stepped into the yard and called upon her, she rolled down her skirt to cover her muddy ankles and rushed to greet him.

"My apologies," she said, out of breath from her dash. "I couldn't hear through the trees." As she wiped the dirt off her hands, she realized that he was a new face. He wasn't Hagg Ali's usual helper, the wiry old Saidi. This was a young man, lanky and gilded, and when he turned to face her she felt as if she were a girl again, standing before Gamal in her parents' home in Abu Radhi.

"It's no problem," he said, averting his eyes with a slight smile.

The man called her *lady* and followed her to the pile of lemons she'd prepared for his arrival. Silently, she watched him scoop the good fruit into his parcel. All the while she scrutinized the way his cheekbones cut his face like the barbs of a feather, the way his muscles moved under his skin as if the latter was made of diaphanous silk. Like the boy in the alley the day prior, this man had the same lone dimple in his chin and the same head of hair that was so lush it looked like a toupee. Like the boy in the alley, he wore a serious look that just barely hid a smirk—an expression that begged her to keep looking. It occurred to her that he could be the boy's father. No—he wore no ring on his finger. Perhaps his brother.

"Does your family live nearby?"

"No, they live in Munifiya," he said, sweat forming under his crown of hair.

The stiff fists at her side loosened as he uttered the word *Munifiya*, lovely Munifiya which had nothing to do with Mahalla, and Suad found herself leaning closer as if she were trying to embrace the soft resonance of his voice—and him, it seemed. When she'd drifted to about a finger's width from the collar of his shirt, she stepped back and patted herself down as if she were hot, and then realized that her hand had made it to the top of her chest and had remained there, resting. She whipped it back at once. She must compose herself. This was not Gamal, nor was it the son he'd created with that bitch cousin that was half his age. He was a stranger, and to celebrate she offered him a drink.

"You must try my lemon-mint juice. It's famous."

As he followed her into the house, she didn't stop him or tell him to wait outside. He simply walked in and left his sandals at the door. Ayah was in her room and the house was quiet except for the television which played state news, a clip of the Qasr El Nil bridge in Cairo lying empty over a calm river.

"Is that from today?"

"Hmmm, yes," said Suad, "Or maybe not. Actually, I don't know." The truth was that despite all her efforts, she couldn't keep track of what was happening down there in the capital city, what was truth and what was fabrication. She thought of that hellish, demonic scream she saw from that man atop a camel in Tahrir and wondered how it was possible that he'd coexist in the same city shown on MisrTV right now, still and placid.

"*Mashallah*," he said, "the army must have cleared Tahrir quickly. Praise God."

"The TV is lying!" Shouted a disembodied voice from behind the wall.

"Pardon me, that's my silly daughter." Suad gave the wall a firm rap to tell the girl to shut up. That Ayah. For a moment she tensed, imagining Ayah sauntering out to argue with this fine man who was not so much older than her. Maybe he had a thing for dirty glasses, for chipped nail-polish and chewed-off nails. For insolence. The same sort that had entangled Suad with Gamal so many years ago. She felt her body temperature reach dewpoint as beads of sweat prepared to burst forth form her temples. But Ayah never came out of her cave.

The Gamal lookalike sat down on the couch as Suad went to the kitchen to fetch him a drink. There was a pitcher of ready-made juice on the counter, but it wouldn't do. So she handpicked her finest lemons, squeezed them dry, and stirred in a handful of minced mint leaves, saving a sprig to stick in the glass like an Alexandrian cocktail. Drink in hand, she returned to the living room to find the young man still sitting alone. His leg was crossed at the knee to show off its length, and a sliver of strong, bronze ankle showed under the hem of his jeans.

"*Sahtein,*" she said, bon appétit. She watched him drink until there was nothing but a stream of pulp left behind. Up close and under the white indoor lights, he looked even more like Gamal, with gleaming teeth and faint lines at the edges of his eyes that lent him a rough-hewn wisdom. She had already seen his ringless finger but asked if he had a wife to confirm it.

He shook his head. "No, but I hope to get married within the year."

She noticed a speck of pulp stuck to the corner of his mouth. If only she could wipe it off with her finger. But he was not Gamal, and Suad was not fifteen, and there were dishes to wash, lemons to peel, a phone to watch. And with an *inshallah*, she took his glass and sent him on his way. Through the window she watched him load the tuk-tuk with her lemons and drive off, back down the road that led into the city.

*****

Before bed, Suad unlocked the bottom drawer at her bedside. She dug through a sea of papers to reach *it*—that thing, the peculiar contraption that had sat there in a wadded-up ball gathering dust for years. It unraveled in her hands. There it was, the underwear. It was a strange pair, bright red and made of lace, and the backside was composed of nothing but a string.

They were three years into their marriage when she found the underwear in Mahmoud's suitcase. She remembered it well—the way she ticked off explanations in her head as if to defend him. Not once did she ever consider saying a word to him, even though it certainly didn't belong to herself or, for that matter, her mother-in-law (though the image of Abla in the red underwear gave her a giggle in that tense moment). She convinced herself—while wincing at the distaste—that it must have belonged to an old girlfriend from before they married. *That's what men do,* she'd told herself. *They're weak.* So she stowed the red underwear away and did nothing but take it out from time to time to marvel at the peculiar design.

Tonight was one of those nights. She laid the underwear out on the bed before her and imagined putting them on. Should she? No, she should not. But why not? Her eyes fell on the Quran by her bed. That was why. She took it off the nightstand and hid it in a drawer, covering it with clothes for good measure. And then, with slow, measured breaths, she slipped on the underwear for the first time.

In the mirror, the red lace dug into her hips, making her flesh look like a rump of veal wrapped in twine. The string in the back felt vulgar, like it was a sin just to wear it—let alone what was meant to be done while wearing it. She was so alarmed with her own reflection that the underwear was only on her body for a matter of seconds before she ripped them off, and back into the drawer they went. She turned off the lights and sank into bed, thinking about how fast time passed and how little things changed. It wasn't so long ago that she was a little girl in Abu Radhi, worrying endlessly that she would never get married—a thought that now amused her, thinking back on that tireless child who never failed to find something to fret. She was so ignorant of the fate that had awaited her all along, like a wall of concrete standing unseen at the end of every road she could possibly take.

In the dark, Suad slipped off her wedding ring and felt the cool dampness of her skin beneath it, free to breathe at last. She always took the ring off at night in order to sleep easier, but tonight, she held it between her fingers before setting it aside. It was a simple gold band with a rectangular faux ruby in the center. Now that she was older the ring finally fit, after the skin of her finger had swelled and deflated for two pregnancies. When she first got married, the band was too big and would slip off constantly. She never had it fixed because she found the cost unjustifiable. Instead she focused on how lucky she was to just have it, this most valuable possession, the most expensive thing she'd ever had, that symbol of the most important event in her life. Material possessions didn't matter, anyway. Marriage mattered. Even if it was to a man who'd been chosen for her by accident of birth, a man who'd broken her heart as if he'd ever had it in the first place.

It helped that she was never one for ornaments anyway.

The ring made a light clink against the nightstand as she set it down. It hadn't changed much in physicality, other than losing a bit of its luster, but its spirit had become something wholly different from the first time it was slipped onto her finger. It was the day of her engagement. She remembered it clearly. It happened in her parents' living room in Abu Radhi. She wore a cream-colored dress, almost a bride. Mahmoud sat before her with a flake of phyllo stuck to his tooth. She wanted badly to reach for his mouth and scrape it off, but she barely knew him and nobody else seemed to notice or care. She supposed it didn't matter—marriage mattered. There was an unexpected comfort in looking down at that too-big trinket. She was *done*, done being a daughter, done being a girl, done being the subject of every pubescent daydream in Abu Radhi. Sometimes she imagined it had come from Gamal, and her heart would go rat-a-tat to match the jangling of his keys. But that was wrong. She would commit to the man with phyllo in his teeth, just as he had committed to her with that ruby-red ring.

Ironically, it was when she found the red underwear in Mahmoud's suitcase that the ring became even more precious in her eyes. The development was unexpected—absurd, even—but she liked to think about it from time to time as proof that God was on her side, despite everything.

It was spring, almost three years to the day of their anniversary. She was pregnant with Ayah and Sami was only a toddler, still clutching her knees with a thumb in his mouth and crying with every bowel movement. Mahmoud still lived with them back then and wouldn't leave for the Gulf until years later, when Sami started primary school. It didn't make much difference though—Mahmoud had grown more remote every day since Sami's birth, and by then he only came around for lunch and a dreaded bout of sex every now and then. Suad didn't really mind until the phone calls started.

One day the telephone started to ring more often than usual. Whenever she would answer, the person on the other line would hang up without anything more than a quick breath. It wasn't unlike that phone call, days ago, when she'd tried to reach Sami. At first, she thought it was some local boy looking for excitement by talking to a woman. It was common back then for boys to dial random numbers until they heard a woman's voice, and then call back again and again just to bother her. For the life of her, she couldn't understand why those boys found it so amusing, but she was content with the explanation. Then one night she awoke to find the bed empty. The sound of Abla's snoring boomed from the other side of the ceiling. Beneath it—in the troughs of quiet between each monstrous breath—she heard Mahmoud's hushed voice down the hall. She got out of bed and followed it to find him sitting cross-legged on the living room rug, talking on the phone. She heard enough to know he was talking to a woman. He called her his darling, *habibti.* He told her to stop calling at such odd hours, when their only cover was Abla's snoring, because Suad was bound to find out. Suad perked up at the sound of her name and found it satisfying, somehow, that the woman knew it.

Then the real atrocity. *I love you.*

The last time he said that to Suad must have been their wedding day. What a joke. She'd never really noticed the absence of those words until she heard them directed at another woman. He said it was because of this so-called love that he wanted her to be safe, safe from Suad, whose undue intensity in small matters like the lemon grove suggested that she was not a woman to be crossed. And true to form, Suad's insides burned with anger on the other side of the wall. She sneaked back into bed, where she lay awake in the dark with her eyes wide open in horror, awaiting his return.

When Mahmoud came back in the room, she pretended to be asleep. She could feel her eyelids pucker from the force it took to hold them closed. Under the blanket his hungry hands reached for her waist, but she shook them away. Why did he want to touch her, all of a sudden? Did he think she was the one from the phone, the one with the red underwear, the one he *loved?* She told him she was sick, just sick and that he should let her sleep. *Khalas*, she said, enough. The next day, Abla found Suad in tears as she made tea over the kitchen stove. Out of the corner of her eye, Suad could see the stout woman wearing her favorite blue velveteen housedress, standing in the doorway with her hands on her hips. She had the same angry look Mahmoud had whenever she said something he found ridiculous. *Really? Really, ya Suad?* She had his eyebrows too, thick and straight, furrowed when annoyed. When she asked what was the matter, Suad didn't respond. She feared that any word that escaped from her mouth would unleash an unstoppable fit of tears. Instead she wiped her eyes as she poured boiling water into a pot of black tea leaves. But she didn't need to say anything. Abla understood completely—in fact, it seemed she had been waiting for this moment all along. A chance to call Suad a silly girl for perhaps thinking she was a grand madam like Faten Hamama or Queen Nazli, entitled to a man who'd go against his own nature. Abla shook her head, as if the real crime were Suad's tears, and waddled away with her backside swaying under the velveteen housedress. Later Abla retired to her room for afternoon soaps. Suad thanked God for the chance to slip away unnoticed. She walked to her favorite part of the river, a dock on a quiet stretch at the far end of a neighbor's plot of sugar-cane crops. The river was narrow there, barely the width of a bus, but the water was as flat and black as onyx, suggesting depths like the night sky. The Nile tended to be much deeper than it appeared, even in its many little fingers.

She cried for a while sitting on the riverbank, dreading having to face her husband that night, or tomorrow, or ever again. It seemed impossible. And thus, the only thing to do was to make sure she would never again have to stir three cubes of sugar into his tea, to iron his favorite brown suit, to feel his clammy fingers brush her skin from under the blanket. She would have preferred to run away, but then what? Where would she go? Certainly not back to Abu Radhi, where Mahmoud would find her easily. And if she went anywhere else, then she would become nothing more than a lone woman selling tissues on the street. There was nothing to do in that moment—nothing to do but die.

She stood up and walked to the dock. Its wooden boards shifted and groaned under her feet, and she could see the water underneath the gaps. At the edge of the dock she stopped and faced the Nile, black and still, deep enough to submerge her. She dipped a toe into the cold water and then paused to look around, but there were only sheep bleating in the distance. As she gazed back down at the water, she imagined that it would be difficult to drown. It would be dark down there. She would only be able to hold her breath comfortably for a half minute or so, thanks to years of inhaling the smoke from Mahmoud's waterpipe. There would be squirming and flailing, a massive battle between a body trying to survive against a mind's resolution to die. She figured she was lucky she wouldn't have a choice once she hit the water, because she couldn't swim.

Suad was staring so hard at the river that it seemed to draw her body downward, as if the weight of her eyes were sinking her—or perhaps the weight of her pregnant belly hanging over the dock's edge. She rationalized that suicide would be best for the baby too. It would be spared a lifetime of misfortune with Mahmoud for a father, and go straight to paradise. Meanwhile Suad would likely go to hell. But she didn't care—hell was well worth the prospect of getting back at Mahmoud. He would hear the news of her death and feel shame for the rest of his life, forever known as the man who made his wife so miserable that she leapt into the Nile. She smiled at the thought. And as she looked down, the river pulled her in.

It happened in slow motion.

In the split second and half meter between the dock and the water, she reconsidered. In that same moment, she lost her footing, she decided that she had made a mistake—that she wanted to live, that she was a monster for doing this to her unborn baby and to her little Sami, that she would never again see her dear father and mother, that she would never again pick ripe lemons from her trees. Oh, how she would give anything to be in her grove right then, with mud between her toes, scent of citron in the air, blue sky above a canopy of branches.

But she sank. The sound of the water was deafening as it flooded her ears.

There was a noise from up above. *No!* She heard splashing, but it couldn't be her own, because her limbs thrashed in silence underwater. Something grabbed her arm and she thought it was death itself, but instead of dragging her down into the river floor, it pulled her up to the surface, where there was light, and air, and breath.

She opened her eyes to see a man lugging her to the riverbank like a sheep too tired to cross. Gulping for air, she collapsed when her feet touched the earth, making desperate and drastic sounds not unlike the animal she felt like. As she coughed out all the water stuck in her throat, she somehow noticed that she'd lost her sandals. The man seemed to judge her as he watched, leaning on a stick. He was past middle age, with gray hair and a stern expression. Behind him, a gaggle of confused sheep waited. And then at once, he dove back into the river.

By the time the man swam back to her, Suad had caught her breath. He held out his palm, and through the mud she could see the glint of faux ruby lying in a bed of deep wrinkles. He asked if it was hers. It was. Stunned, she took the ring and slipped it back onto her too-small finger. She had been in such a fury that she hadn't even realized that the ring was still on her hand when she left for the river with plans to die. She would have preferred to leave it on his pillow, a gift bitterly returned to its owner. But by some divine accident, the ring had slipped off in the water, and now it was back. Now she was back, too.

The man asked if she needed anything, and she told him no. He asked if he could take her home, and she said no again. Not even some tea, a blanket? No. He picked up his shepherd's stick and left with his sheep, leaving her on the riverbank, soaking wet.

Suad was enchanted, dazzled like the breathless women of Abla's soap operas. In her hand the ring became heavier, as if it was turning to real gold and ruby. It was a miracle, that this shepherd had spotted the little fleck of gold in the black river and that he was able to catch it in the palm of his hand. The shepherd had heard her flailing, her stifled breaths. He found her just like he found the ring. And even though at one point, only minutes ago, Suad hadn't wanted to survive, now she was glad she did. It all must be fate, her *maktub*. Surely this was a message from God—that she wasn't meant to die and she wasn't meant to lose her ring. And if that was so, then she wasn't meant to leave Mahmoud. Suad wasn't one to look at plain facts and not attach any meaning to them.

It didn't occur to her that perhaps, out of sheer lack of river breadth and current, that finding the ring wasn't so miraculous after all. Or that, on this stretch of farmland, a shepherd was bound to walk by at some point in the afternoon. To her there was clear meaning in the incident—a meaning that God had spoken to her and had told her to have faith in her marriage and in her life. It meant that not only would she go home and continue being a dutiful wife, but that she would pay thanks as best as she could. She'd never been one to question the existence of God to begin with, but that episode on the river left her so moved, it was as if he had appeared in human form before her eyes.

She was sure of what to do now. She went home and cooked Mahmoud *molokhiya* for dinner, his favorite, and prayed before going to bed. From that point on, her prayers became more punctual until she never missed one. *Fajr, zohr, asr, maghrib, isha.* She had never before felt she was communicating directly to God, like she *knew* God personally. She had never before felt so sure of herself.

When the baby was born, Suad named her Ayah, for miracle.

*****

In the dead of night, a firm knock awoke Suad. She looked up at the ceiling where she used to hear Abla's thumping and hollering so many years ago, but tonight there was nothing but the occasional skitter of goat hooves from the roof.

When Suad heard knocking again, she sat up in bed. It took a second or two to realize that it came from the front door. Swallowing her fear, she slipped on her housedress and veil and walked through the dark toward the sound. She pressed her ear to the door and the knock came again; this time it was hard enough to rattle the wood. Her hand froze over the doorknob as she debated whether she should answer, and in the fog of interrupted sleep, she almost thought she should.

"What's that noise," said Ayah, walking toward her in the dark.

Suad held her finger to her lips to tell the damned girl to be quiet, but it was too late. A man's voice came from the other side of the door.

"Open up, it's the army."

The army? Suad crouched to see two pairs of feet through the gap under the door. There was nothing in the rubber soles of their shoes to prove their claim, but there wasn't anything to prove otherwise, either. Surely a thief would not announce himself the way they did. One of the feet took a big step toward her and there was another knock.

"Madame."

It was probably foolish to go ahead and open the door, but it seemed Suad had no other choice. She looked up at the calligraphic *mashallah* hanging over the door, and with a quick prayer, she opened it a crack. The white beam of a flashlight shot through, blinding her. When her eyes adjusted she saw two middle-aged men in plainclothes, holding out badges to show they were indeed from the army. Squinting, Suad read their names. Ahmed and Nabil. With their bald heads, they looked nothing like their ID cards but she supposed it was the darkness. She let them in, nodding helplessly, and told Ayah to go back to her room.

"Stay," said the taller one, who she believed to be Ahmed.

Ayah stood still. Behind her smudged lenses, there was fear in her bloodshot eyes.

"Please, sit down," said Suad, though she wasn't yet convinced that these men should even be in her home. She switched on the lights and saw that they looked rougher than she'd thought, like the men who worked in gas stations with skin withered from exhaust. They both had thick hands with calluses at the fingertips, nails hacked off to nothing more than paper-thin nubs.

Nabil opened his briefcase and took out a stack of papers. On top was a document bearing Mahmoud's government ID photo surrounded by text so illegible Suad wasn't even sure of the language. "Does Mr. Sukkary live here?"

"No. He lives in the Gulf."

The men looked at each other with glee, as if they had uncovered some secret. "And he's your husband?"

"Yes."

"When was the last time he was here?"

"I don't know, months ago, at least. Maybe last year."

They both raised their eyebrows. Suad noticed that they moved in unison, and they likely thought that way too, because she could tell that neither one believed her.

"Madame," began Nabil. She was glad he at least had the decency to address her correctly while she sat before him in her house clothes in the middle of the night, her legs and arms clenched together in preparation for whatever was to come, because surely, it wasn't good, despite the *madam*. "As you know, there are current security concerns in this country, and it's important that we all, as Egyptians, do our best to protect ourselves and our families." As he spoke, Suad realized she was nodding her head fast and hard, a little *too* fast and hard, so she stopped herself and held still. "We have been informed that there may be items of concern here."

"No, that's impossible. There's nobody here but my daughter, and she's only a little girl."

They looked at Ayah, who sat with arms crossed to hide that damned, godforsaken rack she had inherited from her mother, clearly not a little girl but a young woman with a towel wrapped around her head as a make-shift hijab. She may not be a child, but she was still harmless, despite the chest pangs she gave her mother from time to time.

As Ahmed ran his finger down the paper, his calluses making a scraping sound. He stopped right under Sami's name. "Where's your son?"

"He's in Cairo. Studying."

"Studying what?"

"Engineering."

"*Mashallah*," said Ahmed, praise God. Suad could tell he wasn't being sincere and this bothered her quite deeply, enough to chew on the inside of her cheek, wishing it were a rind. Whatever fear she already felt rose to a fast-beating terror as she imagined what sort of men these were, to use God's name and not mean it.

"So it's just you and your daughter in this big house?"

Suad clenched her fists at her side. It was true, she was alone there, her husband and son had left her, and now she had to deal with this nonsense in the middle of the night. It should have been Mahmoud or Sami talking to these strange men while she remained in her bedroom, a respectable woman. But they were not there, and she had to explain that yes, the house was empty, that her husband and son were gone, and that soon she wouldn't even have Ayah once she got married and left her too. She glanced back at Ayah with that ridiculous towel on her head. It was to her benefit that nowadays, girls were waiting until after they finished school to marry. At least that bought Suad a little more time.

Together the men exhaled, emitting a gust of hot breath that smelled of tahini and whipped garlic. Their eyes darted down the corridor and up the stairwell. "We need to check the house."

It wasn't a question, but Suad nodded as if to give her consent. She joined Ayah at the edge of the room as the men went through the contents of each cupboard and shelf. "There are just plates in there," she called out. "That's for silverware." But they didn't care. They opened anything that would open, lifting each plate and utensil individually as if whatever they were searching for could be hidden between the tines of a fork. "I told you, there's nothing there."

"Yes, Madame, but we need to check anyway."

They looked everywhere—even the bathroom. Nabil flushed the toilet as if to confirm that it was, indeed, a toilet. Ayah snorted at this and Suad nudged her to shut up.

The girl straightened up quickly when they moved on to the bedrooms, headed for hers first. Suad tried giving her a look, but couldn't reach her through those cloudy lenses. Frustrated, she grabbed the glasses off her face and threw them to the ground. The men called out behind them. "Is everything OK over there?"

"Yes, everything's just fine," said Suad, as Ayah felt around on the floor for her glasses.

One wouldn't think the room of a young girl would be of any use to the men's investigation, but it seemed they'd found a treasure trove in Ayah's vanity. It was full of suspicious compartments that somehow warranted scrutiny. Every bottle, every brush, every substance was opened and tested on the palms of their hands, sprayed into the air, shaken and stirred. When Ayah whimpered, Suad grabbed her and dug her nails into her arm. She had no idea the girl had so much makeup—what for? She held her own tongue as the men moved onto the bookshelf, where they found college textbooks interspersed with dolls of her childhood and souvenirs from her father, who should have been there in place of bejeweled camel figurines. Again, the men inspected everything, checking under each plastic hoof. Of course there was nothing. They rifled through her textbooks and found nothing there, either. Suad thanked God for that stupid major her daughter had picked—nothing important, not a single word to give them pause.

Ayah composed herself as they finished with her room and made way upstairs to Abla's. Suad never went up there—she got flashbacks just looking at the old bed atop its regal, curling frame, the old television set in the corner, the window from which she would pester her daughter-in-law in the grove all day. She could hear the brooding bad-news music from *Face of the Moon* playing in her head as she watched the two brutes pace across the floor.

"And how's this? Nobody lives in the best room in the house?"

"It belonged to my mother-in-law," said Suad, pointing to storage crates stacked at the entrance, marking that she wasn't there anymore. "She's dead." Abla never minded hot summers on the second floor if it meant she could be *above* everyone, the true lady of the house. It was the heat that ended up killing her, giving her a stroke at age sixty-six. The men seemed to understand.

In the end there was only one room left to check, and that was Suad's. She hoped they would forget, but of course they did not and in fact, it seemed they had saved the best for last. Thankfully, Suad had returned the Quran to the top of her bedside table. Perhaps that would deter the men from being indecent. Had she learned anything at all?

They began with the Quran, handling it with relative delicacy. Suad had to stop herself from reaching out to protect it as they turned each frayed page. That would look suspicious. She held her breath until they started on the drawers, and then she really had to contain herself, because any politeness with which they handled the holy book melted away as they took time to fondle each pair of underwear, stifling laughter. Suad was mortified but told herself that it could be worse. It could be Ayah, an unmarried girl with quite a bit of dignity to lose. Mahmoud had already destroyed all of Suad's dignity, that was for sure.

When the men reached the bottom drawer, they demanded the key. Suad seriously considered jumping from the window rather than handing it over, but she did—hoping foolishly that the men would quickly see that it contained items too personal not to guard with a lock. Maybe they'd have a change of heart and respect a lady's privacy. Of course, they did no such thing. She almost fainted when they found the red underwear, shaking out its strings and lace from the tip of a grubby finger.

"That's enough, gentlemen."

When they looked back, she could feel their eyes unpeeling her clothes like the rinds of fruit. She thought it couldn't get any worse than that, but she was mistaken. Next they pulled out hundreds of folded papers— all the letters to Gamal that she had written without sending over the years. The men were not so pressed for time that they refrained from going through every one.

"*Dear Gamal,*" said Ahmed, unfolding the first. "Gamal? I thought your husband's name was Mahmoud."

"Those are private. Letters to my … brother." Suad reached for the paper but he pulled it away. She wondered what Ayah was thinking on the other side of the room, staring at the floor, knowing full well that Suad had no brother and hearing for the first time the name of the man her mother had been thinking of her whole life. How would she ever keep Ayah in line knowing something like that, her future doomed, her chastity unenforceable. Those men had ruined everything.

"I swear there's nothing there," she said, but it was in vain—they proceeded to pull the whole drawer off its hinges, digging down to the wood bottoms as sickening smiles crept up their lips.

*****

After the men finished with her room, Suad opened the front door to hurry them along. But there was one last thing.

"Wait," said the shorter of the two. Was he Ahmed or Nabil? Not that it mattered.

He led them to Ayah's desk, where at last, they found items worth taking. The notebook. The computer. As they unplugged the latter and scooped out its hardware, Ayah yelped, and Suad covered her mouth with her hand to keep her from making a scene. She was fine with them taking the computer. Anything to get them out of the house.

By the time they left, dawn was breaking. The night sky had turned to a pale gray. If those men had any decency they would have come by daylight—but they hadn't any, and to make matters worse, it was time for prayer and now Suad would be late, needing extra time to wash off her embarrassment. She wondered if they even prayed and figured it was better if they didn't, for all their hypocrisy. In her head she repeated the sarcastic *mashallah* Ahmed had delivered to her ears, defaming the word. She noticed that the calligraphy framed above the door was now hanging crooked off the nail, as with the framed portrait of the president. She fixed both and turned to Ayah. The seriousness of what just happened seemed to evade her—but then again, they hadn't gone through *her* unmentionables, had they?

Suad sat down with her head in her hands. Ayah seemed more upset about the computer than her mother being defiled before her own eyes. In fact, her attachment to that contraption was suspicious in itself. What was inside it—why had the men hauled it away? At first she thought it was a mere matter of theft, to pawn off in some underground cellar where men of their ilk lurked. But for some reason, they'd left the monitor—which to Suad seemed like the most important part. Wasn't that what made a computer, well, a *computer*? Instead they'd taken only its innards, as if there were something important inside. Perhaps something like the garbage in Ayah's notebook. *In-soor-jens.* She gasped. They had taken that too, hadn't they?

"What have you done, Ayah?"

"I don't know what you're talking about, mama."

"This is because of *you*, you and that *khara* you read all day."

That's what she was reading. Shit. Ayah knew it as she looked down at her bare feet, toes painted purple to match some despoiled bottle on her vanity. Her glasses slipped down her nose and almost fell to the floor. Since the men left, she'd taped them together, but they were still slightly askew. Now they *had* to be tucked into the folds of her hijab just to stay intact. Suad almost felt pity until Ayah looked up from the floor and took in a quick breath, about to say something horrific. "Speak up," said Suad, before she even got any words out. "Tell me what was in that computer. Go on."

"Nothing was *inside* of it, mama. I was just posting things online."

"What kind of things?"

Her eyes darted back to the floor. "Just some … stuff. Nothing important. The news, for example."

Suad threw up her hands. "Oh OK, it's just *stuff*. Thank God! Tell me, what kind of stuff are we talking? Stuff about the weather? Classwork? Football scores? Your own ass?"

"There's a group called the Youth Movement. About the guy the police killed in Alexandria."

Suad crossed her arms. She couldn't recall his name but assumed there was good reason for the police to do what they'd done. Anyway, what did that guy have to do with it? She prodded her daughter to explain, and learned that little Ayah hadn't been as idle as she seemed. Apparently, she'd been running some kind of online gang called a Facebook group—a circle of troublemakers posting stories so obscene they put Nagwa's gossip to shame. She thought of the pictures she'd shown her today, the men on horses and camels tearing through Tahrir with machetes. Oh, Ayah. What had she done?

"They must have tracked me through the IP address."

"The what?"

"It's like, say, the computer's fingerprint."

That didn't make things any clearer. In fact, it made things worse.

"Enough!" Suad got up and fumbled with the remaining wires but couldn't make sense of them. Why on earth were there so many? Blue, red, black. Thick ones, thin ones. In her day they didn't have such things. Children were obedient, men were decent. There was no such thing as BookFace or Tweet-tweet or IP whatevers. None of this would have happened. Suad would still have some dignity, and the drawer would have remained locked. Now the whole world might as well have seen all her letters and the red underwear that Mahmoud had brought into her home to punish her alone.

With a grunt, she yanked the monitor from the wall and carried it to the window facing the lemon grove. Ayah screamed. Suad didn't look back as she chucked it out the window and watched it crash into a tangle of chips and wires. She still didn't quite understand why the men had been after its contents, but she knew enough. They should be safe, and as long as that thing was in her home, they weren't.

As Suad walked back to her bedroom, she heard Ayah sniffling, and the sound of Nagwa's balcony door swinging open. God forgive her.

# 10

Sami spent all morning trying to convince Rose not to go to the beach. It was unsafe. Illogical. Unnecessary. Who cared that it was her birthday? It wasn't even a milestone like her eighteenth or thirtieth. Besides, they were just *at* the beach only weeks ago, when they spent New Years' Eve in Alexandria. Granted, it was a terrible trip, wracked with rain and bickering. Rose shot him a look when he brought it up.

"Look, we already bought the bus ticket, booked the room. No refunds," she said, as if the money at stake *weren't* about the cost of a sandwich back home. But she wouldn't budge. It was her birthday and they would do as she said.

In the end Sami packed his bags halfheartedly, grumbling all the while at Rose's insistence on going—as if nothing had ever happened in Tahrir or even worse, that none of it mattered.

The streets were particularly deserted at dawn. He'd gotten used to this new Ramses, which had steadily decreased in bustle since that first night of the uprising. There wasn't a taxi or tuk-tuk in sight. Clear asphalt was visible from curb to curb and from the north and down its southern direction. He counted five lanes he never knew existed beneath the usual tangle of traffic, which paid them no mind anyway. There were no loitering crowds on the sidewalks, and the kiosks and black-market vendors were gone from their curbside posts. Shops that were supposed to be open 24 hours, like Abu Ali's pharmacy and the shawarma chain across the way, were still shuttered. The overpass in the distance, too, was empty. Not even a single stray cat rummaged through trash. It looked apocalyptic, like some virus had wiped out the millions of inhabitants, like every car, bus, and donkey cart in the entire city had simply vanished in a matter of days.

Even at that early hour, Ramses should have been wracked with car horns, shouting drivers with road rage, random bursts of pop radio, cats screeching and mothers hollering from rooftops. It should have been impossible to pick out any one word or voice over the vast din—and yet today, each breath echoed down the empty boulevard.

"Watch out," said Rose, grabbing his arm.

But it was too late. Sami tripped over a tin can that clanged like a siren against the asphalt. He reached down to pick it up, if only just to silence it, and found it was no can of beans or Pepsi. It was an empty tear gas cannister. He thought it would sting his fingertips but its power had been spent, the tin bent and punctured, full of nothing but air. On its side was etched *made in the USA.*

Rose shook her head but said nothing. She seemed embarrassed but he didn't understand. If anyone should be embarrassed it was him, an Egyptian, victim to imported weapons so meaningless to their financers that they didn't even know about them. A can worth pennies and not even a passing thought. She hadn't even known that she was paying to crush Tahrir. That's how big America was, and how rich. It could change the entire course of Egypt's history without even the knowledge of its own citizens. He knew it wasn't her fault but he couldn't help but feel bitter. It was so easy to be her, to move through life boundless and unaware of the terrible power she held. To make a huge mistake like having a child out of wedlock and not even worry about telling her parents. She was worried about feeding it, bathing it, sending it to school. *Gah!* He'd be lucky if he even survived telling Suad. It was so easy for her, and so difficult for him.

"Jesus. Propaganda much?"

Rose pointed to a massive billboard in the intersection that seemed to have been erected overnight, reading: THE ARMY AND THE PEOPLE ARE ONE HAND. On it was a soldier, two stories tall, with a rifle on his back and a baby in his arms. Sami's eyes fell to the ground, trying to find another tear gas cannister to divert his attention. Babies would not stop tormenting him, even in the streets, at six a.m. and in the middle of a revolution. Nobody mentioned it—not Rose, not even the billboard itself. It was just a baby, held in the soldier's brawny arms over the silent boulevard. Unexplained, unremarkable. Unlike their own. He jerked his head up when Rose laughed.

"Why is it funny?"

"Because nobody asked. It's almost as if the army *doth protest too much*. Suspicious, no?"

"They say they're neutral."

"Neutral is as neutral does."

"Neutral doesn't kill people," said Sami. Though soldiers were now posted all over the city center, they remained on the sidelines of protests, never raising a hand to—well, their other hand. It was good enough for him.

"Well, the show ain't over until ... you know."

"Until what?"

"Until the fall of the regime."

"Shhhh," he said, squeezing her arm.

"Oh, come on. As if the streets aren't screaming the exact same thing."

The billboard's tagline replayed in Sami's head as they approached, trying to make sense of it. If the army and the people were one hand, and the people were revolting against the president, did that mean the army was too? It seemed impossible. The president himself had been an officer and in fact, so had every other president since the last fez-wearing prince was ousted in 1953. Damn. Sometimes it seemed like Sami was the only person in the entire country who hadn't served.

Exemption from military service was the one good thing about being an only son, but Sami wasn't sure if it was worth the expectation in return. Watching friends leave for conscription had always been a little embarrassing—as if he'd intentionally slipped through the cracks to avoid duty. At least he hadn't gotten off using an excuse like sweaty hands or flat feet. Overactive bladder, even. Ailments that were only ailments for rich kids who could enclose a wad of cash with the doctor's note. Those types were never ashamed. But could he really blame them? Who would actually want to serve, other than this twenty-foot-tall soldier standing above him? Sami had heard enough about conscription to know it was even worse than he'd imagined, and *nothing* like the movies. Grueling months spent alone at far-flung Saharan outposts. Horrible food like cold, congealed foul. No beards, no hair longer than the width of a rolled-up grape leaf. One would think he'd be used to all those rules growing up in Suad's household, but on the contrary, it made him intolerant of the kind occurring anywhere else. So, he found himself in the uniquely *Sami* position of feeling guilty for something he was happy to avoid.

He remembered a classmate, Hamza, who did a stint at the Libyan border last year. He'd enlisted as a fat boy with B-cups and pear-shaped hips and returned a reed with cheekbones jutting out of his face. The first thing he did was collapse onto his dormitory bed— a stiff mat covered in scratchy sheets that now felt like a cloud in paradise. Even worse than the army's bad beds and food was that Hamza hadn't seen a single female for seven months straight. Not *one* girl. Not a plain girl, not an ugly girl, and certainly not a pretty girl. Not even a brash, beat-you-over-the-head-with-a-slipper lady like Umm Akbar from the ticket booth at the Mahalla train station. *Wallah el azim*, said Hamza, I swear to God—even all the bugs in the sand had dicks. And when he closed his eyes at night, all he saw was Captain El Guindy's unibrow growing thicker and blacker with each drop of sweat borne from the Saharan sun.

Still, service might have helped Sami atone for his misdeeds. It would have made his father proud, and especially Giddo, who must be looking down at Sami two years after his death, watching to see what his role would be in this sea change. And what would he see? Sami in plainclothes, with not a government gun but a camera from Japan found in a junk pile. Hair a touch too long like he liked to wear it, a style unacceptable to those of Giddo's generation who thought nothing of self-expression and frivolous choices that devalued those of his mother. Like the girl beside him. What would Giddo think? Would he give him a pat on the back for getting a girlfriend in a city full of sexually frustrated youth? And a white girl at that—the kind of girl who, back in his day, would visit the Pyramids in hoopskirts and sunhats and wouldn't mind sharing a camel's saddle with a man pressed up against them, one leg on each side, shameless. Showgirls like the singer Dalida, a former Miss Egypt who wasn't in fact Egyptian, whose photo Giddo had cut out of a magazine and kept hidden in the pages of a book deep in his closet. Sami had found it one day when they were cleaning out his belongings. He didn't like the thought of his grand-father looking at that whittle-waisted bombshell dressed in a leopard-print bikini. Like he was any other man. Men who were less upright, men who hissed at women in the street. Men who wouldn't look the same way at Faten Hamama or Hind Rostom, because they had husbands and fathers and brothers just like them and didn't smile as big and as … shameless. Is that how he would see Rose?

Sami didn't know why Giddo was supposed to be superhuman and why seeing that pinup had disturbed him so much that he took it home and burned it with the end of a cigarette. He supposed Giddo would have wanted that. As would Sami. In time, he would forget about the destroyed photo and restore his grandfather to his rightful status as a national hero, like the soldier on the billboard with the baby and the gun.

The bus station was closed, but somehow still operating. It was full of vehicles for hire, most incoming, carrying protesters from outside the city, dozens at a time. He ignored Rose's I-told-you-so look as they caught the first ride east, got off at Suez, and paid a Bedouin to take them through the Sinai.

It was a seven-hour trip, hellish at parts—winding up mountains, cutting through the desert as the vehicle palpably overheated. Sami had wanted to catch up on sleep, but the radio distracted him. Dalida. Of all the singers, of all the songs, it had to be Dalida singing *my beautiful coun-try, my beautiful country*, reminding Sami of the very things he didn't need to be reminded of—things meant to be buried in a closet, burned with a match. The radio signal cut so frequently that he couldn't tell if it was replaying over and over or whether it was an uncut version that happened to be seven hours long. Yet the driver refused to change it. NileFM was the only station that got signal in the Sinai—sometimes, here and there—and he needed the sound to stay awake.

"You don't want to me to drive you into the sea, do you?"

Sami saw his eyes laughing, lines like tobacco spreading across the rearview mirror. Yes, he thought. As a matter of fact, he did.

The driver had to stop several times to ask for directions to their camp at Ras Shaitan, which was so remote it was unfindable on a map. It didn't help that the place's name, which translated to *devil's head* to match the shape of a huge rock jutting out of its coast, sounded made up—too on the nose given the circumstance. It was favored by people who didn't want to be found—bohemian types and strange lone travelers who backpacked from camp to camp for months on end. There, for a few American dollars you could rent a hut by the night and watch the sea lap at its doorstep. Sami never quite saw the appeal of those huts. To him they were no different from Bedouin camps on the road—four walls of straw tied together around a gravel floor, holding nothing but mosquito nets and cushions for beds. The kind of place only the poor would live.

"Yeah, but you don't have to be married to stay together," said Rose.

"What do you mean?"

"I mean we can stay together in a hut and we don't even have to show a marriage certificate."

He could see in her eyes that she regretted bringing it up, though she didn't stop. She never stopped. Sometimes it seemed she was testing him, pushing to see where he would break, where he would throw his hands in the air and give up, hitch a ride back to Cairo and leave her in her little hippie camp in the desert. Still, he knew their trip would be useless if they stayed at a normal hotel, where they'd have to rent separate rooms. For all the sneaking around they did already, climbing through a window in the middle of the night didn't sound so romantic. It was what usually put him off traveling—that inevitable roadblock when a hotelier would act like the most intrusive of doormen and ask for a marriage document before handing over the room keys. They had found a way around the issue for now, but it was still *an issue*, an issue for not only hotels but above all, Suad. Uncomfortably, he found himself repeating her words, which were of course rooted in the Quran, uttered in her hushed morning voice. *No leaf falls without his knowledge.* In the Sinai there were no leaves, but only the open sky.

And there was plenty of sky. They spent the first day of their trip climbing up a stupid mountain, where the sun was brutal even in its waning hours, flinging rays of heat off sides of rock like prisms. For some reason Rose wanted to celebrate her birthday doing this—this thing called *hiking*—which to Sami seemed like hard labor, something you'd do out of necessity if you were stranded without a car or bike or even donkey. A last resort if you were dying of thirst or running from some bloodthirsty villain on your tail. Certainly not a pastime.

Sami shaded his eyes and stared longingly at the sea way down at the foot of the mountain. The water appeared to glitter as it lapped the parched shore. Cool and crystalline, with low, languid waves. If he were wearing a watch, he'd be counting the minutes until they could return to the beach. For now, he had only the length of his shadow, which told him it was about midway between afternoon and sunset prayers. He was about to say they should head back soon but bit his tongue. Rose shouldn't hear complaining on her birthday, no matter how twisted her idea of fun may be. His complaints were nonverbal, instead—smoking cigarettes, keeping a few paces behind her, saying nothing of the harsh, jagged landscape that enthralled her.

"Imagine," she said, turning to face him. "Millions of years ago, this whole mountain was underwater." She pointed to the cliffside, which was speckled with holes like tiny caves. "See? There was once seaweed and coral and fish. Now it's all gone, wiped out. A mini-Armageddon."

Sami ran his hand along the rocks, feeling grooves for each line of sediment marking layers of prehistory—like wrinkles or fingerprints or, as Rose said, like rings inside the trunks of trees. Today was just another layer of rock, wasn't it? So insignificant it didn't even warrant its own line. Untraceable in the grand scheme of things. One day, both he and Rose would be long gone, as gone as the fish that lived there before, and all their worries would prove to be in vain, turned to fossils underneath layers of rock.

He crouched and grabbed a handful of sand. It was full of hard bits that sifted like grains of rice through his fingers. One piece was larger than the others and remained in his hand. He held it up to the light. Smooth, white. Ridged on one side and tucked into a faint coil underneath. It was only a broken shell—not the bone he feared. He tucked it into his pocket just before Rose could see. Defiling nature? Taking what wasn't his? She wouldn't understand why he took it, why it reminded him of his childhood and of his grandfather. Giddo would have understood.

Rose called out to him from up the trail. He jogged to catch up and found her bent over the ground, hands on her hips. "Look," she told him, and he looked but could see nothing but dimples in the sand where drops of sweat had fallen. "It's snakeskin."

Sami peered closer and cringed. He hated snakes and even just the skin made him flinch. It was long and coiled, as if the snake was about to strike when the time came to shed. He touched it lightly with the toe of his shoe, resisting the urge to step on it and hear it crunch into pieces.

"Snakes are bad luck."

"No, no. Don't fall for that Adam and Eve nonsense. In the ancient world, snakes were good. They protected you. That's why the Pharaohs had snakes all over their tombs."

Adam and Eve nonsense? Rose was usually a little uncomfortable talking about religion, but this time she looked straight at him, eyes aflame in the golden light. When they first met she had told him she was Christian. Well, it was more like *Christian, I guess*. With time he learned that she never went to church and didn't even know if she believed in God. He questioned whether he would have even started dating her if he'd known she wasn't a believer. Not because he disagreed, necessarily, but because it was one more thing—one *major* thing—that made their relationship impossible. Rose as a non-Muslim was bad enough. But Rose as an unbeliever? That would knock his mother dead just at the thought. And Rose could never hold her tongue about it. Just like she could never refrain from questioning everything Sami thought he knew. She was probably right, but he couldn't help throwing out a counterargument, if only to shake the confidence with which she explained his own country to him. All he could think of, though, was something straight out of Suad's mouth.

"That was the age of ignorance. Later, the Prophet said: If you see a snake, kill it."

"That's a little harsh."

"In the Hadith, the Prophet's companions come across a snake while traveling through caves. They wanted to kill it, but it got away. And the Prophet said … What was it?" He squinted in the sun, feeling sweat form in the lines on his forehead as he dug deep into memories of being a boy with the Quran in his hands, his mother quoting verses for every childhood calamity he encountered—scraped knees and cat scratches and the ilk. He'd never really forgotten. "Ah, yes. 'It has escaped your evil and you too have escaped its evil.' So I guess it's complicated."

"I like that. The snake is neither good nor bad. Like all of us." The faint lines around her eyes deepened with shadows, turning her into an old woman for a moment. "Sort of like the ouroboros."

"Aurora-whattus?"

"I'm sure you've seen it. It's an ancient symbol, a snake eating its own tail to form a circle. The beginning and the end. The circle of life, that sort of thing. You know, poetic."

He looked back at the snakeskin and pictured it consuming itself from front to end. It seemed more demonic than poetic. Rose may be right, but he wouldn't want any such thing on his tomb.

\*\*\*\*\*

The sun had fully set by the time they reached the camp. Nothing was visible in the dark—not the mountains, not the sea, not any huts. Only a few lanterns glowed in the distance like fireflies. They followed the firefly lights to the main hut, where a tethered goat bleated as they passed. A lantern approached them, and behind it, the silhouette of a man beckoned hello.

"*Ahlan wa sahlan*, y'all. Welcome."

The accent gave him away. It was the camp owner, Zane, who spoke muddled Arabic with an inextinguishable American twang, product of an upbringing by assimilationist immigrants. Now he'd come back to the motherland after his *koshari* restaurant went under. It seemed to Sami that Egypt was the natural choice for disgruntled Westerners, Rose included. She and Zane got along, but to Sami he was a strange creature, one who was neither American nor Egyptian. Even his appearance confused him, with brown skin and a familiarly Pharaonic face, Crocs on his feet.

"Party's about to start," he said, speaking loudly as if it was important that each mundane word be heard. He whistled and a dog ran to his side, tongue flopping out of her mouth. "Come with me."

A wedding was about to begin. They followed him to a roped-off area on the beach, where a handful of campers sat under gas-and-wick lights. They pushed their way to the front, clapping and trilling, as a man in his best galabia walked around with a tray of tea and date cookies.

Sami was surprised by how young the bride and groom looked—even younger than him. But he wasn't so young anymore, after all. His eyes stuck to the bride, in pink-and-gold sequins. She must be about eighteen, a little younger than Ayah and older than his mother when she got married. She was still in that razor-thin stage between childhood and adulthood, when life branched off into two paths, one for a continued adolescence and one for a fast-track to motherhood and old age and tired eyes. Rose had taken the former route. Maybe they could be together if she hadn't—if she were more like the girl in pink-and-gold sequins.

Both bride and groom appeared to sulk before their guests, who seemed to be having a better time. There was no hand holding, no entwined fingers. Their eyes glinted with uncertainty and not joy. It was the first time Sami was even looking for that sort of thing. He suspected he wouldn't have noticed at all if he'd stayed away from Rose like he was supposed to. If he had followed the rules, he would have gone on with life unaware, not quite blissful but content to pass his nights alone in the dorms. He'd go home on weekends and wile away his youth until the time came to arrange a meeting with a girl and her family, where they would drink tea and eat honeyed sweets and decide, in the course of an hour or so, whether they should spend the next half century together, to create other human beings together, to die and be buried together.

Now things would be harder for him.

After the wedding, Zane brought a birthday cake to their hut. The cook and his son, the busboy, trailed behind, clapping and singing to a bashful Rose, who closed her eyes and blew out each sparkling candle.

When Sami asked what she wished for, she squeezed his hand and said she was too old to have wishes, even though she was only a year older than him and he still had plenty. Like his wish, for instance, that she hadn't squeezed his hand when he asked. He spent some time deciphering the meaning of that squeeze as he waited for Zane and his sidekicks to leave.

Once they were alone, Sami gave Rose the journal. She seemed to love it—from what he could see of her candlelit face, at least. She lay on her belly in the sand beside him, doodling patterns like snakeskin onto its yellowed, unused pages. As she drew, he ran his fingers through her hair and felt strands snap away like thin bands of elastic.

"I fried it as a teenager," she said, not looking up from the page. "Dyed it every color you could think of."

"I saw the blue," said Sami, coughing through smoke. She'd shown him her yearbook picture from tenth grade, unrecognizable with glasses and short blue hair. *Are you sure that's you?* It was, she'd nodded. *Obviously.*

"Oh, there were so many more colors. First I tried red, which seemed less extreme, like I was just dipping a toe in. Red is a real hair color, right? Just not the fire-engine kind. Then it was purple, which was just pretty. Complemented my eyes or something. I wanted to look nice for my first boyfriend, Louie Ramirez. Ah, I remember him."

In the shadows he made out a wistful smile. Louie? That was the first he'd heard of him. Sami already knew she had a past, which he tried not to hold against her despite the fact that he, decidedly, did not. Well, in grade school there was a girl named Sondos who picked jasmine (and got in trouble for it) just to leave petals on his desk. But Rose was his first actual girlfriend. It wasn't uncommon for guys his age, but he still got embarrassed about it when Rose reminded him that he was not hers. Who was this Louie from tenth grade? It seemed so strange to share something so personal—Rose—with someone he'd never even heard of. Were they anything alike? Sami in Louie, Louie in Sami? He tried to act cool, uncaring, not jealous at all, as he blew smoke into the breeze and asked her what happened.

"Oh. He drove off a cliff."

Sami gulped.

"I'm kidding," she said, nudging his knee. "I don't know what happened to Louie. After he dumped me, I was so upset I dyed my hair blue. That was my way of screaming. I guess for his attention. Never got it. Never heard from him again."

"He just ... poof?"

"Yup. Anyway, after that it was green for a little bit. Then it was blonde or black, when I was feeling modest." She picked up the ends of her hair, now a dull brown. "All the colors of the rainbow, and now this."

"Didn't you get into trouble with your parents?"

"At first, sure. My dad even shaved it off once. But later on they were too distracted by the divorce and all. So, they gave up. Now my dad even thinks it's cool."

"No way," said Sami, though he might have had the same reaction. At first, absolutely not. More reasonable in hindsight. As for Sami, his hair had always been the same, short and practical, just long enough to show its curl. He'd never even thought about it before. It was an unconscious choice to remain that way, the same, all the way to his twenties, and probably to eighty if need be. She said it was what she liked about him. He was so pure—and she wouldn't say it, but he knew—so simple.

They laid in the sand until eight p.m. sharp, when the electricity was cut according to schedule. Most campers retreated to their huts, but he and Rose pulled their mattresses outside so they could sleep under the open sky. She fell asleep quickly, as usual, leaving him all alone in the pitch-black night.

From his pocket, he took out the shell he stole from the canyon and fiddled with it in his hands, running his fingers over its roughness to visualize what he couldn't see in the dark. A million years ago, it must have been a full scallop shell—white and fanned out in ridges, with a conjoined twin that had since been lost. It reminded him of a seashell he once stole from a souvenir shop in Alexandria when he was a kid. He must have been six or seven, and had never felt an urge to take what wasn't his until he saw that pretty shell sitting on a shelf. He slipped it into his pocket as his mother bargained with the shopkeeper over teacups. The whole day he walked stiff with the shell in his pocket, avoiding Suad. She gave him a few looks, but he was able to keep the shell undetected until later that night, when he sat before Giddo and wanted to show it off. But when Sami took it out of his pocket, there was only a pile of broken pieces in his open palm. Giddo picked out a shard and as he looked back, Sami burst into tears and confessed.

Sami turned over, smiling in the dark. Stealing was wrong, of course, but that day in the shop he had felt a sudden impulse of *so what* as he reached for the shell. Almost like stealing was something he ought to try sooner or later, anyway, as if he'd have to learn his lesson firsthand. And he did, because the seashell didn't last long in his pocket. That Giddo kept his secret only bonded them more.

The memory swelled his heart until his chest felt like an overblown balloon that could pop with one breath. Why did Giddo have to go? There were so many things he wanted to talk to him about—Cairo and classes and all the new people he'd met, maybe even Rose. Giddo was only in Sami's life when he was too young to know better.

But death was inevitable. That was Sami's only solace—that it was going to happen sooner or later. All the people he loved would one day leave him, just like Giddo and before him, his grandmother Teta, who died of some parasite from the tap that feasted on her insides until all her organs were hollowed out. Giddo changed after she died. He no longer erupted into bouts of laughter when he watched Adel Imam movies, and when he scooped Sami and Ayah into his arms, he smiled in a sad way, as if there was something he wanted to say but couldn't. Day by day he became more silent. He no longer liked to eat, and not even stuffed pigeon would entice him. He stopped watching his films. Newspapers lay stacked, unread at his bedside. Whenever Umm Kalthoum came on the radio he switched it off. Eventually he didn't listen to anything at all.

Sami didn't understand it back then and, in fact, probably complained that Giddo was boring, but now he knew—it was because everything reminded him of Teta. Happy songs, sad songs. Good news, bad news. Stuffed pigeon, *baladi* bread. Tea with three scoops of sugar and mint, tea with nothing at all. There was only one picture of Teta—on her wedding day in 1965—but Giddo gave it to Suad to tuck away, and never asked for it again.

Like everything else, Sami's relationship with Rose was doomed to die. But it could have lasted a bit longer—*could have*, if it weren't for their big mistake. Now there was no way to continue, to what—bring a baby born out of wedlock to a formerly blue-haired foreigner home to meet his mother? Suad, queen of lemons, slayer of weeds, keeper of the Quran. Archenemy of everything Rose was about.

Sami turned back toward Rose, who lay facedown on her pillow. The moon lit the edges of her hair so that it looked silver. He imagined wiping out her shape with the pink tip of an eraser, starting with her moonlit hair, moving down her shoulders and to her toes sticking out of the blanket. What would it be like when she was no longer there? Would it hurt? Would it grip him by the neck, turn the scent of jasmine to a noose? Would he grit his teeth whenever a particular song came on the radio? He probably wouldn't be able to listen to *any* song or hell, even look at any couple ever again. He was screwed. The best he could hope for was to get hit in the head with a shovel and go back to Mahalla dumb enough to be happy.

He sat up and faced the sea, which sparkled with phytoplankton. Like diamonds strewn across the shoreline. What appeared to be magic was nothing more than a horde of microorganisms which, by some chemical reaction, happened to glow a particular way that night. He envied the way he once was, a child who could be enchanted by the sea and take it as a sign that what was written was written and his mother's word was truth. But Sami was no longer a child, and his mistakes couldn't be cleaned up with a Band-Aid and a slap.

# 11

It probably wasn't smart to use her last guineas to get to Tora prison, but Jamila had no choice. She hadn't heard an update from Rose and was too shy to ask before she left for Ras Shaitan. Now Jamila was days away from contact, and waiting was not an option. She reminded herself that what kept her up at night was only a sidenote for others—especially others like Rose, with life-changing secrets in her trash.

What made Jamila's trip even more reckless was that she half-expected to find Tora in the same state as Nilofone—closed, empty, ransacked perhaps. Whatever the equivalent for a prison and not a store. But she had to try. She ended up finding the prison very much in service, and wrapped around its concrete perimeter was a line full of family members of the arrested and disappeared. Many carried portraits of those they were seeking, which made it seem as if they were already dead. Jamila was well aware that she was probably wasting her time. There were a thousand others dealing with the same or even worse right before her, and she of all people would never get what she needed from a building whose entrance was marked with a tank. They'd roll right over her, squash her to dust. Not even St. Fatima's would find out. Nevertheless, she had come all this way, so she took a spot on the wall and stayed until the sun began to set. At that point she gave up and left. She had a house to clean in Zamalek that evening, and a wallet to replenish.

She squeezed into a river-bound microbus with all the others who'd given up for the day—there were many, too many to fit—and found herself pinned against the window like an Eid sheep on an overloaded truck. Glass to cheek, her mind wandered back to Tora. Dealing with the guards required a strong character, a loud voice and a long stride. Like Rose, for example. Her nationality would work in her favor, but that was about it. And Sami? Forget about it. He couldn't face his mother, let alone a prison guard. No, there was one person who could help her, and that person was none other than Miss Fifi Shafik. Rich and well-known, she had the necessary *wasta* to march into Tora and get answers from guards who'd shrink in her shadow. One look at the glamorous woman—jewels dangling from overstretched earlobes, voice thickened not from smoke, but screaming—would send the officers into a servile panic. *Yes, madam, please, madam, as you wish, madam.* Jamila caught herself smiling, lips curling upward against the glass.

Then again, Fifi could just as well smash Jamila's mission to pieces. Her fame wasn't enough to absolve her of a certain reputation. The retired actress, who'd made a fortune in soap operas broadcast from Rabat to Baghdad, was a touch too brazen both on-screen and off with her many marriages and risqué gowns. Her bosom quite literally hung over the 6 October bridge, cleavage bared atop sweetheart necklines on the sort of billboards that made mothers cover their sons' eyes. Not even age could quell her lascivious name—in fact, it only worsened it. She resented getting older and the dimming stardom that came with it, and the vigor with which she compensated made her look even more shameless. Nobody wanted to see all that. She was teetering into menopause, on the brink of old-womanhood, at the age too many twenty- and thirtysomethings associated with their mothers. And yet Fifi was the kind of woman that men thanked God bore no blood relation. One Ramadan, after she was photographed drinking on a cruise ship, a pair of thugs on a motorcycle chucked red paint at the front steps of her villa. Jamila remembered it well—she was the one who had to clean it up. As she mopped the steps, spilling red paint like the blood of slaughter onto the street, she listened to neighbors who came out to watch and whisper. They all knew the target— brazen, shameless, irrepressible Fifi Shafik.

So it could go either way. Either Fifi would help her find Yusuf, dead or alive—or she'd simply get dragged into jail as he had, leaving Jamila without her husband and now, without her pay.

But Jamila was already missing her pay. Fifi hadn't paid her in weeks and she'd already spent the three hundred pounds that had come from Rose. Even in the throes of revolution, there were plenty of expenses. Rent, food, bus rides like these. She took out the last coin from her purse and held it in the palm of her hand, feeling the shape of King Tut's face engraved in gilded metal. Now she was down to this final, sacred guinea. Parting wouldn't be easy, but what choice did she have? It felt like gambling when she reached her stop, trudged to the front of the bus, and handed it to the driver. The only certainty was that the coin was now gone; uncertain was whether she'd return with the five hundred guinea she was owed.

All this time Jamila had been patient with Fifi, knowing her unreliability wasn't malicious. It simply came with the territory of working for a *fannana*, an artist, as she fashioned herself. She was unlike anyone Jamila had ever known, and that was evident from the moment they met, when Fifi greeted her with a glee so extreme it seemed she might burst into tears the next second. Jamila knew, from a lifetime of ups and downs herself, that such feverish delight could only be felt by someone who knew its flipside. It was a bit, dare she say it, like the sunflower man of Kilo 4.5, who both loved and hated her with equal, simultaneous intensity. Neither emotion could exist without the other.

With her finger, she wiped a line through the film on the window, and in the sliver of clear glass she watched the city flit past—singed, ashen, upside down. Much had changed since Fifi came into her life, and much had not. The day they met seemed so long ago that it might as well be fictional, the memory too perfect, too neatly fortuitous to be true. What Jamila remembered, true or not, was that she met Fifi in an alley by El Fishawy, the same pace she met Yusuf—a place so thoroughly entwined with her fate that it must have appeared in her own coffee cups. Back then Jamila had just married, and her hands were covered in bridal henna from fingertips to elbows. Fifi grabbed her upon first sight. She remembered the warmth of her hand, the softness of weekly milk masks. Her nails were

painted a cotton-candy pink. She wore a fur coat, which was obscene for
more than one reason, and an old woman in opaque sunglasses hung on
her arm. An aunt visiting from Dubai, she said, out looking for antiques in
the old bazaar. Fifi ran her hot, clawed hand over Jamila's cheek, marveling
at her beauty—beauty that was *black*, she pointed out—and congratulated
her on her marriage. As they talked, Jamila learned that Fifi's grandmother
was also Sudanese, the daughter of a camel trader who walked his herd
to Beni Suef all the way from Khartoum. This woman in fur was really a
simple girl from the banks of the Nile—and she seemed quite proud of it
in the middle of the crowded bazaar, where she supposed it worked to her
advantage in haggling cutlery.

Fifi was an odd woman, a very odd woman indeed. But when she
invited Jamila for tea, she accepted. They shared the same Nile water in
their blood, after all, and Jamila was in need of a mother-figure. What she
found wasn't quite that. She should have known better—it was all written in that overjoyed grin, held taut by surgically filled cheeks like a dam
about to spill over.

*****

One afternoon tea turned into an invitation for work, and three years
later, Jamila was entering the Shafik villa for the thousandth time. She left
her shoes at the door and disrobed down to the braids on her head. Fifi
always insisted she remove her hijab in her home. *We're all girls here*, she
said, *sisters*. She didn't count her teenage son in the other room, though he
was getting to the age that it was inappropriate.

Jamila had learned quickly that Fifi was more than just an aging
eccentric—she was a big-time soap star. Faded portraits lined the walls
documenting each serial's theme. There was Fifi in Pharaonic headdress, Fifi
in lace, Fifi in galabia, Fifi in black and white. Magazines bearing her image
with headlines like: FIFI SHAFIK: BELLE OF THE NILE, EMPRESS OF AFTERNOON
SOAPS, 20TH CENTURY CLEOPATRA, ORIENTAL MERYL STREEP. She was a mega-
beauty back in the day, with black hair running down to her famous, tireless
rear-end. Now that hair was largely sewn onto her scalp, and the rump

"Beautiful," said Jamila, returning to mopping the floor.

Fifi knotted the flag around her bulbous hips and twirled before the mirror, stood up close and then backed away to the wall. Finally, she threw it off with a huff, still undecided. She switched on the television to satellite news—the only channel broadcasting from Tahrir—and said nothing but *yalla* to the youth amassed on screen.

Jamila wasn't sure what Fifi thought about the protests. She seemed to thrive off the drama but wanted to get likes again. *Yalla*, she said, do your thing and leave, enough unrest. *Yalla*, there were clips to post, dinners to host. The studio had been closed for a whole week and she'd barely left the villa because of it. Fifi was so cut off that it didn't even occur to her that she'd put Jamila in harm's way by asking her to cross a city in mid-revolt to reach her, distended belly and all. But Jamila forgave her. Fifi just didn't understand.

All she had really seen of the situation outside was that there were checkpoints at every intersection from one end of the island to the other. They terrified her. She said she had a phobia of guns due to a bad experience when she was younger, which set Jamila's imagination reeling, though she didn't ask for details and for once, Fifi didn't offer any. It did occur to her that, for all the checkpoints, guns weren't exactly new to the streets of Zamalek, where there were armed guards for each of the island's fifty or so embassies. She suspected it was just Fifi's excuse to avoid taking the dog out. She'd rather weather the odd indoor piss or shit than cross a single checkpoint.

Today Coco had spared her. In truth, Jamila looked forward to walking the dog. Even though Coco stank, and she preferred keeping contact to the absolute minimum—Jamila loved their outings, which not even a revolution could tarnish. She could walk the streets of Zamalek forever, all around the perimeter of the island and up and down its alleys, under the trees and along the Nile, well into oblivion until her legs gave out. But her legs couldn't give out now. There was business to attend to—and walking Coco turned out to be the perfect cover.

Jamila clicked on Coco's rhinestone-studded leash and took her to her favorite tree at the corner of Shagaret El Dor street. She let the dog take her time to sniff each piece of trash on the curb. Despite the litter, the air outside was delicious, smelling of leaves and not smoke. It felt like the first time she'd breathed in days. She even lifted her veil for a moment, as if she could taste the freshness on the tip of her tongue. The revolution was undetectable on that shady street, all its sound and smoke muffled by the thick canopies of trees. The only sign of it was the checkpoint at the end of the block, where a few men and boys sat around a dying bonfire. It was never not frightening to see armed men—even those wearing hair gel and house slippers, like these. Maybe Fifi's fear of them was true after all.

Jamila tensed as they turned to look at her, and Coco must have felt it too, because she started to bark. She hushed the dog and waved at the men as if to excuse herself. To her relief the men waved back, never once rising from their posts.

She tugged Coco along in the direction of the corniche. She could have sworn she'd seen a Nilofone there once before. That side of the river was quiet, anyway, facing not Tahrir but Giza, where the peaks of the Pyramids hid behind clouds. Despite all the rusted billboards and the dilapidated slums in the distance, the water was so still and the city so silent that it looked like a painting. She and Coco passed the Nileside cafés where Fifi spent normal days lunching with better friends than the one who took Mr. Shalaby. Jamila wanted to climb over the fence and spend the day on a couch by the water. There was nobody there, after all. But not before she settled this Nilofone business. She decided she'd allow herself rest if she could get those phone records.

When at last Jamila found the Nilofone shop, she tied Coco to a bench and walked to the door. With each step, she tempered her hopes, telling herself there was no way and no reason it would be open. But to her surprise there was a light on inside and, as she got closer, an actual person hunched over the counter. He must have seen her glide up to the storefront, black swathes rippling in the breeze, but he kept his eyes on the inventory before him as if he hadn't. Would she be better off removing the veil over her face? Those types of veils were unusual in that neighborhood, where women like Fifi Shafik walked the streets in high heels. Then again, showing her face would reveal her as a foreigner, and Sudanese at that. They'd never help her then.

She took deep breath and raised her fist to the glass, knocking softly until finally, the man looked up. He said something, but she couldn't hear him through the glass. She got the message from his shaking head. *No, sorry, we can't help you, go home, give up.* When she remained, he came to the door and opened it a crack, as if he were afraid she'd barge through.

The first thing he said wasn't a word but a lengthy sigh, so furious it ruffled the tail of her veil. Then, the expected, "what do you want?"

And from her, the customary plea for help.

"Look, I've heard this story before. Your child is sick. He's in the hospital. He needs a kidney transplant but you don't have the money. If you don't cough up fifty-thousand pounds for surgery then he will die. Die! And now it's my fault that your son will die because there's a cash register right in front of me, and in the middle of the revolution I could easily hand you the money and claim looters took it. But I won't. You know why? Because I've heard these lies before. I won't fall for your Sudanese tricks."

Anger bubbled up from the pit of Jamila's stomach, but she tried her best to quash it as she inched closer to the crack in the door. He needed to hear her—just hear her. She'd settle for just that. She took her phone out of her pocket and switched on the screen to show the Nilofone logo, blinking and bright.

"I don't need money. I'm a customer, sir, and I need my records."

"Why the hell do you need those?"

She didn't know what to say. Should she explain everything right there, in the one-inch gap between the door and the wall? Where should she begin— Sudan? Yes, she fled as a refugee, settled in Cairo, was stalked by a sick man with sunflower seeds, changed her number, and filed for resettlement—only to find that it was that phone, and not the sunflower man, that would determine her fate. She didn't know what came over her when she finally opened her mouth.

"I'm the widow of a martyr," she said, cringing at the sound of her own words. "Please help me."

The man huffed and took the phone, then he shook his head briskly. "Only headquarters can help you. You'll need to go to Mohandeseen."

"What?"

"I said Mohandeseen." He stuck his skinny arm through the gap and pointed across the river, where the headquarters stood, ready and able to help her. Supposedly.

Jamila walked back to Coco, untethered her and made her way back to Fifi's, no longer in the mood to take rest at that deserted café. Seventy-seven more to go.

*****

The house was unusually quiet when Jamila returned. No music, no Fifi. All she could hear was the television and the sound of frenetic tapping on videogame controllers coming from Qandil's bedroom. She left the leash on the entryway console, where it joined a half-empty glass of wine, lips imprinted in pink gloss. On the floor there were two furry slippers—the presence of which, without Fifi's feet, seemed ominous. Jamila put them back in the closet, noticing how tiny they were. Fifi was just a mortal, a village girl after all.

She walked down the corridor, Coco trailing, until she reached the bedroom door. She pushed it open to find Fifi engulfed in white tulle and ribbon. As Jamila turned to greet her, she realized that it wasn't just any dress, but her wedding dress, veil and all, tufts of white cascading to the floor like whipped cream.

"Jamila. People are getting married in the middle of Tahrir. Can you believe it?" She pointed to the TV, which showed marchers moving in waves swaying to and fro like the tide, banners held high, and in the center of it all—a bride and groom trading rings in the crowd. "Everyone loves a bride, don't they, *ya* Jamila? And a dancing bride?" She twirled before the mirror, threw her hands in the air, and praised God in her own honor, *mashallah*. Just then, something ripped. She spun around, contorting her arms to reach the zipper of the dress.

Jamila approached cautiously, as if any slight movement might rip every ruffle to shreds. Time hadn't been kind to Fifi's physique—even her third and most recent wedding dress was not having it with her new shape, and the zipper gaped over the soft rolls of her back. She tugged lightly at the fabric, careful not to catch her skin, which was warm and dewy, about to break a sweat.

"*Khalas*, just cut it," she said, fanning herself.

Slowly, as if waiting for her to change her mind or somehow wriggle free herself, Jamila took a pair of scissors and snipped away the caught fabric.

Fifi gave a long *ahhhhhh* as she released her belly to go where it pleased. She sank into the couch with a plop, tufts of gown rising all around her like petals in bloom. "God has spoken, *ya* Jamila. Jamila?"

"Yes, Miss Fifi," she said, propping up her leg to sweep glitter off the floor.

"God has spoken and said: Fifi Shafik will not perform tonight. Not even for our friends, the bride and groom in Tahrir."

Fifi's eyes followed her as she waited for a response, a reaction, a nod, a shoulder shrug, *anything*. But Jamila had nothing to say tonight, just as Fifi had nothing to wear.

"Can you just scoot over so I can reach underneath—"

"What a shit wedding, poor things."

"That's not what I—"

"Sweetie, I've done a lot of weddings in my day—from the streets of Imbaba to the Four Seasons Hotel. I'll dance on the Titanic just as well as Abu Himar's dinghy down the river. But I've never seen a wedding that … that *awful*. Tahrir? What, will they catch the El-Wahab bus on the way home?"

Jamila tried to cover her amusement with a sneeze. It was the glitter. Yes, that was it. She shouldn't encourage Fifi. But it was too late.

"Imagine, a wedding smelling of trash and gasoline. No music except for car horns, *beep beep*. You want Nancy Ajram? More like Mohammed Badie with a bullhorn. Seriously, Jamila, as a woman, as a young lady, as a *jewel*, imagine getting married like *that*. Standing in a crowd of hoodlums. Why, there must have been a hand on the bride's ass the whole time!"

There was a ripping sound as Fifi burst into hoarse laughter. Jamila leapt toward her—a vain effort to save one more inch of seam—as she continued.

"Trust me, Jamila. I know an ass-grabber when I see one. And *that* crowd? Was full of them. No wonder the bride looked so sad. If it were me, if *my* in-laws threw me a wedding like that … Oh, you don't want to know." She shook her head, left and right, for seconds after her last word until finally the dam broke, and she started to cry.

Not again. Jamila wanted to console Fifi, to get her out of that dress and tuck her into bed to wake up anew the next morning. But in that moment, out of fear of saying something to make it worse, she just handed her a box of tissues.

As Jamila went on with her chores, she heard the tears subside. Eventually Fifi's whimpers gave way to the sound of crunching wrappers. When she returned to the room, she found Fifi chomping chips two at a time. It seemed the food had lifted her spirits for now. As she bent down to pick up a wrapper, a stinging pain struck her belly. It had grown so heavy it threatened to topple her over—one wobble and she would be on the floor, bent and bruised as the wrappers at the madame's feet.

Fifi didn't notice. Her eyes were now engulfed in a tub of halva, which she ate with a spoon like a carton of Chinese food. The sound of her lips smacking with sesame paste grew louder, deafening almost, as Jamila stared back in disgust. Fifi wasn't hungry, and she didn't even like halva. She was racing to empty her kitchen cabinets as if it would soothe the old wound dug up in the tufts of that wedding dress.

"Miss Fifi, I need to go home before it gets too late."

"Very well," she said, not looking up from her halva. "You go back to your husband, I'll go back to my cake."

Jamila bit the inside of her lip as if to temper her tongue. She'd kept Yusuf's disappearance from Fifi but now wanted to throw it in her face. It was what she deserved for being so wrapped in her own chaos that she couldn't tell the difference between halva and cake. She should hurry up and ask for her pay before the night descended into even more disarray.

"Oh," Fifi yelped, as if she'd just remembered. "I've gone to the Crédit Agricole *a thousand* times now. It's still closed. I'm so sorry, but I'll have to pay you when it reopens, *God willing*."

Jamila could feel her face getting hot as she restrained herself from turning and shutting the door in her face. But as if she were dealing with someone right thinking, someone sane, she took a breath and explained.

"I don't have enough money to get home."

Fifi looked up, confused, spoon still stuck in the brick of halva.

"How much does the bus cost?"

"One guinea."

"One guinea! You don't even have that?"

Jamila shook her head, not knowing what to say. All she knew, already, was that she'd made a mistake telling her—not expecting the mix of alarm and ridicule she received in turn. Didn't Fifi know the price of water or a loaf of bread, the cost to rent a single room in a slum like Kilo 4.5? No she did not, it seemed. Fifi reached for her wallet and pulled out a single coin with a smile, as if it would take her to Dubai and back on a private jet.

"Alright, here's your guinea. I'll deduct it from your pay. Oh and Jamila—you really should be more careful with your money. Don't throw it around, dear. Be wise."

Jamila took the coin and fled the villa, so livid she forgot to grab her veil by the door. To think—just hours before, she'd thought this woman might help her. Now it was clear that she would have to find Yusuf by herself. Somehow.

*****

Jamila's cheeks were still taut with anger when she reached Ramses. She had never tried so hard to hold back tears—in the street, on the bus, up the stairs to apartment 702—but when she finally had the chance, she couldn't.

The hall was so dark she had to feel her way to the door, running her hands along walls coated with filth. She wasn't used to being there without a streak of light beaming beneath the door, the sound of the TV coming from the living room where Sami and Rose sat in a perpetual love daze. When she left for Tora that morning, she hadn't bothered leaving a light on to pretend they were home, thinking it might invite troublemakers. She wanted the door to blend into the cavernous hall, just another abandoned unit like all the rest inside the building. Now the place was even more frightening—the ceilings high and looming, the spiral staircase a hellish, endless length, each floor full of doors sealed shut by decades of grime. What an odd place for two living youths to call home. Even the cramped, dilapidated apartments of Kilo 4.5 seemed more welcoming. Rose was no movie star like Fifi Shafik but Jamila was sure she could afford a place in a nicer part of town, because she paid her more, and always on time.

As Jamila opened the door, she reminded herself that she was doing Rose a favor, just like she did her a favor when she discarded that pregnancy test and said nothing about it. She bolted the door shut and went to the kitchen to warm up rice in silence—that was all she could tolerate right now, silence—but she couldn't even have that. A wailing drew her to the kitchen window, where she saw the silhouettes of tussling cats through the frosted glass. She cursed under her breath as she tried to shut out the horrible sound. Normally she would have more sympathy but tonight was not the night. At once she threw down her spoon, grabbed the broom, and struck the window. The cats dispersed with one final, ear-shredding screech.

Jamila scraped burnt rice into a bowl and took it to the living room. It was strange to sit on their couch. Even stranger to turn on the TV, as if it were hers. She kept the volume low, lest some ghost overhear, and flicked through all three-and-a-half channels only to find nothing but kittens flocking through fields of dandelion on each. The cats had followed her even there. She switched to the half channel, preferring its scrambled nonsense, only to hear a cheery ringtone cut through the mind-numbing fuzz.

It was Sami's phone.

As it continued to ring, Jamila followed the sound to the bedroom, where she found the phone in a pile of dirty laundry. On the screen flashed his mother's name. Not again. The ring seemed to grow louder as she wondered what to do. She could answer it like she did before—maybe this time she would get the chance to say something. But what would she say? Nothing—that's what she had to say. Nothing.

She wrapped the phone in a dirty T-shirt to muffle the sound as it rang and rang. It felt like she was burying the thing alive. How could she do this to a woman who was worried sick over her son? Her ringing deserved to be heard, whether or not anybody answered. She unwrapped the phone, set it on the table, and went back to her bowl of rice. Hungry as she was, Jamila couldn't eat. Her hands shook so hard that singed grains dribbled off the spoon and onto her belly.

The baby kicked as she dusted the rice off. She held her hand to her belly and the shaking subsided. In a few months' time, the baby would be in her arms—a moment she'd looked forward to until Yusuf disappeared. Now she dreaded it. The child would not only face a fatherless, wandering life, but would surely inherit the strife she'd endured throughout her pregnancy. It would seep into the blood through the womb. And there would be blood. She imagined giving birth in the corridor with seeds beneath her back and between her toes, neighbors hovering, the sunflower man shouting obscenities as the baby's first words. She hated the thought of raising a girl in a world full of men like that.

What was it that people said? *Watch out for your daughters, or …* Or what? It seemed to her that people should watch out for their sons. Boys were so fragile—a threadbare line between victim and perpetrator. Many grown men would fall apart if they went through just a sliver of what she'd seen—and her story wasn't even exceptional. Far worse testimonies were ringing through the halls of St. Fatima's at that very moment. Women's were different. Men suffered traumas with a timeframe. Prison sentences. Bouts of torture. War. But women fought a losing fight until the day they died—in the streets, in the home, at work. On buses, even. In elevators and bathroom stalls. Everywhere.

Jamila guessed from the low-slung shape of her belly that she was carrying a boy. A son like Sami. Sighing, she envisioned this boy-to-be, born to a lone woman and a disappeared man, named Idris or Ibrahim after her brothers, or maybe even Yusuf if it didn't seem so hopeless—a confirmation of death more solid than a mutilated body. He would be handsome, no doubt. Tall like his mother, eyes fringed in heavy lashes like Yusuf. If he was anything like his father then he'd have girls chasing him from an early age. God only knew the kind of trouble he'd get into when he was old enough to live on his own, like Sami, to find a girlfriend or twenty, to do … that.

She stopped with a spoonful of rice in the air midway between her mouth and the bowl, thinking of that pregnancy test and how it had laid, positive result face up on the dirty hallway floor. Just the thought was enough to give her a flutter of panic. Sami was a good man but what he'd done was inexcusable. She couldn't imagine having a son who did that— and on top of everything, being unable to reach him.

When the phone rang again, Jamila dove off the couch so fast she nearly slipped and fell on the freshly waxed floors. Something compelled her back to the phone—as if it were some involuntary, instinctual response to the ringing—and she went to the bedroom and closed the door. It was still Sami's mother, of course. Her hand jittered as she watched the phone vibrate in her palm. Whatever it was, it wouldn't stop. She could have slaughtered and defeathered a whole chicken in the time she'd been stand- ing there, deciding what to do. And still, it rang.

Through the window she heard voices down on Ramses Street. She peered out to see a group of young men carrying rocks in their T-shirts as they walked south toward Tahrir Square. Boys causing trouble. Even then, in the middle of the night. Imagine the terror Sami's mother must be feel- ing, no word from her son in the middle of this unrest. Sami could easily be one of those boys on the street, rocks in his hands, rocks in his head. And on the last ring, her finger found its way to the right button and clicked.

"Who's this?"

Jamila hadn't even gotten a *hello* out when the woman interrupted, barking quickly as if it were her fault that Sami had kept her waiting, ignoring her through all six thousand rings.

"This is ... Jamila."

"And who are you, Jamila?"

"I—I'm a maid, madam. I just wanted to tell you that your son is fine. He's traveling and left his phone behind, but he'll be back soon, *inshallah*."

"A *maid*? Sami has a *maid*? Is that boy living in a dormitory or the Royal Semiramis?"

"No, no," she said in his defense. Now his mother thought he was throwing guineas out the window like Fifi Shafik downing a whole bag of chips. "I'm not Sami's maid."

"Then who's maid *are* you, young lady?"

She didn't know why this woman made her so nervous, like a child slapped in front of the whole classroom—a stuttering, stammering mess, incapable of giving the right answer. She was only trying to help. She had nothing to hide. So, when she opened her mouth to speak, at last, she said the truth.

"I work for Miss Rose."

The woman began coughing, like something was stuck in her throat. Jamila thought of hanging up but couldn't. Before she knew it, her throat had cleared, and she was onto the next, obvious question, the words peppering out like punches.

"Miss Rose? Who is Miss Rose?"

Jamila realized she'd made a terrible mistake. She realized it before they got to this point—perhaps when she picked up the phone. Now she had to explain, somehow, this woman with whom her son was living, sharing a bed, making a baby, and now, traveling the Sinai desert. She was a foreigner—should she start there? Maybe that would make it better. It's understandable, she could say. It's how foreigners live. She might be shocked out there in Mahalla, but that's only because they come from different planets—this woman breathing fire into the receiver, and the woman in question. Who. Is. Rose.

"She's from America, you see, and she's his … uh, friend. Anyway, I just wanted you to know that he's safe and sound and you shouldn't worry and actually, I should get going."

A gust of breath crackled through the receiver, but the woman said nothing. Jamila checked to see if the line had been disconnected, but it hadn't. She wished to evaporate completely, to not exhist and to never have existed in the first place.

"Hello? Hello?"

When there was still no answer, she hung up.

As Jamila set the phone down, she realized that not only had she made a mistake but what was coming would be far worse. Eventually Sami would come home to that phone of his and find out she had blown his secret. Quiet, dumb Jamila. Who never said anything unless it was the worst thing possible to say. How could she have done this? And Rose was pregnant. Look at this trauma she had caused them before even the birth of their baby.

Jamila still couldn't bring herself to turn off Sami's phone—knowing it would make his mother lose whatever shred of sanity she had left—so, she buried it at the bottom of the laundry basket, dragged it into the closet, and shut the door. She gathered all her things—slippers, paperwork, pins from her hijab. Back in the kitchen, she washed all the dishes and wiped down the counter. She set a sheet on the couch and climbed into its pillowy tufts, exhausted from the years' worth of troubles she'd encountered today. But the phone wouldn't let her sleep. Somehow she could still hear it ringing for hours as she lay in the dark, and it seemed to get louder as the night trudged forth. Was she imagining things? Surely, the sound of the phone hadn't penetrated layer after layer of cloth, through the closet door and all the way down the hall. Surely this was all in her head—a literal ringing in her ears. An effect of what Dolores had explained to be PTSD. All the refugees had trouble sleeping, she'd told her. Yes, PTSD. That must be it.

Jamila didn't sleep a wink. Tomorrow, she would have to go. PTSD.

## 12

In the last hour of darkness before dawn broke, Sami awoke to the sound of an engine. He turned to face the road, where a car approached, puttering. Its headlights illuminated the mountain until a snakelike, reptilian beast took form in the shadows of crags. In his half asleep stupor he almost laughed. He and Ayah used to cast shadow puppets with their fingers against the walls as kids. Camels, crocodiles. Now a snake. But this was no puppet—its silhouette was exact, like stencil. As the car rounded the bend, the beast contorted out of shape, shadows shifting like the revolving insides of a kaleidoscope.

The image remained firm in his mind as he sank back into the sand. Mouth open and snarling, claws curled over the rocks. In the moment he'd been certain of what he saw, but the longer he stared at the blank, dark mountain, the less could believe even his own minute-old memory. He thought of the phytoplankton that looked like glitter in the sea. Likewise, this was not magic but only an effect of headlights hitting the rocks. But if that were the case, then wouldn't that shadow appear any other time a pair of headlights hit the mountain at the same angle and time of night? This spot was remote, but even Bedouins had trucks. Thousands of others—well, hundreds or rather dozens at least—must have driven past to create the same shape. Surely he wasn't the first person in the million-year history of the mountain to witness that shadow. It seemed strange he hadn't heard anything of it. That semi-natural phenomenon should be a world-class attraction, planting billboards every kilometer on this strip of coast. *The great midnight mountain demon.* Maybe then there would be more than grass huts to stay in.

But the absence of all of that seemed to mean one thing—that only Sami could see it. He asked himself why. There had to be a reason. He cracked his knuckles like boulders colliding against the quiet night. He knew why. This was because he'd done a very bad thing, many bad things, and here was a divine warning. Like the snakeskin on the mountain trail, splayed across the ground as if to trip him. There was no neatly scientific explanation like that of glowing phytoplankton. No reason except for the fact that this demon was what he'd become, for not only doing what he did but for contemplating ways to get out.

Until now, he'd been in denial over the constant nagging in the back of his mind. *Get rid of it.* They could find a doctor in some far-flung hospital who'd take care of it for a few hundred guineas passed under the table. Then there would be no evidence and nothing to confess. He'd find a way to scrape up money. Would Rose help pay for it? He thought of *Nadim* scribbled onto notebook paper. No, she would never agree to it. And yet she had to. He took a deep breath and closed his eyes. Then he would have to dope her up and take her by hand to the operating table, give her some kind of elixir to go to sleep and wake up no longer pregnant. He didn't like thinking about it. It was awful to even entertain the thought. But somehow it seemed more humane than letting her go through with the birth. Rose had no idea what hell awaited them when a secret like this came out. That terrible whisper of a thought that had lay dormant at the back of his tongue was teetering at the tip now, and at any moment, he'd scream through the canyons. *Get rid of it!*

What an awful person he'd become. A waste of Suad's righteous upbringing. A demon like the one on the mountain. He knew that was why he saw it.

Of course, he couldn't go back to sleep. All he could do was wait for another car to pass, the way he might wait for a ghost to reappear just to make sure he'd actually seen it. This must be what Rose referred to as the witching hour—the last moments of darkness before dawn. When paranormal activity was at its peak, reality blurred in the transitioning night. In Cairo, the muezzin would be calling out the day's first prayer, and birds would be chirping even in the still-dark sky. Back home he'd hear the churn of factories, the constant whirl of the neighbor's cotton wheel. But here, there was no muezzin or birds or wheel. The mountain had disappeared. The sea was undetectable except for the slow lick of the water, itself too faint to hear without trying. Even the sky, crowded with stars, couldn't dispel the beast in his head. He grabbed the sand in his fists as he stared above, feeling as if the galaxy could suck him into the ether if he let go.

*****

He woke up on a bed of flattened sand, the roll-up cushion lying beside him. He was alone. Rose must have left to take a shower. He lit a cigarette and stared at the sea, savoring this moment before he'd have to face her.

The water was flat and shallow, so transparent he could see all the coral sprawling under the surface. How different it was from the Alexandrian coast just a few weeks ago, where the sea had been gray to match low-hanging clouds. To be fair, January was a bad time of year to visit. That a local church had been bombed during the same weekend—on New Years' Eve, nonetheless—only helped set the tone for a terrible trip. Sami remembered hearing the warbling voice of Umm Kalthoum on the radio as he and Rose sat at a seaside café, holding hands under the table, and the way it faded into white noise when she told him. The loosening grip of her hands as she realized the extent of his horror. The water reddening from the blood of spearfishing. The foam capping the waves like a rabid mouth coming for them. Those words, *I'm—you know*, had morphed the whole coast into a hellscape.

That feeling was still with him here. Maybe it had nothing to do with the weather after all. In fact, he was even more bothered by the brightness of the sun in Ras Shaitan, and the pink glow of the hills on the opposite coast. It all seemed to taunt him. *Look at all you'd enjoy if you hadn't gotten into this mess.* He tried to orient himself—if Mahalla was west, then Dammam was east, and that meant his father was somewhere over those eastern hills, watching, judging. Though he stared, cigarette burning, he felt no longing.

When he reached the cigarette's filter, he realized Rose had been gone longer than expected. She'd left the journal among her things in the sand. Now was his chance. He looked over his shoulder and reached for the journal. Before opening it, he took time to admire it in his hands. It was a rare find, a classic beauty bound in leather imprinted with a floral pattern like henna. Made for her, made for him to find in Khan El Khalili. He cracked open the cover with the tip of his finger, then shut it and opened it again. It wasn't right to read her journal, but he figured there were no boundaries between them now, and after all, he'd bought it.

On the first page, she'd written her name in both English and Arabic, the latter with exaggerated curls. Then the line, *once you drink from the Nile, you are destined to return.* It was an old fable, a cliché among foreigners. Amusing to Rose and concerning to Sami. A returning Rose seemed like more trouble than he'd anticipated. Strange that she'd copied that line onto the very first page, as if declaring the journal's purpose, the way he might write *physics* in a school notebook. It hadn't been funny when Sami tried using it to cheer her up between heaves. Now it was a mantra.

All Sami knew was that expats loved it. He couldn't blame them—expats *did* seem to always come back. Freshman year, Hamza kissed a British girl behind the library at lunch hour. He cried when she went home at the end of the semester—and again when she returned a year later on holiday. Even his hydrocarbon professor, Mr. Schlum, who you'd think would be immune to such superstitions, had come back to Cairo after growing up in Maadi with his diplomat parents. Eternal return. Was it magic or a self-fulfilling prophecy? All roads will lead back to Cairo if you believe it. Even the literal act of drinking Nile water was unavoidable—after all, it ran through the taps. When he first met Rose she was so worried about her delicate stomach that she brushed her teeth with bottled water. Now she used the tap like him. Sometimes she'd play it safe by ordering sodas and fruit cocktails and beers, only to unwittingly suck up the melted remains of ice cubes through her straw. Tap water. And how many feluccas had they taken up and down the river? Surely, at *some* point *some* droplets of river had spurted out of motors to land on her lips. Straight Nile water.

In fact, there was one night last summer that she ingested far more than a stray droplet. After drinking too many Stellas on a dinner cruise, she was so out of it that when a man from the street handed her a tin cup of tap water from a fountain by the river, she drank it. Rose always told the tale with a smile creeping up her lips in amusement, like one hell of a morning-after drunk story, the punchline being the simple fact that she drank from a communal cup on the side of the road, full of water pumped from the river where dead donkeys and other carcasses lay to rest. By the next morning, not much of the stuff remained in her body, but surely some worm or microorganism must have made its way into her bloodstream and stuck. That meant she'd one day return to Egypt. Without Sami. He turned the page to find his name at the top, then braced himself.

*Sami teases me for sleeping so much, as if it means I'm at peace some-how, like all is fine and dandy, peaches and cream. Even Jamila judg-es me for it. I could see it in her eyes in the kitchen the other day. If only she knew about the pregnancy. I want to tell her.*

He set down the journal. If he had an eraser, he'd wipe those words off the page and pretend he'd read no such thing. If the words didn't exist, then what happened hadn't happened, he could toss the journal into the sea and tell Rose a falcon swooped down to snatch it. But the words were there, and there was no eraser, and what happened had happened. Slowly, he breathed in and returned to the page.

*I want to tell her. Woman to woman, both young and pregnant, both pretty much alone. But it was that look that stopped me. She looked tired – tired of work, tired of me. Like she wanted me to just leave her alone. So I did.*

*I wish they knew that there's no rest in my sleep. I wake up covered in sweat, sheets soaked to the mattress. And there are only bad dreams. Maybe it's a side effect of pregnancy. Maybe it's the hash he's always smoking. Maybe it's everything.*

*The dreams keep getting worse. An injured palomino pulling a cart full of bricks uphill, limping. A coyote trailing us up the mountains, waiting till we tire out enough to be his dinner. We're riding a rollercoaster holding champagne glasses, trying not to break them. I'm about to miss my flight home and I'm still packing, trying to stuff all my things in a suitcase that can't hold it all. Crowds bidding on a goat in Souk El Gomaa, spitting prices based on the quality of the meat.*

*The last takes place in the Diesel. It's dark and smells like trash, and I can feel grime under my bare feet as I give birth in the open hall. Sami's sitting between my legs, eating a bowl of koshari or something. Nonchalant. He doesn't even help as I push and push. He just stares down at me with that weird, distant look, like he doesn't know what to make of the mother of his child. A non-Muslim, non-Egyptian, non-virgin, nonentity. Unsuitable, unreasonable, impossible, implausible. Godless and rootless and youthless. He's known it all along, pressing it down, but every once in a while, it'll dawn on him. I can see it in his face. Even while giving birth to his child. In the dream, I pull it out of myself while he sits there watching, judging, chomping on chickpeas. When I see it, I scream. It's deformed, face like a fruit fly. Skin gray, like it's not even alive. And when I look at Sami, all he does is shrug.*

Sami held the book open for a few silent minutes, stuck on a page he desperately wanted to turn. The dream was disturbing, yes, but so was what she thought of him. He supposed he could have brushed it off, called it nonsense from the subconscious mind, but then he'd be lying to himself. What she described was truer than any waking moment—his distance, all the worries he suppressed, even his judgment (which to be fair, was more his mother's than his own, but racked his mind nonetheless). He might have had a word with her if there were anything he could say. What? That she's wrong—that she is indeed suitable and reasonable and possible and plausible? No, then he'd be adding to his list of mistakes. It was a long one, growing by the minute.

When he heard the door swing shut from the main hut, he set the book down where Rose had left it, went back to his own, and tried to act natural. Smoking—no, staring at the sea.

They spent the rest of the day passing time under a straw canopy. Rose continued writing as Sami sneaked glances, hoping he hadn't left behind an eyelash or fingernail to prove his lurking. On his lap sat one of her books on ancient Egypt, earmarked and highlighted like a textbook. *In the Time of the Pharaohs*. She read that stuff for fun. It must be how she knew all that mumbo jumbo about the snake on the mountain trail. He dusted off sand between the pages and flipped to the index to look up *S* for *snake*. His eyes flitted up and down the list of entries. *Snake, god. Snake, ouroboros. Snake, uraeus.* He flipped to the first.

Apep, or Apophis to the Greeks, was a freakish serpent god, ruler of chaos and conflict, frequent antagonist to the big god, Ra. To think, there was a time when there were not only multiple gods, but imperfect gods, gods with names and personal beef. Gods like Apep who slithered up from the underworld and ate the sun. Sami cringed, picturing jaws unhinging. He learned that the ancient Egyptians prayed to keep Apep away, and priests wrote manuals on how to fight him. *There*, he thought, fingering the page. In Apep, Sami found vindication for his fear of snakes. Here was proof that his fear was ancestral, perfectly natural. It ran through his blood the same as genes for big eyes and curly hair.

He looked over at Rose, whose pencil moved furiously across the pages of her journal. She hadn't mentioned Apep before. Probably because it didn't support her contrarian argument. She had already read about the snake god—he could tell by the creased pages, dog-eared at the corner, the circle she'd drawn over *antithesis of order and light*. Yet she was still unafraid, or at least pretended to be. *Snakes have a bad rep*.

Beasts in his head, he couldn't help thinking of the mountain demon. Up on the cliffs, he tried tracing the crags to find the missing beast. But there was no demon in the daylight. Not even bits and pieces he could

draw together like a constellation. All he saw was a mountain, unremarkable except for its beauty, rocks like any other.

*****

Today the cook served an unfortunate lunch of roast goat, stewed Moroc-
can style with cinnamon and raisins. Rose refused, saying she felt nauseous.
Sami tried not to think of her nightmares as he gorged on two servings
too delicious to turn away. Besides, it would have looked suspicious. His
eyes scanned Rose periodically as she picked at a bowl of coagulated foul.
It seemed she hadn't noticed him snooping.

In the main hut, he found more campers than he'd thought were
there. An Australian with blond dreadlocks. A pair of sunburnt Europeans. A guitarist in a reggae band, stranded on his way to a show in Cairo. A
month ago. They all blamed the revolution for their extended stays, saying
the roads were unsafe. And if the revolution never ended? All the better.
They thought Sami and Rose were crazy for planning to head out that
day, but their reaction only fueled his urge to go. He needed to get back
to Cairo, where a revolution continued without him, where the chaos
crushed his own thoughts, where even the blast of a gunshot was about as
significant as a penny splashing into the sea.

The news blared from a radio in the kitchen—something about
bombs, something about revolution, something that had set the sleepy
camp abuzz. Everybody huddled around Zane, who sat cross-legged with
a fresh scarf tied around his head, taking questions as if he were an expert.

"Is it true that the Islamists are behind this?"

"What do you think will happen if the regime falls?"

As Sami sawed off a sliver of goat meat, he wondered if Zane had ever
seen the cliffside demon. Probably not. The man was too busy running his
mouth, spreading false information just as deftly as state news. According
to him, there was no youth movement and there was no Tahrir. There was
the regime and the Islamists, and your choice was one or the other. Sami
spoke up when he couldn't take it anymore.

"I've been to Tahrir. It's not like that."

"Don't be naive," said Zane, cigarette dangling from his gesticulating finger. "This country is much bigger than whichever corner you staked out in Tahrir. Where were you, by the KFC? Kind of says it all, doesn't it? There are places that don't even *have* a KFC. You're in one right now."

Sami didn't need to be told of such places, and by an American at that. He reminded him that he was from Mahalla, a place Rose might call "the real Egypt," and that he may not have been everywhere, but he'd surely seen more than Zane had. At least, in his head he had. In his defense, it was hard to get a word in with Zane yammering away, impressed with his own voice and stature among the clueless campers—all foreigners except for the guitarist, who was too high to care.

"If the regime falls, it'll be Saudi Arabia up in here in a month, *tops*. Your girlfriend's going to have to wear a burka and you can kiss your Stellas goodbye. So enjoy this place while you can."

Sami looked around, hoping to find just one fellow skeptic, but there weren't any.

"Stability is key," said the cook of all people. He was a poor man from Kafr El Sheikh, the sort who should be fighting for bread, freedom, and social justice in Tahrir. Maybe he didn't want to go against his boss—the boss who thought he had flesh in the game despite his ability to fly back to America the second the shit hit the fan. Yet the cook seemed sincere when he leaned in and said, "But if anything happens, I hope America puts a good president for us."

At this the other campers laughed. One of the Europeans chimed in. "That's not how democracy works, my friend."

"That's the thing," said Zane. "Egypt isn't *ready* for democracy. When my illiterate housekeeper can read the difference between bleach and detergent before she does my laundry, then maybe I'll consider it."

Sami's head spun. Dictatorship is good. Freedom is bad—they'll fuck it up. Democracy is impossible, untranslatable. He lit a cigarette without realizing and swiftly butted it out when he noticed. He shouldn't look nonchalant like Zane, no—that was the difference between them. Zane was a spoiled pseudo-Egyptian who didn't get it. Sami was the real deal, from fucking *Mahalla* via Tahrir Square. He was about to jump in and set everyone straight, but Rose beat him to it.

"That's because of the poverty. Squatters living on rooftops. Kids selling tissues on the street. Donkeys in the middle of traffic. It all goes back to that."

Zane stood up and dusted sand off his knees. "Poverty sucks, Rose, but let's face it. This is a third world country. If some people are poor but the country is at peace, then it's worth it. Maybe you've been brainwashed by country folks, people who wouldn't mind the beards taking over. And now you're asking for too much, just like them. Last year the Brotherhood finally got permission to run for office and then they *still* bitched. Sorry, y'all won five seats. The year before, it was what—*prison time* for even thinking of joining? So, get over it. Everybody needs to think about how bad it could get. Let's not push it."

Zane had wanted the last word, but Rose—sweet Rose and that baby-induced nausea—wouldn't let him. She keeled over to the side, covering her mouth, and inched like a slug toward the sea, where she retched.

*****

Hours later, as they stood with their bags on the desert road, Sami realized what the radio had been blaring about in the main hut. A church had been bombed in Rafah last night, which was why the bus station was closed. Now the only way home was to hitchhike.

They sat on their bags with a scarf draped over their heads for shade. Long intervals passed between any signs of life beyond a distant car or tumbleweed. Beads of sweat became puddles between their skin. To stay awake, they found entertainment in anything that stirred—a strange insect carrying a twig across the road, a big bird flying past (sign of a carcass somewhere near), wild dogs barking in the mountains. When a pickup truck appeared on the horizon, Sami jumped to his feet to flag it, but the driver made no move for the brakes and simply drove on, elbow sticking out the window. This would be harder than he thought.

He turned to face Rose from his spot in the middle of the road, where he straddled a blank space that should have been painted with a dotted line. As he walked back to her, the words of Zane and the other campers rattled through his head, imprinted on the mountains and the sea.

"Why did you move here if it's so bad?"

"What do you mean? I love it here."

"You know what I mean. The poverty. The backwardness. The *army.*" When he realized he was using air quotes again he snapped his hands back to his sides. Rose and her Americanisms were seeping into his every move whether he liked it or not.

"It was the best of cities, it was the worst of cities."

"I don't think you understand this place."

She jerked her head up, looking straight at the sun. "What do you mean?"

"Maybe it's a language issue."

Her mouth formed a vague snarl, as if she would pounce if it weren't for the heat. "Explain."

"Well, for one, you keep calling Tora Prison as if it's going to do anything for Jamila. It's *not.* You're just dragging this out, getting her hopes up that she's going to find Yusuf's body or better yet, find him alive. So stop. She's going to need to make peace with not *ever* getting an answer, because she never will."

"How are you so sure he's dead?"

"Come on, Rose. You saw what they did to Khaled Said—and that was a regular middle class kid from Alexandria. Imagine what they'd do to someone like Yusuf. A refugee from Sudan. A worker. Black. You might think we're all the same—"

"I don't."

"OK," he said. Sure. "What I'm trying to say is, there are things you don't see as an outsider. Things that I guess make it easier to say stuff like that. *It was the best and worst city.* Whatever. It's just Cairo."

She looked down at her shadow on the road. "I'm just trying to help."

Somehow they were both defeated. He was about to sit back down when a red speck approached in the distance, traveling fast on a rough engine. Sami waved his arms frantically. This time the vehicle stopped. He shouted *Cairo* across the road, the driver nodded, and they were off.

Sami didn't wake Rose when they reached Cairo's city limits, where they were greeted with a text message:

> To the young people of Egypt: beware of rumors and be reasonable. Egypt is above all else, so watch over her.

# 13

Kilo 4.5 greeted Jamila with a gap-toothed sneer. Here she was, back again at the edge of Cairo—at the precise point where the city crumbled into slums, where sand took the place of asphalt and only tuk-tuks could pass. With her face covered, she walked through dusty alleys praying she wouldn't find a single sunflower seed in her path. The place bore little resemblance to the teeming neighborhood she knew—it was still—without so much as a motorbike passing through. The shoddy, lifeless buildings towered over her and seemed to grow, brick after brick without even a window to interrupt the monotony. She shuddered, almost smelling the dank must of those seed-strewn corridors inside.

When Jamila returned there, nights ago, she'd hoped to find some of her flatmates—like Khadija, the old woman from Dongola who'd raised six grandchildren within the four blocks of that slum, or Said, the brick-layer who got Yusuf his first job building a hotel overlooking the Red Sea, or even Abu Mikdad, the grumpy amputee who hobbled up and down stairs without a cane. But there was no one. Had they all gone to Tahrir, to the Nileside villages they came from? She figured it was just her luck—to be in a slum like 4.5, where each room was so packed that the floors sagged, and find herself once again, all alone.

In the morning, she walked to the highway and hitched the first micro-bus headed for Giza. As the bus sped onward, a text message screamed from her pocket, startling her. She was still jumpy from that last night in Ramses, when Sami's phone rang for hours. Now she had Rose to ignore—ever since she returned from the Sinai, she'd been trying to reach Jamila with the same feverish persistence of the mother. And Jamila treated each attempt just like Sami did—by ignoring them. She swiftly deleted each message without reading it. There was a high chance Rose had found out what happened the other night, and Jamila didn't want to hear what she had to say about it.

Jamila could never set foot in Ramses again and didn't want to explain why. *I spilled all your secrets to Sami's mother.* Well—not *all* of them, but she might as well have brought up the pregnancy too. The shame was so intense and her need to run so urgent that she even thought of changing her number again. If she ever could get ahold of Nilofone.

It was a relief not to find Rose's name when she reached for her phone. Instead, it was a text from the far more preferable Supreme Council of the Armed Forces:

> The army is guarding your safety and will not resort to using force against the great people.

The army again. They'd been texting her for days now. At first Jamila was confused—maybe they had the wrong number—but as the phones of passersby dinged in unison, she realized that the army was texting *all of them.* That relieved her, somewhat, of her fear of the inbox. It seemed less like a real message than something to fester in her pocket, like used tissues. Almost amusing in its lack of sense. She imagined mortal fingers punching those words into a keypad, pressing once, twice, thrice for each letter, one phone and one pair of hands to represent the entire army. An army so big it had planted tanks on nearly every street corner, full of skinny-boned soldiers so insignificant they fell asleep with guns in their laps. To think—those were the boys who would supposedly protect the people, *all* of Egypt's people. *The army and the people are one hand,* or so it was said. But if that was the case then whose hand would grab her tonight?

A group of boys jumped off the back of the bus when they reached the outskirts of Tahrir, where bottlenecked crowds slowed traffic to a standstill. The rest of the passengers followed. Then it was only Jamila. As the bus rounded the square, she pulled her veil taut across her nose to avoid the smell of burnt rubber pouring in through cracked windows. It was the "Sunday of Martyrs," she learned, and Tahrir was flooded with faces of the disappeared and deceased, their portraits bobbing solemnly above the crowds. She scanned each face, subconsciously looking for Yusuf's—once again, she caught herself putting him in the same category. Martyr.

"Hey, honey."

Jamila froze. Martyrs faded to sunflower seeds and rotten teeth, sweaty palms against her backside. She spun to see a boy blowing her a kiss through his open window the next car over. Maybe he knew the sunflower man. Maybe that's why he used his nasty words. Maybe they were both in on this scheme to terrorize her from one end of the city to the other. She reminded herself that this was a city of twenty million, probably half harassers in their own right, and the likelihood of those two knowing one another was about the same as finding a diamond in the sea—or more aptly, a flea in a dumpster full of shit.

When she turned back even more boys crowded the window, snickering like rats. What did Dolores call them? Pieces of shit. It was a wonder their tongues weren't hanging from their mouths as they feasted on what—her browbone? Any morsel of flesh was fair game, it seemed, and it never ceased to amaze her what little the veil did to curb any leering. The boys seemed amazed too—amazed that she looked back instead of cringing like every woman besides maybe their mothers, surely the only living females who'd stomach their piece-of-shit faces.

The thought of Dolores and her cigarette-puckered lips gave Jamila courage for some reason. There was someone she could share this with—someone who'd turn these pieces-of-shit into gold for her resettlement case. She wanted to stick her tongue out and taunt them, boast that she was going to America, and that they'd be stuck in that Tahrir microbus for eternity, sweating between vinyl and a dozen fat men. Instead, she had another idea. She slipped out her phone and held it up to the window. The

boys nudged each other, excited. Then she took a picture. *Click.* A photo
of dual purpose—to build her resettlement case and to see the looks of
confused horror as she clicked.

Finally the bus broke from the traffic and they left the boys behind.
She got off at the corniche, ready. *Click.*

*****

It was an unpleasant surprise when Jamila answered an unknown number
the other night to hear the voice of none other than Mr. Salem, a former
employer that she'd thought she was free of. New phone, he clarified. She
bit her tongue as she imagined a thousand Nilofones throwing open their
doors for him of all people. She would have hung up if she weren't sleeping on a dirty floor in Km 4.5, empty bellied, holding her nose to suppress
the stench of festering trash. She needed the money. That it would come
from his sweaty, nasty hand was of less importance.

Jamila had been working for Mr. Salem for a year when he was arrested
and sent to prison months ago. The wife took out her anger on Jamila and
fired her swiftly—her work was no longer needed, *aslan.* Not one bit. Jamila
never thought she'd hear from them again and was quite OK with it. But
somehow, amid all the unrest, the riots, the *revolution*—a judge reopened Mr.
Salem's case and slammed down a gavel in his favor, dropping all charges of
money laundering and terrorism. Now Mr. Salem was back, so Jamila was too.

She rationalized her decision to return to the Salem house with one,
her desperation for money, and two, its proximity to the Nilofone headquarters in Mohandeseen. Before heading there, she stopped by the store,
where she found a harried employee sorting through a three-foot stack of
receipts. To her shock he let her in, which gave her a swell of hope that she
tried to stifle just as quickly.

She said the usual, "Excuse me, sir, I need help." Words she was tired
of repeating.

"Well, I can't help you," said the man, shrugging.

She searched his eyes for the slightest sign of hope, but there wasn't
much to work with. He was an odd-looking man, with two small eyes

set deep in the center of his face, like a plastic doll with its head smashed in. As he returned to the receipts, his forehead formed horseshoe-shaped trenches that deepened when he looked back up. Jamila wasn't budging.

"What's the matter, lady? Power's out? Tap's run dry? Out of cash? Loved one's missing? Join the rest of us."

"That's not it." She looked directly into those tiny eyes of his, just as she had looked at the boys in the bus, and told him exactly what she wanted. Phone records. Every last one. Now.

"Are you kidding?" Now his face wrinkled up like a sundried date, as if what she needed were so absurd, so outlandish, that it had aged him in a split-second. "There's a revolution going on and you want your *phone records?*"

"Well, yes."

"Look, lady. The computer's not working. Printer's out of ink. Network's down. The whole world's coming apart. All of our employees have either disappeared or gone on strike, or both. The backlog from the past week has me swimming in paperwork. It's impossible."

"But the other Nilofone said headquarters would have what I need."

"Who told you that?"

"The man in Zamalek."

"*Zamalek?* If there's any store with the capacity to help right now, it's that one. They'd never inconvenience the rich and the foreigners, and the *rich foreigners*—you know, all the people that got us in this mess we're in today. The reason a kilo of tomatoes costs more than a carton of cigarettes. The reason I'm thirty-five and can't afford to get married. The reason I have a business degree and yet, here I am."

She stepped away from the glass. Now it was getting political. Maybe she should just agree with him—yes, flatter his woes.

"I'm sorry," she said.

He nodded. She bit her lip.

"So, what can I do?"

"Go back to Zamalek and tell them the boss demands they give you your records. The president said everybody should go back to work, after all. It's an order."

"Are you the boss?"

"And you're Nefertiti."

Sighing, she slipped her phone back into her purse and walked away. Emptyhanded, still. But she was getting closer. One day she'd hold those records in her hands—even if she had to bash her way in and loot the place herself.

*****

Mohamed Salem's home was unusually chipper that morning, festooned with fresh carnations on every table and console. Both TV news and radio Quran played over the crunching of newspaper pages, forming a static wave that rushed her as she walked through the front door, passing under a brass plaque bearing all ninety-nine names of Allah.

Abeer nodded to acknowledge her arrival. Mr. Salem greeted her with a sick grin. If he weren't ... well, *him*, then she'd almost feel sympathy. Postprison, he was relishing his newfound freedom so much that he seemed incapable of knocking that smile off his face. He wore a sharp gray suit instead of his usual house galabia, and he glided around on the pads of his feet, as if he were dapper as Omar Sharif. He took every opportunity to catch his reflection—in the hallway mirror and the TV screen, even in the metal handles of the refrigerator door, which distorted his shape to make it thinner. And he was thinner indeed, after months of diarrhea and runny bean soup.

While he was locked up, Abeer had hired an Egyptian girl named Bayan from the slums of Manshayet Nasser who lived in a closet beside the youngest daughter's bedroom. Today Bayan would work alongside Jamila—it turned out Mr. Salem really did need extra help, and it wasn't just an excuse to see her. That night they were hosting a party that had set the whole house aflutter. There were guests to entertain, dishes to wash, rugs to beat. A pound of *basbusa* sat in the kitchen waiting to be served on their best gilded dish, and myriad teacups needed washing. They sent Bayan to the dry cleaners to pick up the rest of Mr. Salem's suits as well as any spare chairs she could find on the street. Jamila eavesdropped as she cut the pastries into small diamonds, if only to distract from her hunger.

In the other room, Mr. Salem sat on a plastic-covered couch with his wife. He wore a pair of glasses on the bridge of his nose and another perched on his forehead—one for TV and the other for the newspaper—switching between the two as he and Abeer muttered excitedly about the news. *Aho, look here. Listen to this. Can you believe it?* It seemed the news had been good to Mr. Salem and his comrades—a regime man had agreed to meet with them to negotiate the demands of the revolution. Tonight they would host him along with senior leaders of the party. Jamila almost laughed imagining the vanity of all the chubby, bald men who would soon crowd the room. They would make sure to look their brotherly best—suits pressed, beards trimmed, many newly svelte after freshly cut prison sentences. She lit a stick of incense, waving the scent of *oudh* all around as if in protection.

Bayan came back with three strong knocks. Jamila opened the door to find her in working stance, crouched on bent knees. She handed over a bundle of warm, folded suits, and then ran down the stairs to return with two chairs stacked on her back, like a donkey. The two of them covered each seat with brocade cushions and arranged them along the walls of the living room, so that Mohamed Mohamed Salem's guests could sit in a circle with their *basbusa* and tea and look each beaming, prayer-bruised face in the eye.

"This moment is ours," said Mr. Salem through coffee-stained teeth. As Jamila collected his cup, she counted rings of residue on its rim. He'd refilled it four or five times that morning. It would be a long day, longer than she knew.

*****

Jamila should have seen the red flags. Mr. Salem had employed her upon recommendation from a broker in Nasr City—one who specialized in maids, and Sudanese ones in particular.

At first she was relieved. Mr. Salem seemed nothing like the bosses she'd been warned about. He wouldn't even look her in the eye out of so-called piety, and he was jovial and treated her kindly. She found solace in the framed scripture hanging on his walls, the prayer bruise on his forehead, the lack of liquor in his cabinets. He seemed to be a real man of religion—more like an uncle than the frightening preachers on TV, who

wagged the holy book in threat. That sentiment lasted a good week or
so, until Mr. Salem's hand made its way to her knee, and then her thigh,
and then between her legs and to her breasts and even her swelling belly,
which didn't deter him. This upset her even more than if he was the usual
suspect, a typical hair-gelled street specimen with no pretensions of piety.
Just as she thought she'd found something she dearly lacked—someone to
watch out for her in the way Fifi couldn't—she lost it, just like that.

Mr. Salem's imprisonment brought Jamila a sweet respite, and she
wouldn't let herself feel bad about it. Besides, he'd been jailed and released
many times before. She learned it was routine. Every couple of years—whenever there was an itch of unrest in the populace—policemen would come to
the Salems' door bearing badges. They would rifle the duplex for the man
himself and all his paperwork, phones, and hard drives. Once, they held him
down over the sink and shaved his beard with a dull razor before putting him
in handcuffs, slapping him all the while. The most recent arrest happened
just before parliamentary elections. This time his location was kept secret.

Jamila had thought he was dead. She assumed his family did too. And
yet here he was today—two weeks into the revolution, and the only sign
of his imprisonment was the belt pulled tight to keep up his pants.

"A man without a belly isn't worth a penny," he said, using the newspaper to muffle his laugh. Everything was a laughing matter now, even
the memory of the arrest—and as such, he treated himself to more coffee,
*basbusa*, and Jamila's rear end.

She was bending over the table with a washcloth when she felt pressure on her backside. Not again. She tried giving him the benefit of the
doubt. Maybe it was the backrest of the chair, for instance, or maybe
it was only her imagination. But of course it wasn't. The same terrible
scenario was repeating itself just like the police rounding up bearded men
to fill some monthly arrest quota. She was sure the police would be back
again. It was only a matter of time. But he wasn't thinking of that as he
grasped her left cheek in his hand.

From the corner of her eye, she saw Abeer talking on the phone across
the room. If she looked up at that moment, she would catch him in the
act—or rather, catch *Jamila* and kick her out again. Abeer was jealous,

somehow, as if she would rather be a maid groped in broad daylight, and not a relatively well-regarded wife. But Jamila couldn't get fired—not before she got her money. So, she stood up calmly, broke free from his grip, and shuffled to the kitchen.

He followed her and placed a syrupy plate beside the sink.

"Here you go, *chocolata.*"

She could feel his eyes stuck to her like the damp legs of flies. For a man who wouldn't make eye contact, he was remarkably comfortable looking at her body. In the end she was saved by Abeer, who shouted for him from the living room.

"Mr. Hegazy is calling. *Yalla.*"

Mr. Salem took one last look at her swollen, tired body, his gaze as sick as a tongue's lick.

*****

Jamila survived the day by thinking of freshly baked bread and the clang of guineas. Mr. Salem came through in more ways than one. In the evening he handed her a few American bills, assuring her that the exchange rate worked in her favor.

"Nobody wants Egyptian pounds anymore. We want dollars, dollars, dollars."

But there was one more thing before she could go. His two hands swam around her veiled body to find her backside, which he squeezed while looking at the wall over her shoulder. She imagined vomiting right in his face, ruining that new suit he'd already stained with crumbs and coffee. While his hands were on her ass, she thought of the crisp bills in her purse, estimating their worth in loaves of bread. Three loaves, four loaves, five loaves, maybe even a dozen if she went for government *fino* instead of the standard *baladi*. By the time Mr. Salem was satisfied, she'd settled on a larger quantity of cheaper bread, which she'd buy later from the souk under the 6 October overpass.

Free at last, she flew down the stairs, horrified at her ability to tally off errands under the grip of his grimy hand.

# 14

When Suad gave the butcher her order, she almost said *Jamila* instead of the whole rabbit she was really after. Luckily, she caught herself in time. It would have been an odd word to utter over a steel countertop smeared with blood—a name meaning *beauty*. Jamila, Jamila. She repeated the name in her head as she watched the butcher pound meat with a mallet, one syllable for each beat. It was thanks to that woman that she'd learned what her son was up to.

That night on the phone, she'd been speechless, unsure of what to make of her claim. *He's with her.* Rose. One syllable to house the catastrophe unfolding. After that call she couldn't bring herself to dial Sami again, though she tried many times, punching in the numbers and then hanging up before it would let out even one ring. She'd rehearsed what to say over and over: *Look, I was young once too. I know it might be fun to run around town with that woman, but it's not proper. It's not correct. Who do you think you are, Omar Sharif? You think we're in* Ba-rees? *You think you can lie to your mother,* ooh la la, *and get away with it?* Even her rehearsals devolved into breathless tirades. She thought she might compose herself better if she used the words of the president himself. *There is a thin line between freedom and chaos.* The latter would come inevitably the longer he strayed. He would turn into some kind of wild animal, like that man swinging a machete from a camel's back in Tahrir.

But Suad remained tongue-tied when her lips met the receiver. In the end she decided to sit back and wait, see how long it took for him to reach out—the same game she tried playing a hundred years ago when he never called on the anniversary of Giddo's death. And she thought *that* was a tragedy. Now look at this mess in her hands—a son turning fast into a Tahrir hooligan.

The butcher finished hacking off a leg of lamb, wrapped it in paper, and handed it to her along with a kilo of rabbit. When he said goodbye, she almost answered with the name again, *Jamila*. Oh, that woman. She didn't know whether to curse her or sing her praises for delivering the news.

Suad walked through the dust-choked alleys of the souk until she reached the vegetable stand, where she needed to buy a bushel of *molokhiya*. There, she found an assortment of leaves gathered in bunches with rubber bands, and she fondled each, one by one, to find the best batch. She knew to look for dark leaves, quenched with a good winter rain. When she picked the winner, she gave it to the vendor to weigh. Her mind wandered to Sami again. What would she do about him? She needed to find him a wife, marry him off before he gave her a heart attack. It wouldn't be hard to find a more desirable partner than that *Da-lee*. A girl from the family, or the daughter of a friend. Someone who'd never embark on a premarital romance, let alone take a sordid holiday during revolution. A girl with upright morals and the bloody sheets to prove it. Sami wasn't thinking of these things now because he was still a foolish boy. One day he would, and she was sure of it, because mothers knew best.

"Here you go, Umm Sami," said the vendor as he gave her the *molokhiya*. It was as if he could read her thoughts. Disturbing.

An album of girls flipped through her mind as she dug through her purse. Who had she missed? There was Basant, the daughter of Mona, with thick hair that was rumored to flow down to her plump bottom. Soon she would graduate from university, prime time for engagement these days. And there was Salsabeel, the neighbor girl. She wasn't quite ideal herself, having recently discovered the garish style of pop stars in billboards and—God forbid—prostitutes in the cabarets. Face smeared with a pallor, eyelids dusted in alien shades of green and blue, inky brows strong as tattoos. Even her hijab was a problem—massive and showy, always in tart hues of candy. She followed the awful trend of pinning her hair with clips and pom-poms and God knows what else—*koshari* takeout boxes, for all Suad knew—so that it looked like she had endless mounds of air piled under her scarf. Then there was the spandex that clung, wrist to ankle, to every curve of her hourglass figurine. Such fashions didn't exist in Suad's day. Back then, the only way to show off the goods was with an open window and an outgrown dress.

Anyway, Suad would consider her. There was nothing like the discovery of *that woman* to make a girl like Salsabeel look suitable. What man could say no to a girl like her, with her long lashes and curves?

*****

El Shoun was a nightmare, as always. Once again, Suad found herself in that vast dust pit, arm in the loop of a shopping basket and head stuck in a haze of unpleasant news. No, it wasn't a haze, because a haze could dissipate even in the industrial zone of Mahalla. Rather, she was stuck in a cement mixer jammed to a standstill, and all the news choked her like the grip of hardening concrete. She couldn't grasp what was happening; it grasped her.

As if this Sami business wasn't enough to drive her up the wall. Now it seemed that the Cairene disease had sufficiently infected the whole populace—except for her, that is—and the workers were on strike. Mahalla, a city always in motion—looms and sewing machines ticking, wheels and conveyor belts running—had fallen still at the assembly line. Factories empty for days. Lights off, looms disengaged. Not one thread spinning. The cooling towers that should have been oozing black smoke into the sky had no breath today. And the factory workers—who should have been, you know, working—had instead filled El Shoun like multiplying cells, swelling and spilling out onto highway ramps and train tracks. If Suad were a doctor, she'd declare, scalpel in hand, that survival depended solely on a full-on excision. A fatal prognosis. And the tumor, El Shoun.

She held her hand over her chest to feel her heart race. With each beat she heard the butcher's mallet smash flesh into sludge. It was cruel, all of it. She watched protesters tear down a poster of the president, stamp it with muddy shoeprints, and hoist it like a carcass of victory over the square. Oh, that damned square. The place where order turned to chaos just as the streets spilled onto an intersection of donkeys, tuk-tuks and trucks. Where on days like this, crazed factory workers left their looms to converge with the singular aim of disgracing their president. It filled her with the uncouth urge to throw her body over the front lines, to shield the president from those dirty shoes and the wild, demonic fervor that had swept over the country despite all semblance of logic and morals and manners.

Terrible as it all was, Suad didn't know why exactly she was surprised. There had been a strike like this one the year her father died. Even in his weakened state—the cancer having spread to the lymph nodes by then—he shook his fist at the lazy, spoiled youth filling the streets. Back in his day, workers wouldn't dream of showing up late, let alone go on strike. A man would give his right arm for a decent job behind a factory loom. When pay was overdue, they'd protest by *working*. They'd stay in the factories for hours and hours past dismissal, spinning cotton into threads of gold until their bosses were compelled by shame to pay them. Was it any surprise? People had manners back then. Politeness was an actual value. People wouldn't so much as whisper a complaint of the president, and now—look.

All around her, the citizens of Mahalla huddled around radios, debating aloud and in broad daylight, cursing the president's name, not one shred of shame in their voices that raised in decibel with the dial, up, up, up. They could crank the volume high as they wanted—it wouldn't make a difference. Couldn't they hear? The president promised all would be well if everybody would just go home. If the hoodlums would leave the square and stop rioting, then their demands would be met. Suad was certain. The president was in his eighties now, ancient even by Egyptian standards. He was a full decade over the national life expectancy, though you wouldn't know it, because he was well preserved by winters on the Red Sea and the formaldehyde lacquer on his head. And now, in his final years, this mess had to go and take hold of the wrongheaded youth. Would they treat their grandfathers like this? Their disrespect was appalling.

There were rumors that the old man was dying, bedridden in a hospital when he wasn't addressing the masses in a suit. He was so sick that his dear wife had to write all his speeches. Suad imagined the woman perched at the edge of his hospital bed, pen in hand, transcribing his calm wisdom until, with enough morphine, he could buck up the strength to go on TV. He delivered each speech in a low, droning voice, which to her sounded like the call of a muezzin, and ended with a plea. All he wanted was to die in his beloved Egypt. Didn't they all?

Despite Suad's qualms with his regime, and there were many, it was wrong to treat an elder this way. Giddo wasn't even his age when he died. She wished she could march into Tahrir herself and drag the protesters out by the scruffs of their necks, starting with her son.

*****

In the afternoon Suad tried to nap but wasn't able to sleep. Under the drawn curtains of her window, she turned over for the millionth time on the sway-backed mattress, still thinking of Salsabeel and her obscene body, the tiny waist and hips like a gourd. Suad once had the same figure, but she always hid it—except for that first Monday of each month when she would prepare to greet Gamal at the end of his gas route. Those days she always wore a dress cross-stitched with roses, though it was several sizes too small—so tight she needed to hide the gaping zipper under her hair. The dress had since disappeared, likely at the hands of Teta who had intercepted her laundry basket with the singular goal of destroying it.

In the dark blotted-out light of her bedroom, she raised her bare leg in the air. Now her flesh was as loose as milk pudding and jiggled with even one strong breath. The tops of her thighs were strewn with brown stretch marks from her second pregnancy, when her whole body had blown up to bring Ayah into this world. After all that bodily expansion, the girl was born premature, weighing less than a leg of lamb. Abla had blamed it on all her time spent in the garden, saying that all that bending and squatting had induced labor before it was time. Mahmoud, of course, had no opinion other than his mild disappointment that it was not another son. No doubt, the new wife would bear nothing but sons. No doubt, the new wife was as young and ripe as Salsabeel, as all the fruit hauled off by Hagg Ali's man the other day.

When Suad remembered the young man, it filled her with a longing for what had been lost. There was a time when she was his age. There was a time when she would have been a good match for the tall man with the nice hair and the dimple on his chin. There was a time when he would have looked at her with shyness and not the same comfort with which he'd greet his mother—a time when he'd find it shameful to follow her into her home alone when her husband wasn't there. And it was now that she realized, as if the decades had only just been erased, that that time was gone.

Giving up on her nap, she rolled over and opened the drawer at her bedside. Crumpled papers emerged from the compartment like bread rising. She cringed imagining what Ahmed and Nabil had read that night. *Letters to my brother.* Suad had never been so embarrassed—not even Mahmoud could humiliate her like that. And to think, the whole drawer was his fault to begin with. He was the one who brought the red underwear into their home, and it was because of that red underwear that she started writing letters to Gamal, not ever feeling bad about it. The memory almost made her slam the drawer shut again, but a magnetic nagging drew her hand to it.

Some letters were much older than others, with yellowed paper and red ink from a pen that had long since dried up and disappeared. The newer ones had been written in haste, with letters slanted at an inscrutable tangle. She'd forgotten to dot the appropriate places—the dot for *gim*, first letter of Gamal's name, and the dot for the *ba* at the end of the word for *love*. If it weren't for the predictability of her constant ruminations—of men and lemons—she'd never be able to decipher them. She hoped that it had been these new, unintelligible letters that the officers had found. Their jeers would have been much worse if they could read what was actually written.

Suad grabbed her reading glasses from their spot beside the Quran and began with an old letter, one with edges wrinkled stiff from some long-gone glass of water. The folds were stuck together and had to be ripped apart carefully, and inside, red ink had dribbled out at the edge of the paper, leaving a stain like dried blood on the margins. The writing had imprinted itself to the opposite folds of paper, so that each word was marred by the ghost of its neighbor. It was hard to read, but she could make out the message using her instinct and memory, as if she'd written it yesterday, as if she'd never forgotten what she wrote—as if each letter was imprinted to the insides of her skin, in smudged ink that only she could read.

*Dear Gamal,*

*Remember me? You're probably wondering where I went. They took me away to the other side of Nahr El Bared Street, near the Bassiouny sugar farm. If it's possible, please change your gas route to include my new place. Our gas man is named Tarek Salah El Din, and he comes from a family of Saidis on Katora Street. Maybe you can switch routes with him. With that kirsh of a belly, he would probably appreciate the shorter distance between houses.*

*The girl in the flowered dress*

The paper crunched as Suad folded the letter back up. From the drawer she dug out another scrawled in the red ink. This one had been folded several times over. It seemed to have never been reopened because the paper was still crisp and smooth, and the lines between the folds were singular and strong. Whatever was inside must be something she hadn't ever wanted to revisit. She opened it to find she was correct. It contained the story of Ayah's birth and why she chose the name—from the red underwear to the river to the ring. She even told Gamal about jumping into the Nile, assuring him that she hadn't been thinking straight, that some jinn had come over her and possessed her pregnant body and pushed her into the river. She wrote of the midnight phone call and asked Gamal if it really was normal for a man to do what Mahmoud did, as Abla had said. Were all men disloyal? No, they couldn't be. Because Gamal had showed up at their door each week just when she expected him. Until he didn't anymore.

Had she been wrong all along?

Suad pressed the letter to her chest, thinking back to the last time she saw Gamal. He took no time to even say hello. He rushed toward her, and in his lips there was more haste than tenderness. She would have been alarmed but there was no time to think as he moved, ravenous, the way she raced against weeds in the grove—as if each second behind were a second wasted, as if he'd been staring at her through the window and at once was set loose, and all the fingers and sweat and heat washed over her like the sand carried on western winds during the *khamseen* season. He seemed to know it was the last time.

But Suad did not. The only reason she allowed Gamal to even touch her—other than that exceptional resemblance to Abdel Halim Hafez—was because she believed there would be no last time, that this was the start of a big love that would become marriage and children and burial in Mansoura cemetery where their bodies would become one with each other and then with the earth, and then one day a tree would grow from their bones and bear ripe fruit for grandchildren and great-grandchildren to come. She knew nothing back then. She didn't know that the tip-tap of her heart when he touched her meant nothing at all—that it was no precursor to marriage and not even a courtship. It didn't even mean he liked her. And it was this prospect that wracked her mind the day a ring appeared on his finger and he melted into the door instead of her arms, and the words exchanged between them shortened to a point of absurdity, as if they had never laid eyes on one another and were nothing more than strangers exchanging glances in El Shoun Square. She was tempted to say she should have known better but how could she? She was only a girl, and she believed it when he said he loved her. She drank every word like a glass of sticky-sweet *Qamar El-Din* juice.

That day—the final day—their tryst was cut short by a door slamming shut. That stupid, stupid door. If she could get her hands on it now, she'd break it in two over her knee. Funny thing was, back then, it hadn't even bothered her. She wouldn't have cared if a pigeon shat on her head. All she could think of were Gamal's hot lips and the way his breath smelled like menthol Halls. Just the thought made her smile to herself like a neighborhood loon. Teta had noticed, of course, and from that day on she was on a mission to marry Suad off. Within weeks she became the wife of Mahmoud, a man whose touch felt like just that—a touch, no different than a slab of cold meat bashed with a mallet into a butcher's block. Bang, bang, bang, the two of them were melded together by force, turned from living flesh to ground meat and packed into Styrofoam tubs for refrigeration.

Teta had said it was Suad's only option. That turned out to be a lie. As years went on, she realized that at worst, she would have become a spinster like Hagga Ibtisam, who ran the only woman-owned kiosk in town, and who swore that the key to longevity was keeping away from men. Or maybe, just maybe, things could have turned out differently if she ever actually sent one of these letters to Gamal. She would have folded one into a paper plane and sent it flying through the alleys of El Shoun and into his bedside window. Maybe he would remember her as she was back then, waving from the window with her *bazaz* pressed against the sill. Maybe he would return to her, leave behind that woman and the son who looked just like him.

She'd been jealous that day she saw them in the alley by Hagg Ali's shop, but there was comfort at the thought that he hadn't gone anywhere. It had been decades since she saw him, but one never knew—maybe one day she would run into him in that same alley, or on the streets of his old gas route.

And as if the latter hadn't ever occurred to her, she leapt up from her bed, got dressed, and made her way to the street. It was a Monday afternoon.

*****

Suad walked in the direction of Abu Radhi, watching the buildings become denser, the clotheslines heavier. The shadows under palm trees grew darker as the sun set. She saw Gamal's shadow on the ground beside her own, his broad shoulders ticking with each step. She quickened her pace and he did as well. She stopped to let a car pass and he did, too. As she hopped over a puddle, she heard a splash and imagined mucky water seeping into his shoe. They scaled the alleys together, passing strangers who knew nothing of what had been between them, all the fools who had no clue of what plagued Suad, the woman with eyes locked ahead.

First came the sesame. She hadn't even reached the pharmacy door and could already smell the sesame ointment she used to buy for Giddo, who was always coming home from the cotton factory with scratches and burns. He liked it because it was natural, but she couldn't stand the stench. She hadn't so much as opened a tube in years, but it didn't take long to remember. And if there was sesame then that meant her old house was near.

She scanned the building facing the pharmacy but couldn't yet find it. Abu Radhi had grown older and with time came repeated beatings from sandstorms, leaving it browner than she remembered. She counted windows to the fourth from the ground, which seemed right, and her eyes stuck. That was her window—*hers*—and yet the new tenants had installed a panel of frosted glass to obscure the view. Now it would only let light in. She would never be able to sit there again and watch the street, waiting for the sound of that dangling keychain, and it filled her with rage. It didn't matter that the house belonged to someone else now, and that Suad was no longer a girl and that for all she knew, Gamal could have changed his gas route or quit the business altogether. All that mattered was that her youth was gone, and now, there wasn't even a trace. Soon even the memories would dissipate, like Gamal's shadow in the dark.

The balcony was still there, though those senseless new tenants had covered it with glass too. They didn't deserve to live there if they couldn't even appreciate the view. To think, they had no idea this was the home where Suad was born and each of her four sisters; where she learned how to bake date cookies and stew lentils with turmeric; where Giddo had died on a cot by that same window; where Mahmoud slipped that faux-ruby onto her hand. And she realized what was in her heart no longer mattered—if it ever did.

Under a dying palm tree, she found a doorman's chair that seemed to have been placed right there for Suad and Suad only. When she sat down, it gave her a perfect view of the intersection leading to El Shoun. Gamal would likely come from that direction. But as she sat there, her eyes never left that fourth-floor apartment. She could picture clearly the day of the engagement, Mahmoud in his brown suit, pastry stuck in his teeth, breath smelling of nicotine and not Halls. And she pitied him—yes, pitied him—because while he was slipping a ring onto her finger, she was thinking only of Gamal. Despite everything that came later, Suad was the one who messed up first.

As she rose from the chair, the evening wind swept in and rustled the tree's dry leaves, sounding like rain. It was too dark and too late to search for Gamal now. She got up, steadying herself on the hollow tree trunk, and took one last look at the place where she grew up. Then she went home—her *new* home—the only one, after all.

# 15

Sami had never seen Abu Ali in this state. As he restocked his medicine cabinets, pills dribbled out of his wobbly grip and hit the countertop like pellets of hail. They scattered across the floor and his eyes followed, bouncing to and fro like atoms, as if he couldn't focus on a single thought, or pill. Sami supposed he should cut him some slack. Looters had bashed in the pharmacy's storefront last night and had made off with a good chunk of Abu Ali's inventory. The only sign of normalcy was his trademark sky-blue galabia, though he normally reserved it for Fridays (joking, on better days, that it would ensure God saw him in the mosque).

Abu Ali greeted them with a terse, "good morning." The words came out right but his hands jittered behind the counter. If it were up to Sami, he'd just wave and go on with his day and leave Abu Ali to tend to his ransacked store in peace. But Rose insisted.

"Where. Is. Jamila." She spoke loud and slow, making a strenuous effort to separate her words as neatly as the pharmacy shelves—cough syrups in the corner, antihistamines beside the saline sprays. Sometimes she talked to Sami that way, as if he were one of her eight-year-old students, needing help to understand. "Su-*dan*. The girl. From Sudan."

Abu Ali's eyes returned to the pill-strewn countertop. He picked a stray aspirin tablet from a pile of spilled Tramadol, as if to change the subject.

"The looters ... they took this week's shipment from Alamein. Fifty crates, gone. Ten thousand guinea, gone. It seems Tramadol is the new gold."

There was something off about him, Sami had to admit. This wasn't the face of a man who'd simply lost a few crates of inventory. Had they made him uncomfortable? Had he seen something he shouldn't have seen? Perhaps a kiss in the stairwell, an embrace through the upstairs window. Rose always kept the damned curtains open and would even get undressed in front of the window if Sami wasn't there to stop her. That must be it. My God, he'd have a word with her later.

As Sami watched Abu Ali lock the cabinet door, his eyes drifted to the shelves, which had never looked so depleted—half empty, bottles askew. Only the top shelf was in good shape, full of pink boxes. He squinted to read the labels. *Pregnancy test*, over and over again, *pregnancy test*. There must have been a hundred, untouched. Of course they were untouched. Who would walk into this place and ask for one of those? He looked at Rose standing beside him. *Her.* He imagined her facing Abu Ali eye-to-eye and pointing to that shelf as if it held nothing but Band-Aids. It would be a nightmare if it wasn't so believable.

Impatient, Rose unleashed a *huff* in response to the pharmacist's story, as if she knew better than he did about his own store. She knew everything, didn't she? To her it didn't matter that eyes watched them from every corner, nor did it matter that now, the man they had to face every day, at the foot of their own door, knew exactly what they'd been doing up in apartment 702. Now Abu Ali couldn't even look them in the eye.

"I know just as much as you," said Abu Ali, his eyes never leaving the countertop, which he wiped clean with a rag. "Jamila just disappeared."

Rose gave one more huff. "How can you not know? Don't you sit here all day watching the street? Isn't it your *job*?"

The pharmacist unfurled his rag onto the counter with a slap, then looked straight at them. "Look, I'm not your doorman. You should go get one if you want those kinds of answers. I can't help you." His voice lowered, quivering like spilt tablets. "How could I even think about that woman? My son is gone too."

Rose backed away from the counter, looking embarrassed for raising her voice. So *that* was what embarrassed her. Not the baby, not the open window, but a harsh tone. Sami was so busy trying to figure her out that he almost didn't realize what Abu Ali was saying. His son was gone.

"Gone? What do you mean?"

"I mean he's *gone*," he repeated, voice quivering like spilt tablets. "Gone in the way people are *gone* during revolution. Taken, disappeared, hauled off by the police or whoever it is with the batons and big trucks nowadays." He asked if they'd heard anything, a withering hope in his underslept eyes, but of course, they had not.

"We've been in the Sinai," said Sami, relieved at what seemed like a good excuse. But as he watched Abu Ali's eyebrows contort to form rings of skin around the prayer bruise on his forehead, he realized how ridiculous he sounded. Abu Ali must be wondering why his son was the one who was gone and not them, two sinners careening reckless like a loose tire across the desert—sinners hiding the biggest sin of all inside Rose's womb. Sami looked at the portrait hanging on the wall behind him, which showed three identical boys varying only in size. It was the eldest, Ali.

The pharmacist's eyes fell to the counter again, and his tone softened as he shook his head. "I knew something was wrong, I *knew* it. It was too late at night—much too late for a phone call. I was home in Abassiya watching MisrTV when some boys called the house. I'd never even heard of them before—Kimo, Gindo, Bibo, Hashisho, whatever—but when they said they were friends of Ali, I knew something bad had happened. They said he disappeared on Mohamed Mahmoud Street, and the air was so full of smoke that they lost him in the split-second it took to blink. One of them—Mimo, Kiko, whoever—said he thought he saw men in plain-clothes drag him off, not a uniform in sight."

Sami asked him if he'd tried calling, as if it were possible he might have forgotten. The sight of those pregnancy tests must have turned his mind to sludge. But Abu Ali nodded, not minding the silly question. In fact, he seemed glad he'd asked, as if he himself had been asking that same question over and over, as if in each repetition there was a chance he'd discover some news. Ever since the phones came back, he'd called and called, dial tone on loop, then Ali's phone was switched off, and then there was nothing.

Just then Abu Ali's phone started to buzz, rattling the countertop, and they all leapt toward it. But it was only his wife. The bitch. He hit ignore, tightening his grip on the phone as if he might chuck it across the counter.

"She's going crazy, crying nonstop like she's got two burst pipes for eyes."

"Can you blame her?" For a moment Rose sounded genuinely sympathetic.

"I can't," he shrugged. "It doesn't make any sense. Why Ali? The boy isn't political at all. He could name you more Al-Ahly players than members of parliament. So why?" He looked for an answer in their vacant stares, but there wasn't any. That was the worst part—not knowing if his wife should put on her black mourning clothes and sink into the outstretched arms of wailing women, or if their son would one day show up at their door, messy-haired, sunken-eyed, and in need of a bath.

There was nothing Sami could say to help him. Even his presence was a slap in the face. Sami was there, despite his poor decisions, and his son was not. Just a child, just a boy who played football in the streets. He forgave Abu Ali for not knowing about Jamila. Rose held her tongue as she watched him buy a packet of aspirin to pay his condolences—for his missing son just as much as the pregnancy test.

*****

The streets were buzzing about a bombing the night prior, but Rose's mind was still stuck on Abu Ali.

"Calling the police all day, isn't he? It's almost as if there's nothing worse than not knowing. I bet Jamila can relate."

"Alright," said Sami. Alright. He would let her have this one and keep calling after Yusuf as if it would make any difference—because it wouldn't. Unlike that baby and her decision to flaunt it for all of Ramses. He lowered his voice as people skittered past, beating them to the square. "Did you use a test to find out about ... you know ... that?" He looked down at her deceptively flat belly, not knowing how he'd been able to avoid this question until now. Unconsciously he sped up his pace, trying to escape the conversation he started.

"Yes. I pissed on a bag of wheat."

He slowed down. "What?"

"I did as the ancient Egyptians did. I took a bag of wheat and a bag of barley, and I pissed."

"Can you answer the fucking question?"

"Yes, Sami. Of course I used a test. The modern kind."

"OK. That's, uh, great. They're what—ninety-nine percent accurate? Miracles of science. Anyway, where did you get this test?"

"A pharmacy."

He gulped. "Abu Ali's?"

"Probably."

*Probably?* As if she didn't remember—as if it didn't even matter? Sami paid more attention buying cigarettes. He closed his eyes to keep from hurling as the ground seemed to loosen beneath him. He imagined Ramses Street splitting down the middle, the crack growing wider until it reached the doors of the Diesel, sucking them all into the ether—she and him, Abu Ali and his pharmacy, all the cats living in trash heaps and every speck of grime lining the walls like prehistoric sediment.

"Are you OK?"

He opened his eyes to see there was no crack but the one between them. Rose stood tall, hand on her hip as if yet again, she knew better. He wanted to shout, grab her by the shoulders and shake, but couldn't. There were people around. People everywhere, watching. He bit his tongue and vowed to say something when they returned home later, if he could ever face that place again. The Diesel didn't even have a backdoor he could use to avoid Abu Ali. There was no way in but the big, open front door—and no way out just the same.

*****

They walked without speaking until a hubbub around the shuttered falafel shop drew them down the alley to Café Tasseo. There, they found a ten-foot stain of soot marking the entrance, where a bomb had exploded last night. It had even taken out the Ramadan garlands that had hung across the alley—those same stars and moons that nobody had bothered taking down the year prior, to Rose's joy. The café's sign dangled from its last attached cable, frazzled wires poking out of each broken bulb. Somehow the acacia tree had remained intact except for some leaves that had been singed off, lying blackened on the ashen ground.

Rose gasped. Sami was too shocked to even do that. So, this was the bomb the street had been buzzing about, here at Tasseo, the last place he'd expect. What sense was there in bombing a café? It wasn't a government building, nor was it Tahrir. In the middle of a revolution, somebody had taken the time to make a bomb—it was homemade, he guessed from all the nails riddling the ground—and set it off at a harmless coffee shop.

The asphalt glittered with broken glass from the café's windows. Sami could feel them under the flimsy soles of his knock-off Chucks. He peered inside to find an empty space where the cash register once sat, its wires yanked out of the wall, a plaster gash behind. He saw the charred remains of the napkin-covered walls, all the drawings turned to blackened film like fish scales. The ibis was surely a goner. Who knew? They'd outlived that piece of paper after all.

As Rose poked around, Sami stood back, nostrils burning from the stench of soot. The morning drifted away with all its trauma. There was no Abu Ali, no pregnancy test, no baby. He held his breath as he remembered the day he met Rose a hundred years ago, right in that same spot. It was in the spring. He had a feeling something good was about to happen and kept catching himself smiling at strangers who smiled back. He was mid-step across the threshold when he saw her standing there staring at him, as if she'd been waiting for his arrival.

And now, look at this place.

There was no blood, but there must have been. They learned from passersby that the bomb had killed a father of six from Dokki who happened to be zipping by on his moped at the precise moment it exploded. It must have been right at that spot where the black cloud engulfed the door, and his life, but had spared the sign that still dangled, beat up but nevertheless, alive. Café Tasseo. It had survived to remind him.

What had happened was absurd and yet made perfect sense. Of all the places in Cairo—enormous, eternal, endless Cairo—that bomb went off *there*. Of all the street corners, blocks, and neighborhoods on this side of the Nile and the other, of all the slabs of sidewalk and curb, that bomb went off at *that one*. Of the city's six thousand square miles, that bomb exploded in the *one* spot where *one* of those twenty million Cairenes decided, for once, to do what he wanted and not what he was supposed to do. Of all the thousand years of Egyptian history, it was *that* year in which *that* café was bombed. It was one of those moments, like the night he saw the beast on the mountain, that made Sami feel like the only person in the world—as if all the heavens and the earth were created around his own existence and all the forces had conspired to make *that* bomb go off *there*.

And someone died. Someone died in the spot where in one moment, ages ago, everything began and everything ended.

*****

Not even Tahrir could lift Sami's mood, though it tried. The demonstration was dubbed the "Day of Egypt's Love," and the square was lit up like a carnival, with popcorn and sing-along songs and bullhorns passed around in open hands over the crowd. Sami took a date cookie from a woman handing out snacks and gave it to Rose. They'd barely spoken since Tasseo, but he could tell by the sour look on her face that she was hungry. She opened it to find the cookie crumbled.

"Date cookies are always like that," he said.

"I don't want a bunch of crumbs."

Crumbs. That sounded familiar. He remembered the blank quiz he'd grabbed, another lifetime ago, on his way to Khan El Khalili—the shopping list that stuttered, the deranged repetition of the word *crumbs*. She didn't know he'd tried to bring her those crumbs, only to find them scattered like guts all over Ramses Street. Maybe that's why she lashed out the way she did, embarrassing him in front of Abu Ali. He took the cookie back, wrapped it up, and tucked it into his pocket for later—perhaps when hunger superseded the quality of what he could give her.

Without a word between them, they watched a young man hop atop a car with a guitar. He seemed to be some sort of Tahrir celebrity. As he sang to the crowd, the crowd sang back, knowing all the words as if they were Amr Diab or Umm Kalthoum songs and not lyrics scribbled in haste on the backs of protesters. *Bread, freedom, social justice.* Bread. Not crumbs. He watched joy emanate from faces painted with the flag, signs waving, cameras flashing, girls shrieking for the hunk with the guitar.

Rose looked straight ahead at the singer. Something about her unnaturally steady gaze told Sami that she knew he was watching her, and her refusal to look back was just that—a refusal. Was she swooning inside, rapt by the singer with the corkscrew curls, just like all the others? After all, the man sang of bread—bread and not crumbs. He could provide her with what Sami could not. And as the girls of Tahrir squealed on, he could think only of how miserable he had made her. There were a million people shouting but all he could hear was the word *crumbs*. Crumbs and not bread.

Sami needed to get out of there. He needed it so bad he didn't think twice about returning to the Diesel. He was about to nudge Rose to go home when a white light swooped in and stuck to his face. He held his arm over his eyes but couldn't see the source of the light. Was it a headlight? Was the mountain demon about to reappear? He imagined its serpentine shape taking form—this time not in the crags but in the crowd, shoulders and elbows and hands tessellating into claws outstretched. He took Rose's hand to steady himself, but now they were both blinded, and they stumbled together.

When at last the light shifted, he made out the silhouette of not a demon, but a man. He was pointing a camera straight at them, with a light beaming above the lens as if the flash were stuck. *You jerk*, thought Sami, but nothing came out. Sami swatted at the man but missed, and he saw the taut line between his lips curl upward. The bastard was smiling. This must be one of the regime goons he'd heard about in Tasseo—thugs paid to menace the square, like those who took Abu Ali's son. Until now, Sami never believed they existed. He turned away from the lens, but the light clung like a tick, and it spun with him as the crowd blurred to a black curtain.

Somehow, they emerged from the crush and broke into a run, pushing bodies out of the way that fell like dominoes to the edge of the square. *Forgive me*, he thought as they ran north on Mohamed Mahmoud. *Forgive me, Rose. Forgive me, Abu Ali. Forgive me, Suad.* They weaved through rubble until the streets darkened and tall buildings dwindled into shoddy apartments with blankets for curtains. It was quiet—too quiet, and in the breeze, he could have sworn he heard the name *Ali*. Was it his father, searching at all hours, in the very spot his son disappeared? Was it the goon, taunting them with the possibility of ending up like the boy—gone? Sami shuddered at the thought of that thug trailing them all day—from the bedroom to the pharmacy, Tasseo to Tahrir, and now, here.

They had to go. Sami grabbed at Rose, catching only her sleeve, and dragged her into the alleys, where the labyrinthine darkness might give them some cover. God willing, there would be places to hide, doors to duck into, safety in the narrowness of walls closed tight around them. He pulled her through a passage between buildings, where runoff from pipes formed a stream down its length. Each time there was a splash, he winced, and under his breath he cursed the cats darting out of their way, complaining.

At last it seemed they'd lost the camera man, but Sami still didn't feel safe. He remained paranoid, scanning each nook and shadow for that light, the thin-lipped smile, the camera lens. But Sami didn't need to see him to know the goon was still watching—he was sure of it. He could feel the warmth of that camera light boring a hole into his back.

The rest of the way home, they exchanged few words other than the odd *wait up, come on, turn right, now left*—words that stung worse than any insult. He knew what Rose was thinking—*it's over*—but he didn't address it or even make eye contact. He was too tired, and so was she. She'd slowed since the chase, stopping to take breaks under streetlights, catching her breath with a hand on her abdomen, feeling the air flow in and out with a pained look on her face. He would have asked but he didn't want to acknowledge it. And she also said nothing.

*****

When they reached the Diesel, the fluorescent lights of the pharmacy were still on. Sami didn't even look to see if Abu Ali was there. He kept his eyes ahead until they were inside, then up all seven floors to apartment 702. Rose darted through the door first, leaving her key dangling from the lock.

Sami bolted the door shut and flicked on the lights, moving slowly, savoring every moment he didn't have to look her in the face. Fortunately, Rose seemed to be in the bathroom, buying him a few more seconds alone. He took a cigarette to the balcony and felt the cold night grip his bones, the tingle of tear gas on his lips. By the time he was down to the filter, she still hadn't come out of the bathroom.

"Rose," he called out, "is everything alright?"

She didn't answer, but he could hear her fidgeting, the lid of the toilet clanging. Still mad, wasn't she? He stubbed out the cigarette and went to see what was the matter.

In the hall he spotted a small red stain on the ground. It seemed to be blood. Was it Jamila's? For some reason his mind leapt to her first, fearing her disappearance was the worst kind—like that of her husband. But he touched the blood with the tip of his finger to find it wet, too fresh to be hers. As he stood up, he noticed more droplets leading to the bathroom door. He knocked softly.

"Everything OK?"

No answer.

He opened the door a crack, just enough to see Rose slumped over the toilet with bloodied underwear at her ankles. At first, he didn't understand—a period was nothing to cry about. Her irises glowed like absinthe against the bloodshot whites, slick with tears, and when she looked up and into his eyes, black as the hole coming to swallow them all, he realized this was no period. It wasn't about that date cookie or the goon with the camera, either. It was the baby.

"It's gone."

Sami didn't know whether it was devastation or relief that struck him still, shocked in his spot on the tiled floor. He inched toward Rose and lifted her bloodied body into the bathtub. The faucet made an animalistic squeak as he twisted it open, and she cried out as if it hurt her ears. *Please let there be water, please let there be water*, he thought, and when water emerged, he exhaled with an *elhamdulilah*. The water came out strong and steaming rather than its usual cold trickle, with all the noise of the Aswan Dam. He was grateful, feeling less pressure to say something, *say anything*, when any word would drown in the sound.

She bled into the tub as it filled with water. He thought of the Alexandrian sea in the winter as he reached into the bloody water to peel off her clothes. He threw them into a pile of dirty laundry, to be washed some day in the near future when he'd no longer be there. Strangely, there was no attraction in her nudity, even after all the blood washed away. Somehow, he'd moved on already. He'd made his decision and accepted it. Rehashing any feelings would set him back, and he couldn't go back. This was the end. Now Rose was like a patient in his arms, a professional duty, and he rinsed the blood off her legs with clinical detachment.

He wrapped her in a towel and moved her to the couch, where he propped her up like a doll reclining, legs outstretched. He asked if she was comfortable. Again she didn't answer. Now what? He wished she would just go to sleep, but judging by her vacant, wide-eyed stare, sleep was far off, if not impossible.

The only thing to do was drink. The liquor cabinet was packed full of all the drinks Rose had forgone lately, and inside he found a bottle of Spanish rioja that a friend had brought her in December, cork still sealed with wax. Odd she hadn't drank from it—not even a sip. He wondered how long she'd been pregnant and if she knew then. Come to think of it, she hadn't had anything to drink for New Year's either. Back then, he'd thought she was trying to impress him, acting the part of a good Muslim woman—someone Suad might like, and someone Sami would not. He felt ashamed remembering how he'd thought less of her because of it. Now it made sense—Rose had never changed for him. Rose had always been Rose, the decision her own, just like the decision to keep the baby no matter how much it destroyed his life.

He set down a bottle of gin, making a heavy clunk, along with a half-empty carton of mango juice from weeks ago. He didn't care. Old mangos wouldn't matter, getting sick wouldn't matter, drinking himself to death wouldn't matter. None of that would ever matter now that the baby was gone, their relationship too, and worst of all they were *out*, sealed onto celluloid for all Tahrir to see. Sami gulped straight from the bottle as he imagined the goon's film playing out in some police station, fat officers picking lint out of their ears as they watched their two faces, marked together for eternity in the middle of an insurrection they had not caused, but fell into the same way he'd fallen for Rose—by accident, going with his gut, following the vibes of the street which pushed them together just like throngs in the square.

There was no hiding now that Abu Ali knew everything, and the goon, whoever he was, had found them in the square and shone a spotlight on their faces for everyone to see. And they *all* had seen—every last one of the million-plus people who stood in Tahrir for the so-called Day of Egypt's Love. What love? Egypt had no love for Sami and Rose. She policed them in apartment stairwells and straw-hut camps in the Sinai desert, and tonight, in the middle of Tahrir Square. She chased them through streets strewn with ash, forced them into alleys where they would again end up cornered. Egypt might have love for football and *molokhiya*, for Umm Kulthoum and Naguib Mahfouz, for the desert and the sea—but it had no love for Sami and Rose. Not together. That was for sure.

Sami put the bottle straight in his mouth, imagining it to be a gun. What would happen if he just … pulled the trigger? The gin sank like fire into his belly. He winced at its chemical bitterness but kept drinking until there was only an unreachable droplet left at the bottom. Finished, he let the bottle drop and roll off the table, crashing into pieces on the floor, making it glitter like the sea, like the sidewalk of Tasseo. As he stared, the floor pulled him in. He inched closer to the ground, growing heavier, mouth numb, brain barren, until finally he sank. Now the memory of the goon was funny, along with all his worries over a baby that had ceased to exist before it even existed. A shard pinched through his jeans, and he laughed harder.

"Take me to bed," said Rose. Her tone was so firm it snuffed out his laughter. Even in his stupor, he could tell she was angry, calculating the time it would take her to clean up his mess in the morning, when he'd be gone.

He picked himself up off the floor and carried Rose to the bedroom. As he lay her down, he thought of spending one last night beside her, then leaving before dawn. He searched for the answer in her eyes—those eyes that had sparkled days ago, set alight in the sun, eyes that tonight were dull and lifeless, emerald turned to murky Nile water. There it was.

# 16

Jamila didn't know why she was in a good mood. There was no news from Tora, nor St. Fatima's, and nights spent in Kilo 4.5 were predictably long, wracked with nightmares about that phone call that blew everything for Sami and Rose. But for some reason, she awoke that Wednesday morning smiling, a slight giggle even, as if someone were tickling her. She could see through the cracks in the bricks that the sky was blood-orange—unusual for this time of day. For a second she panicked, thinking she'd slept until sunset and had missed her appointment at Fifi's, along with another day's wages (which were promised to come today, for the hundredth time). It was only when she heard the call to prayer, crisp against a quiet that could only belong to morning, that she realized she hadn't.

Just one more moment of sleep before facing stir-crazy Fifi. But as Jamila closed her eyes, a tapping sound pried them open again. She smothered herself in blankets to escape it. What was that? It seemed to come from the wall above her head, like a fingernail drumming concrete. As she sat up, the sound stopped. She stared at the still wall, bare but for the uneven plaster between bricks. This tapping was shy. This tapping was surely in her head. This tapping persisted. When it started again, she threw off the blanket in a huff, and as she stood up, she noticed that her hands were covered wrist to fingertip in wet henna.

At first she was terrified. Had somebody come to her in the night, painted her hand while she slept? Had she painted it herself and forgotten? Was she losing her mind? She dabbed her finger against the ink, blotting out a swirl with a smudge. It seemed to be real. As real as the scent of sage in the air which, as she sniffed, reminded her of that day years ago in Khan El Khalili, when she met Yusuf in the alley by El Fishawy. She always wanted to relive that day until she drew her last breath. And here it was—the henna, the sage, and ... him?

She whispered his name into the dark. *Yusuf.*

And she swore on the graves of her mother and father and each and every one of her siblings that he spoke back.

*Jamila.*

She lay on the floor with eyes wide open. The tapping had stopped, and she could feel the warmth of his body, the weight of his hand. *Jamila.* That voice was unmistakable. Calm, soft as a muezzin's hum. The lolling last syllable that he always drew out, *laaa*, as if to savor each moment her name touched his tongue. She buried her face in her arm, cringing. That *laaa* could kill her. That *laaa* was a knife slashed across her throat. A boulder dropped onto her stomach. A shovel scooping out every last one of her entrails. A seed on the floor, fruit of flowers turned to horror. It taunted her, *laaa*, dangling his scrap-like memory before her, out of reach. She wanted more than a scrap. More than a memory. More than a ghost. That's what he was, wasn't he?

She coughed, the truth settling like particles of dust in the air.

Yusuf was gone, his body no more, and she could do nothing about it. She could spend her life searching, crawling on hands and knees rubbed raw against the ground, trail blood drop by drop until there was none left—and still, find nothing. She could call Tora each hour until her last, stand in the queue wrapped around its perimeter forever and never get an answer. One day, by some miracle, she might find his corpse, dig it out of some mismatched grave. And he would still be dead.

But Yusuf existed, nevertheless. Right there in that moment. In the cement hellhole of Kilo 4.5. With her head against the bare floor, feet curled up to the wall. Bricks all around, the stench of garbage never too far. And yet, his ghost was still there, breathing beside her. All she could do was surrender. She closed her eyes and saw the corpse she never found float away on a piece of driftwood on the Nile. And she gave it one last push.

*****

When she woke the henna was no longer there, nor was the sage or the warmth of Yusuf. She traced the top of her hand from wrist to finger and felt nothing but the scales of her dry skin, not even the faded imprint of petals and swirls. As she exhaled she remembered that Yusuf was dead, and that all she could do was whisper *good morning* to the memory in her head.

*God is great*, called a distant muezzin. She rose and walked to the window at the end of the corridor, which wasn't so much a window but a gap where bricks had been knocked out between the beams to let in light. Bending through, she peered out to trace the sound to its source, but couldn't—beyond the slums, a thousand minarets speckled the horizon, from Shobra to Fustat and all the way to Ain Shams, and one by one their muezzins joined in the chorus. It was the first time she realized Cairo was beautiful. Despite its brick slums, its festering garbage. The catcalls and leering, the rats blowing kisses. Air made of smog and exhaust. Rooftops crowded with shacks and satellite dishes. Hands on her ass, hands in her pocket. It was all true, all Cairo—but so were those minarets and the citrine sky. So were her walks in Zamalek, the shady streets where roots jutted out of the asphalt. Her flatmates in 4.5—those who'd defended her from the sunflower man and those who'd given her shelter when she ran from him. And all the case workers at St. Fatima's, from Dolores to the pimply-faced teenager who after all, had tried.

As a flock of pigeons whipped past, Jamila ducked beneath the window, startled. A neighbor must have released them from some unseen rooftop. She crept back up to the light and watched them fly in circles, up to the tallest roofs and then dipping low. When they came close she could feel the wind stirred by the beat of their wings, feathers fluttering out like petals over the rubble.

*God is great*, repeated the muezzin as the birds flew farther out, circling wider.

When the pigeons' orbit began to shrink, she leaned over the bricks to find their owner calling them back. Like a dancer, the man waved a red sash in the air and in an instant, the birds changed directions midair. As they made their way home, the circles shrank slowly to the width of a satellite dish until finally, there were no pigeons. And as the muezzin finished morning prayer, she said, "God is great."

*****

Before leaving for Zamalek, Jamila slipped the testimony out of her St. Fatima's file to make sure nothing was missing. It was so thick it felt like a book in her hands. To think, a book about her life (or at least, all the bad parts). A pile of papers that could change everything and which she never went anywhere without. At night, she slept on top of it. By day, it accompanied her to appointments from this end of the city to the other, and every boarded up, looted Nilofone in between. It wasn't exactly safe, but then again, neither was anyplace else.

Carefully, as if just breathing the wrong way would destroy all the papers and thus, all hope, she flipped through. On the cover there was her name, Jamila Abdesalam, and a photocopy of her refugee ID card. The following pages were more difficult, detailing everything that happened from Omdurman to Kilometer 4.5. It was strange seeing the names of Mama and Baba and Yusuf in print, scattered among all the terrible things that she'd never think of telling them. The rebels. The smuggler. The broker in Nasr City and the man he brought her to, Mr. Salem. Her secrets were out now, shrunk down to mere ink and paper. What the testimony didn't contain, though, were the secrets she'd kept from Sami and Rose—the pregnancy test, the phone calls, the self-imposed eviction. By now they'd probably found out about how she unwittingly exposed them, as well as her disappearance. They'd think it was good riddance.

She reminded herself that with hardship comes ease. Maybe this was all her preparation for some big reward ahead. A reward like resettlement. When she closed her eyes she dreamed of being someplace far away, far removed from all the ghosts that haunted her along the Nile. A blank slate where she could look at the horizon dry-eyed, no bodies to find, no questions unanswered. Where she could finally rest her sore bones that had searched so long for Yusuf's. Where there would be no past outside the pages of her testimony, which she would tuck away somewhere out of sight to never come out again. Or better yet, burn it. What use would there be, anyway, once the testimony served its purpose and got her out of here? It was a diamond in the sea, as Yusuf said—but if she learned anything in these past weeks, it was the speed and spontaneity of change. A life up in flames, a city falling. Presidents faltered. Nobodies became martyrs. Bodies lost, bodies found. It took seconds for a single canister of tear gas to blind a whole city block. There was no telling what lay ahead of her at any given moment. She only had to try.

*****

As Jamila stepped into Fifi's apartment, streamers of red, white, and black fell over her face.

"Long live Egypt," said Fifi in place of hello.

It seemed she'd changed her mind about the revolution. In its spirit, she was decked in patriotic gear, with a flag tied around her waist and an Al Ahly cap perched carefully on her head—so as to maintain the integrity of her month-old hair extension tracks. Jamila approached her with caution. She knew the need when she saw it. She walked forth slowly, not sure which Fifi she'd get today—the actress, the mother, the crier, the binger. It could be any one of those or all of the above.

"I need your opinion, young lady," she said. "Today I'm posting in honor of Egypt, mother of the world, and I don't know what to wear—the flag or the hat?"

"Both are nice," she said, playing it safe. No matter what, Fifi would somehow end up wearing them both anyway.

Throughout the day Jamila kept one eye on the TV. It showed the usual flood of demonstrators in Tahrir, faces shouting through balaclavas, flags waving in the air. And from the outskirts, tanks watching. Would this ever stop? She remembered what the junk collector had said, the

# 17

...ed Ayat al-Kursi to Suad's lips that morning, because she
...words in her head. She reached for the Quran and flipped
...ead it so often that there was a smooth sheen to the page
... the text with her finger, time after time, year after year.

...e of God, the Beneficent, the Merciful. Say, 'I seek
...the Lord of daybreak against the harm of what he has
...e harm of the night when darkness gathers, the harm
...when they blow on knots, the harm of the envier when

...s particularly apt nowadays. She drew back the curtain to see
...len was wet from an overnight sprinkling of rain, and small
... accumulated in the trenches between lemon trees. As she
...ver her bed, limbs cracking and squeaking like Nagwa's cotton
...estimated how many weeds must have sprouted since dawn
...least one for each tree, which meant a dozen, times two to
...c. She looked forward to plucking each jinn out of the freshly
... earth and carved out an extra hour to weed that morning.
...t now, she had other demons to dispose. She looked at her
...drawer, which stared back today in a particularly harsh manner,

revolutionary demands and the wormy guava. She wanted to agree with him. She wished him wormless fruit. But she couldn't help fearing what all of this would mean for her resettlement case. Now that Yusuf was gone it was all she had to carry with her, quite literally. And what good was a legal case in a city that was stuck in a state of upheaval? Parliament was closed and would remain closed until the fall of the regime. There would be no one to read her testimony and even worse, her testimony wouldn't mean anything. Of what worth was her story when people were setting themselves on fire in public and not getting more than a passing mention in the news? She tried to imagine what it might take to be heard but could not.

When Fifi called for her again, she tore her eyes away from the TV. She found the woman standing over the remains of Jamila's torn-open purse, gripping the torn cover of her testimony in her acrylic-clawed hand.

"Coco did it," said Fifi. "That means she loves you."

Jamila cried out as she dove to collect her things. A strap here, a cookie wrapper there. A pair of keys, one to her own flat and one to Rose's, which she'd left behind without thinking. A dried-up tube of lipstick that had sat unseen in the depths of her bag since her wedding day. Frantically she tossed item after forgotten item aside as she gathered all the loose pages of her testimony. She flitted through to make sure she had everything, and she did, *elhamdulilah*, from her date of birth on the first page to the assortment of signatures on the last. Only the cover was torn, but she could easily tape it together. Her heartbeat slowed to a normal pace and the sweat at her temples abated.

"What is that, anyway?" asked Fifi, pointing at the papers.

"It's my ... story."

"Your *story?* Oh Jamila, you never told me you had a story."

She explained that it wasn't *that* kind of story—whatever fairytale serial that Fifi had in mind—but rather documents from St. Fatima's Refugee Aid, a charity she'd most likely never heard of that operated out of an abandoned villa down the street. Refugees? Asked Fifi. Yes, refugees. Like her.

"Why didn't you come to me if you needed help?"

Jamila almost let out a snort. If Fifi wanted to help her, she could start by paying her the guineas she was owed. Besides, what else could she possibly do? Iron her hair? Donate a couple of sequined gowns? She remembered the time she thought Fifi could help her find Yusuf, as if it would make any difference to his fate. She was glad she never asked. Glad, and yet it dawned on her that there was something that actually *could* turn things around.

"Well, I've been trying to reach Nilofone …"

"The one on Abu El Feda Street?"

"Yes. Well, all of them."

"And?" She tapped her fingernail on the back of a chair, not unlike Yusuf's ghost on the wall.

"St. Fatima's needs my phone records for the past year. For my, uh … paperwork. But the people at Nilofone won't help me."

"Say no more," said Fifi, grabbing her phone. "I know the boss. A very nice man. Very. He'll do *anything* for me," she winked. "We'll get you your record, whatever that is. Tonight."

Surprisingly, Jamila didn't need to explain why she needed the phone records. She didn't tell her she had a pending resettlement case that they would somehow help. She explained this was all because of a man who stalked her so relentlessly that she changed her number and hid her face in a veil. She just spelled out her name and listened as Fifi rang up this man who—praise be to God—liked the shape of her ass, or the sway of her hips, or whatever indecent feature Fifi had to offer. It didn't matter. Fifi requested her records on the tail of a few compulsory pleasantries. *Her records*—that elusive, faraway concept that would soon materialize like gold in her hands. And to think, all it took was one phone call. From the right person, of course.

"He's sending his boy to deliver it right now."

The good deed seemed to put Fifi in an even more manic mood. After hanging up the phone she fell onto the rug, squirming to the beat of a familiar song, the white stripes of her leggings making serpentine lines to match her shapely rump. *My beautiful country, my beautiful country.* The song was playing on TV, on the radios, on phones. Yet Fifi couldn't get enough.

"Turn it up," she said, but the song was already over by the time she got to the remote. She pouted, lips coming together in one glossy mass.

"Oh,
the next t
At once
belly as if he
was somewha
an ambulance?
returning to his
behind him. At t
harder, until they
Something str
howling at the mo
ing each piece of tra
today what Jamila wa
her eyes and for a mom
mad like Fifi? It made n
urge that bubbled up in
to laugh, to look at all th
once seemed inappropriate,
streaked tissues, mercy for he
taut for too long.
Jamila's cheeks still hurt fr
day, humming *my beautiful cou*

The sun was setting when Jamila re
baking bread wafting from alleys stre
the clotheslines zigzagging between
changing, winter to spring, the time o
the desert to coat the whole city with gra
the better the harvest, as her mother used
distance she found herself smiling at noth
all at once.

revolutionary demands and the wormy guava. She wanted to agree with him. She wished him wormless fruit. But she couldn't help fearing what all of this would mean for her resettlement case. Now that Yusuf was gone it was all she had to carry with her, quite literally. And what good was a legal case in a city that was stuck in a state of upheaval? Parliament was closed and would remain closed until the fall of the regime. There would be no one to read her testimony and even worse, her testimony wouldn't mean anything. Of what worth was her story when people were setting themselves on fire in public and not getting more than a passing mention in the news? She tried to imagine what it might take to be heard but could not.

When Fifi called for her again, she tore her eyes away from the TV. She found the woman standing over the remains of Jamila's torn-open purse, gripping the torn cover of her testimony in her acrylic-clawed hand.

"Coco did it," said Fifi. "That means she loves you."

Jamila cried out as she dove to collect her things. A strap here, a cookie wrapper there. A pair of keys, one to her own flat and one to Rose's, which she'd left behind without thinking. A dried-up tube of lipstick that had sat unseen in the depths of her bag since her wedding day. Frantically she tossed item after forgotten item aside as she gathered all the loose pages of her testimony. She flitted through to make sure she had everything, and she did, *elhamdulilah*, from her date of birth on the first page to the assortment of signatures on the last. Only the cover was torn, but she could easily tape it together. Her heartbeat slowed to a normal pace and the sweat at her temples abated.

"What is that, anyway?" asked Fifi, pointing at the papers.

"It's my ... story."

"Your *story?* Oh Jamila, you never told me you had a story."

She explained that it wasn't *that* kind of story—whatever fairytale serial that Fifi had in mind—but rather documents from St. Fatima's Refugee Aid, a charity she'd most likely never heard of that operated out of an abandoned villa down the street. Refugees? Asked Fifi. Yes, refugees. Like her.

"Why didn't you come to me if you needed help?"

Jamila almost let out a snort. If Fifi wanted to help her, she could start by paying her the guineas she was owed. Besides, what else could she possibly do? Iron her hair? Donate a couple of sequined gowns? She remembered the time she thought Fifi could help her find Yusuf, as if it would make any difference to his fate. She was glad she never asked. Glad, and yet it dawned on her that there was something that actually *could* turn things around.

"Well, I've been trying to reach Nilofone ..."

"The one on Abu El Feda Street?"

"Yes. Well, all of them."

"And?" She tapped her fingernail on the back of a chair, not unlike Yusuf's ghost on the wall.

"St. Fatima's needs my phone records for the past year. For my, uh ... paperwork. But the people at Nilofone won't help me."

"Say no more," said Fifi, grabbing her phone. "I know the boss. A very nice man. Very. He'll do *anything* for me," she winked. "We'll get you your record, whatever that is. Tonight."

Surprisingly, Jamila didn't need to explain why she needed the phone records. She didn't tell her she had a pending resettlement case that they would somehow help. She explained this was all because of a man who stalked her so relentlessly that she changed her number and hid her face in a veil. She just spelled out her name and listened as Fifi rang up this man who—praise be to God—liked the shape of her ass, or the sway of her hips, or whatever indecent feature Fifi had to offer. It didn't matter. Fifi requested her records on the tail of a few compulsory pleasantries. *Her records*—that elusive, faraway concept that would soon materialize like gold in her hands. And to think, all it took was one phone call. From the right person, of course.

"He's sending his boy to deliver it right now."

The good deed seemed to put Fifi in an even more manic mood. After hanging up the phone she fell onto the rug, squirming to the beat of a familiar song, the white stripes of her leggings making serpentine lines to match her shapely rump. *My beautiful country, my beautiful country.* The song was playing on TV, on the radios, on phones. Yet Fifi couldn't get enough.

"Turn it up," she said, but the song was already over by the time she got to the remote. She pouted, lips coming together in one glossy mass.

"Oh, no," said Jamila. "You'll have to wait two whole minutes until the next time it comes on."

At once Fifi broke into a fit of laughter, rolling around and clutching her belly as if her glee were painful. Jamila hadn't meant to make her laugh and was somewhat alarmed by the intensity of it. Should she call for help, perhaps an ambulance? She looked to the kitchen, where Qandil rolled his eyes before returning to his room. Fifi roared even louder as the door slammed shut behind him. At this Jamila started to laugh too, and Fifi noticed and laughed harder, until they were two women gasping for air on the living room floor.

Something strange had come over Jamila. She felt like a wild animal howling at the moon for no particular reason, like Coco the dog, sniffing each piece of trash on the curb because that's what she wanted. And today what Jamila wanted was to laugh. Tears spurted from the edges of her eyes and for a moment, she thought she was crying too. Had she gone mad like Fifi? It made no sense, but it felt good to finally succumb to the urge that bubbled up in her gut whenever she was with Fifi—the urge to laugh, to look at all the pain and cookie wrappers and *laugh*. It had once seemed inappropriate, now merciful. Mercy for Fifi and her mascara-streaked tissues, mercy for herself and that stern face of hers that she'd held taut for too long.

Jamila's cheeks still hurt from laughter when she left Fifi's house that day, humming *my beautiful country, my beautiful country*. If only.

\*\*\*\*\*

The sun was setting when Jamila reached Kilo 4.5, streets quiet, scent of baking bread wafting from alleys strewn with trash. A faint breeze rippled the clotheslines zigzagging between buildings—as if the seasons were changing, winter to spring, the time of year when winds swept in from the desert to coat the whole city with grains of sand. The bigger the storm, the better the harvest, as her mother used to say. And as she gazed into the distance she found herself smiling at nothing in particular, or everything all at once.

# 17

God must have willed Ayat al-Kursi to Suad's lips that morning, because she woke up with the words in her head. She reached for the Quran and flipped to the verse. She read it so often that there was a smooth sheen to the page where she'd traced the text with her finger, time after time, year after year.

> In the name of God, the Beneficent, the Merciful. Say, 'I seek refuge with the Lord of daybreak against the harm of what he has created, the harm of the night when darkness gathers, the harm of witches when they blow on knots, the harm of the envier when he envies.'

The verse was particularly apt nowadays. She drew back the curtain to see that the garden was wet from an overnight sprinkling of rain, and small puddles had accumulated in the trenches between lemon trees. As she stretched over her bed, limbs cracking and squeaking like Nagwa's cotton wheel, she estimated how many weeds must have sprouted since dawn prayer—at least one for each tree, which meant a dozen, times two to be realistic. She looked forward to plucking each jinn out of the freshly quenched earth and carved out an extra hour to weed that morning.

Right now, she had other demons to dispose. She looked at her bedside drawer, which stared back today in a particularly harsh manner, knobs like fisheyes. With a huff she yanked it open and watched the letters spill out. This time she didn't reach to unfold any—there had been enough of that. Instead she grabbed letters in bunches and stuffed them into a shopping bag as if it were her garden sack. There must have been a hundred of them, and they filled the bag like dead leaves, crisp and withered with age and all the calamity that came with it. Through paper folds she caught a glimpse of his name, *Gamal*, and winced. She couldn't wait to be rid of them, and rid of him.

Ayah was still sleeping, so Suad walked softly to the kitchen, trying not to wake her for perhaps the first time. There she dug out an iron pan, like the one she used to make date cookies for Gamal long ago. The cookies he refused, just like he refused her. Apparently being delicious was just enough to sample and not take for his own. She envisioned those crumbly, powdered morsels beneath her fingers as she crushed the letters down into the pan to make them fit. Then she slid the pan onto the oven tines and lit a match. She didn't even flinch when the flame reached her fingertips— she just shook it out and watched the fire lick the letters and then engulf them entirely, turning white to black, paper to ash, words to just—zilch. Just before the last shred of paper blackened, she saw his name once again, *Gamal*, only this time it shriveled into ash as it should have long ago.

After the letters were sufficiently destroyed, she marveled at how it had only taken seconds to demolish three decades of fruitless longing. The charred scraps were like corpses, soulless and vacant. Nothing was left of them, no letters, no names, no ink. It was a relief and yet she also felt foolish—foolish for giving so much weight to mere paper, foolish for holding onto a man of whom she knew nothing but glimpses. She poured water over the embers and watched them sizzle and hiss and release a pleasing smoke into the kitchen, and with it, she exhaled thirty years of pent-up breath.

She tossed the remains in the trash and then thought for a second with her fingertip in her mouth, as if she'd caught her daughter's loathsome habit. Deciding that she didn't even want the ashes in her house, she tied up the garbage bag and took it for disposal. But instead of leaving the sack at the door as she usually did, she took it all the way out to the street and to the next corner, where she dumped it in a stranger's pile of trash. As she walked away she felt better, but figured that she wouldn't rest until even that pile was removed from the street. Tomorrow morning, God willing, it all would truly be gone.

*****

That evening, Suad's kitchen counter resembled a canvas that was a work in progress. Sprinkled across the white tiles were piles of red sumac and paprika, earthen allspice and coriander, yellow wedges of lemon, black pepper, and greens chopped into pieces as small as grains of spice.

Mahmoud was due back by nightfall. She was making *molokhiya* stew for him as he'd demanded, careful to watch the time so it would be ready just as he walked through the door. At the edge of the counter sat the Al Fakher tobacco he preferred, and cans of strawberry soda. She'd searched downtown to the riverbanks for pomegranate, but it seemed Mahalla was all out—thanks, no doubt, to the so-called revolution. In the end she went with strawberry, hoping that its red color would fool him after a long day of traveling. And it would be a long day indeed—he'd arrive in Alexandria at three and then take the train to Mahalla, and with all the chaos in the country, there was no telling if the trains would run as scheduled. It was so strange, she thought, that he would suddenly go great lengths to reach her. Perhaps the revolution had stirred his heart for his *baladi* girl, Suad, who despite the dirt under her nails, came from the same sugarcane blood as he did, after all. And she, freshly free of decades-old paper, would be ready to welcome him home, a fresh start between them, both pairs of hands wiped clean of their other lovers, whether real or imagined. Yes, *imagined*. Imagine that.

As she sank a handful of chopped leaves into a boiling vat, she eyed Ayah across the room. Once again, the girl was bathed in the electric-blue glow of the TV, phone in hand, though she promised she was no longer up to no good. Her hair, uncombed for days, resembled the matted pelt of a wild beast, and Suad could already hear Mahmoud's complaints. *Why do you let her go about like this? How will she ever get married? A head like the ass of a buffalo. Nobody will want her, and if nobody wants her then she'll be ours forever, and with gas prices going down there's no more money, and I can't afford her or you either, and I think I'll stay in Dammam next time, and the time after that, and in fact I'll never come back, because who wants to come home to a bunch of women with their heads up their asses, who, on second thought, probably* should *put their heads up their asses, it would be better that way. Better to stay.*

Suad stepped away from the stove and fanned herself, worked up from the spiral of doubt that still resided in her despite all her attempts to heal. Perhaps she could distract herself by fixing Ayah's hair. She warmed spoonfuls of castor and olive oil over a low flame, then came at her with dripping hands.

"Come here." She grabbed the girl's hair in bunches, like leaves of overgrown *molokhiya*, and parted sections to slather in the hot elixir. All the while Ayah groaned, her eyes never leaving the TV. When her head was slick and black as an oil spill, Suad gave her a pat and instructed her to leave it in for an hour—enough time, God willing, to sufficiently tame it before her father arrived.

Ayah didn't get her hair from *Suad*, that was for sure. All her mother needed were a few curlers to restore a bit of the body of her youth. She dug them out of a dusty corner of the closet, set her hair, and returned to the kitchen, where the messy part was about to begin.

From the freezer she took out the vacuum-sealed rabbit she bought from El Shoun the other day. She grabbed it by the ears, still covered in fur, and threw it onto the bare countertop as Ayah stuck out her tongue from the corner of the room. As Suad dismembered the rabbit she pondered the cruelty of life, looking into its round black eyes that lay open and afraid, as if it had known its fate in the second before it died. "This was written," she said under her breath, as if to console the dead animal. Before long, all that remained of the rabbit was a bowl of marinated meat, which she submerged into a frothing green stew.

Mahmoud was due to arrive shortly, so Suad covered the pot and returned to her room, where she scrubbed herself clean of the herbal stench that clung to her skin and clothes. The tips of her fingers smelled of coriander, in particular, and would need to be soaked in vinegar and soap.

She'd never spent so much time in front of the mirror—not even when she was young and could still attract men. Every errant hair, scar, and wrinkle appeared stark and glaring on skin more blemished than she'd realized. Had she really been walking around like this—white hairs growing out of her chin, lines fanning out from the corners of each eye like an accordion? And her eyebrows, which she'd thought she could get away with leaving be, were now two rectangular masses above each tired socket, almost joining in a faint bridge at the middle.

She felt oddly satisfied as she got to work with the tweezer, as if she were weeding the grove. When she was done, she wiped away all the dislodged hairs and took in her new reflection. The last time she looked this way she was much younger, a different person, and for a second she couldn't wait for Mahmoud to see.

In Ayah's room she found the drawer full of unused makeup that had been of such interest to the two marauding officers the other night. She peeked out the door to make sure Ayah was still preoccupied. The girl was back to *tic-tacking* at her phone, of course, hair oiled and gathered in waiting. Suad sighed at the sight of her. She would be mortified if her daughter caught her dolling herself up, though soon it would be no secret.

First she powdered her face, turning toasted wheat to not-unbecoming gray. She didn't have much of a set of eyelashes, but she brushed on mascara and watched them bloom like her garden after the rain. Finally, she removed the curlers and basked in her new face, and the only reminder that she was still Suad, girl of Abu Radhi, were her drab clothes. Loose and plain, they were clothes for prayer or gardening. They were certainly *not* for meeting her husband or any man for that matter, and definitely not one like Hagg Ali's delivery man. But it was not the latter who'd visit that evening, so she straightened her hem, rolled down her sleeves and took a last look in the mirror. Though she felt like an imposter with her face made up, she was determined to greet Mahmoud that way today—a new day and a new beginning, a new wife and a new country.

When she walked back into the kitchen, it was enough to rip Ayah's eyes away from the TV.

"*Mama.*"

But there was no time to bask in her new look. Suad dragged the girl into the bathroom where she washed out every last trace of oil from her hair and smoothed the unruly bush into a mass of waves. With a light slap on the bottom, she sent Ayah back to the TV and returned to the kitchen. There, she scooped the *molokhiya* into a porcelain bowl along with a rabbit leg and a mound of rice. Mahmoud would walk through the door at any moment, so she readied his drink and tossed the can so he wouldn't see it was the wrong flavor. His shisha pipe, now polished and gleaming, was packed with tobacco and topped with a coal. A booklet of matches sat beside it—the same set she'd used to destroy the letters. She didn't feel guilty about it—in fact, she felt it was right.

The clock now struck seven, but Suad didn't worry because she had learned to give her husband a time window of several hours. She refused to sit, however—Mahmoud shouldn't find her idle, thigh meat splayed wide on the couch—so instead she stood on her two strong farmer's legs, hands on hips, watching the door from the kitchen. When the clock ticked past the window of allowance, she decided to show a hint of disapproval by proceeding to serve Ayah her portion of *molokhiya*. The bowl was still in her hand as a car door slammed shut outside. But through the curtain, she saw that it was only Nagwa's husband, who had returned from work. At once she ducked, almost dropping the bowl splat on the floor. She'd drop dead just the same if either he or his wife saw her looking like that, a powdered-up hussy awaiting a husband who was late again. Uncomfortably, Suad noted that there was no sound of spinning cotton. Somewhere out there, Nagwa was up to her old games.

*****

Night was announced by the barking of street dogs. By then, the *molokhiya* was cold and stiff. Suad scooped it into containers for refrigeration and emptied out the glass of flattened strawberry soda. She'd done nothing but stare at the door for hours, vaguely listening to the evening news program, which she hadn't realized had ended, now succeeded by a broadcast of fuzzy yellow chicks running through open fields.

"Come watch" said Ayah, jumping up from her seat. "The president is about to speak."

Suad leapt to join her daughter on the couch, where they both hunched toward the screen, fingernails in their mouths. When the old man appeared, she gave Ayah a preemptive slap to keep her mouth shut. They couldn't miss a second. Behind the podium the president looked like his usual self, dapper, with hair lacquered in black dye around a face lined with time. He looked good for his age and for all the trouble he was dealing with, and she mouthed a well-deserved *mashallah*, almost bursting into tears as he began.

*My sons and daughters, I was once young too.*

Indeed, she had also been young at one time. But she didn't know where he was going with this introduction. It was already too conciliatory for her taste. Maybe this was his way of luring hooligans to his corner, starting with a fiber of relatability. Who *couldn't* relate? It was hard to grasp but there was a time when even Suad was ripe as a yellow-green lemon, with clear eyes of black velvet and a heart foolish enough to think anything would last. But nothing did. Not her youth, not her hopes, and certainly not the outright sham of a relationship she had with Gamal. She would have thought that the president's insistence on this shared experience—youth, and all its idiocy—would bring him down harder on the rioters and looters of Tahrir. But the words that ensued didn't make any sense.

*Your demands are legitimate, your movement is honest . . .*

Suad reached for the volume, but it was already cranked as high as it would go. She could feel her own forehead crinkle as the president conceded, *mistakes can happen in any political system.* Mistakes? It was like watching parent tell his child he was right, right for knocking over a dish of *molokhiya*, right for painting the walls in crayon, right for tossing tissues into the air just for the fun of making a mess. He littered the speech with numbers—*76, 77, 88, 93, 179, 189*—articles of the constitution that he promised to repeal. Who said anything about repealing? She couldn't fathom the words she was hearing. Was up down? Was left right? Was yes no, black white?

If it were up to her, she would waste no chance to tout the accomplishments of her rule. The house was tidy. The *molokhiya* sweet and smoky. The children were in school, the prayers counted. There were many things that really weren't that bad, and many things that could fall apart in an instant if the youth had their way. Business was booming in the Delta, cotton wheels spinning, factories puffing black smoke into the air, the smoke of productivity. Sure, there were bombings here and there against the odd church or tour bus, but really, it could be much worse. It could be like Iraq or Afghanistan. Things were not so bad that tourists had stopped coming; in fact, they still flocked to the Pyramids and to the temples of the Said. There was much to boast, but the old man didn't.

"He's very humble," said Suad, desperate to eke out an air of pride to hide her confusion. She set down her tea, as if it would help her think. The bits of lemon pulp in her teeth felt like boulders. Using her fingernails, she picked them out of every crevice before leaning back toward the man in the dark suit, presentable.

And then it happened—the very thing she'd dreaded all along, the outcome that inched closer with each word. Transfer, transition, delegation. Peace, transparency, elections.

"Stop," said Suad, her voice emerging rough and throaty, like an involuntary grunt or the first words of dawn, unprepared.

*Dear youth of Egypt, dear citizens—*

"Stop," she said again, her voice picking up strength. But he didn't stop. She fell to the ground and assaulted the volume on the remote again, pressing the buttons over and over like a crazed child in an elevator. But it didn't do a thing to aid her aging ears. She almost tore the damned buttons straight off the box, destroying yet another electronic, while all Ayah could do was lay a hand on her arm as if to hold her back. The girl was too distracted, too rapt with the catastrophe her revolutionaries had brought upon the nation.

*I am not going to run in the upcoming presidential elections …*

Suad repeated the words in her head and then aloud and then started to weep. How could this be? She pressed her face to the screen, almost kissing it. To her horror she hadn't misheard because she was getting old, or perhaps misunderstood because she really was just a farm girl. It was true—come elections in September, he would no longer be president. He'd be gone like all the men she'd ever known, leaving her alone to answer the door in the night, with nothing to save her but the scripture etched into her mind. Her only solace was that elections were a good six months off. It was ample time to change his mind, despite his promise to *adhere* to this decision—*gah!*—the way her dress adhered to her rear end, soaked in a panic-sweat.

All he wanted was to die in his beloved country.

Tears fell from her eyes as he went on to praise Egypt, ancient and eternal, the country he'd served for three decades. *Three decades!* When he came into office, Suad was still tottering around in that too-tight dress, chasing Gamal in Abu Radhi. The thought of ever having another president seemed absurd—such a departure from life as she knew it that she might as well die. Surely it was even more traumatic for her kids, who'd never even *known* another president. But Ayah sat like steel beside her. Maybe this was yet another trait she'd inherited from her father's side—a coldness where for Suad, there was nothing but hot tears.

"Darling, it'll be OK," she said, prodding to see if she bit. *"Inshallah,* he'll stay."

Ayah scrunched up her face, befuddled. "No, *inshallah* he will *leave."*

*"Eh,* silly girl, he said he'll leave in September."

"No, there is no September. There's only now." She leapt from her seat and ran back to her room, where Suad could hear her type furiously at the keypad of her phone.

"Back to Tweeter, back to YouToo. Go get lost, crazy girl."

*****

Not even a national tragedy could distract Suad from her regular roster of worries, but around midnight she gave up on watching the door and retreated to her bedroom.

What was taking Mahmoud so long? Had he even landed or was he still suspended in the sky, nonexistent for a few hours more?

He once said that flying into Alexandria was a real sight to behold—the Nile Delta opened up like a verdant lotus spilling petals into the sea, and you could find Mahalla as a lone spot of sand within it, surrounded by green. He could even find their house, he said, because it stood on the borderline of the city, where it transitioned abruptly from factories to farms, brown to green, beside channels of the river that flowed black and deep. She had never seen this, of course, and took only his word for it. Suad never cared much for traveling, but her husband never seemed as remote as when he spoke of experiences to which she couldn't relate, whether it was the look of their hometown from above the wing of a plane or a sip of beer in his uncouth youth.

Suad lay wide awake in bed, staring at the black ceiling above her, until eventually the sound of her daughter's typing ceased, and the night settled into silence. She listened, but there was no key in the door, no tires crunching on freshly raked gravel. Not even the sound of Nagwa's cotton wheel. She waited for headlights to flood through the windows, but they never came. And in the darkness, she rose to pray.

*In the name of God, the Beneficent, the Merciful.*

# 18

In the morning Sami walked the corniche, restless. Here he was again, Zamalek. Where he was supposed to be. With the eastern wing of the river rightly between him and Rose. The island bore no resemblance to Ramses, with streets full of trees rather than the wreckage of protest, grand villas in the place of the exhaust-choked Diesel, and looters warded off by neighborhood watchmen sipping tea at the end of the block. But not even a change of scenery could get Rose's voice out of his head.

It was strange how many women suddenly looked like her. By the bus stop, he spotted the same heart-shaped face, but plumper; under the bridge he found the lank curl of her hair; a little girl selling tissues had her poison-green eyes. Yes, it was poison—she poisoned every place he went, appearing between blinds, in air conditioning vents, in every fiber of every rug and curtain drawn in vain. As if she'd never been gone, as if he hadn't walked out of her apartment with a bag full of his things as she slept. As if the buzz of the ceiling fan hadn't sounded like a fighter jet as he closed the door. As if each memory took place only seconds ago. She was hours gone but each step he took was in her shadow. At times he even felt her breath casting dew onto his skin, and he shuddered, shaking it off.

He would have to avoid any place they ever dined or met, anywhere they once walked the streets, any tree from which they'd stopped to pick off buds, any building on which she'd expressed an opinion, any café where she once breathed the coffee-tinged air. Tasseo had been destroyed, at least, but to be safe he probably shouldn't set foot in that alley again. The ghosts of those blown-out Ramadan garlands were still too near. From now on he would hate the sight of flowers, which would all bring to mind her name regardless of type. He would have to avoid Ramses altogether, which would be a challenge considering it was where the train station was and remained, un-bombed. And Khan El Khalili. The little hole-in-the-wall antique shop. Any taxicab, any time-defining Umm Kalthoum song. *All* of Cairo was uninhabitable now.

On his way to the dorms he diverted his path for the corniche, thinking the Nile might bring him some peace. As he walked he gazed with envy at the grand balconies above him, where he wished he could be sitting instead—overlooking the river at a distance that seemed safer, more abstract. He wondered which type he'd prefer at this moment, when nothing seemed to please him. Some were sealed with windows, some open. Some were shaded by the branches of trees, some bright. Some were full of potted plants, some bare and unused. Here and there, Egyptian flags dangled from railings, either as a nod to revolution or the regime—he wasn't sure. On one such balcony he saw a woman posing for a photo with the river behind her. In the doorway stood a maid who resembled Jamila with her skinny limbs and coffee-bean skin, holding the camera with an uneasy look on her face. Sami stopped and watched the camera flash, once, twice, a dozen times. The posing woman laughed and then the other laughed too, and their laughter fell like petals to the street, a light and joyous mass. It couldn't be Jamila.

Still, he made note of the building, an old villa with wind-whipped shutters. Above the door, tiled letters spelled out *Pyramide House*, the *H* missing. There was a bench in front of it, facing the Nile. He slung off his backpack and sat on the bench, hoping for a second of rest before someone came and shooed him away.

The Nile looked so different nowadays without all the usual feluccas, the bridges crowded with cars and idle youth. And yet Sami saw nothing but Rose reflected on its flat, still surface. How could he not? She loved the river more than he did. She was the foreign one but somehow it ran through *her* veins. He thought of that tired old saying—*once you drink from the Nile, you are destined to return*—etched onto the first page of her journal as if to define it. No wonder it had come to mind on that first day of the revolution, National Police Day, when he was trying to cheer her up through sickness, to give her a smile between heaves. The memory was almost comical now—the way he pretended she was only sick from water, the way he uttered that line she loved to no response. That must have been the moment it all fell apart. When all the cracked pieces, held together like Abu Ali's shattered storefront, finally gave out.

Somehow the fable seemed less absurd now, in the aftermath of the breakup, as the entire course of their relationship—from the moment he opened the door to Tasseo to the moment he left apartment 702—ran through his brain on constant loop, like the film reel that had caught their faces in Tahrir. With each pulse, a pang, another snag in the cellophane. Their first date at Galaxy Cinema, cups of coffee on the balcony over-looking Ramses Street, wading in the warm waves of the north coast last summer and the shallow Red Sea that winter, the venomous glow of her eyes when she was sick. He wondered if Rose would ever come back now that they were over and the baby was gone and she had nothing to bind her to Egypt. It had once seemed obvious. Now he wasn't so sure.

*You are destined to return.*

That night Jamila read her coffee cup seemed like a different era, one that warranted its own line of sediment in the canyon. What did she say? *You keep going in circles.* Like drinking from the Nile and coming back. Why would anyone return? All he saw was the traffic and pollution, the beggars and the noise. The heartbreak. Closing his eyes, Sami tried to see Cairo the way Rose did. He tried putting himself in the shoes of an expat like her, someone who ran away from a modern country with basic human rights to find refuge in Egypt. Perhaps once you left, all you remembered was the good stuff—all the incongruities that gave the place its ineffable beauty. If he squinted he could see it too. It was a beauty that some people didn't get—people like his mother, who needed fresh air and clean streets and the kind of peace you could only find under a canopy of leaves. People with the constant itch for cleaning and pruning and weeding and ablution. No, it was not for them. It was the kind of beauty with flaws like dust and wear and cacophonous sound, flaws that somehow made every speck of prettiness even prettier, like Umm Kalthoum singing over bleating car horns and bougainvillea buds glimmering against walls caked in grime. Those who protested the loudest would be the first to return, Rose included. She knew the place well. She couldn't live there but she couldn't live anywhere else.

He pictured her returning one day, an old woman with strands of gray in her once-blue hair. Like him right now, she would sit on a bench by the river and see the past in each ripple on the water's surface. She might think of calling Sami, maybe she'd write his number on the back of her hand. Through wrinkles it would be hard to decipher. She'd have to pull her skin taut to make out the numbers which, as she read them, she'd realize she'd never forgotten. She would punch them into her phone—some new, razor-thin gadget from the future—and with each ring think of hanging up. But she wouldn't because she was Rose. Braver than he, and too curious for her own good.

He didn't know whether he would pick up. He supposed time would tell.

*****

The loss fell over him once he unlocked his dorm room and collapsed into bed. It would be nice to sleep for the next month, or maybe forever, but who was he kidding—there wasn't enough hash in the world to shut his eyes. Instead, he kept busy by unpacking. There was his toothbrush and his pajama pants and the hoodie that had hung in her closet. Even the cans of soda he kept stocked in her fridge. He'd taken it all—not out of stinginess but because it seemed kinder. Kinder for her and crueler for Sami. Now he had to live with all this junk that reeked of Ramses—like cedar floors, like gasoline wafting from the train station, like roasted peanuts, like tear gas from those first street battles for Tahrir.

Sami ran his hand through his hair, dragging his nails along his scalp as hard as he could, and then his neck started itching and he scratched that too, and soon he had red gashes beneath his jaw, as if he'd been trying in some backward, impotent way to strangle himself. When he realized what he was doing and that it was crazy, he stopped and stared at himself in the mirror. His eye sockets were dark and cavernous, as if he hadn't eaten or slept in days. His face hadn't seen a razor since before the beach, and now hairs had sprouted along his jaw, giving him an older look. He could barely recognize himself. He could barely remember who he was just a few weeks ago.

This new Sami would do what he was supposed to. This new Sami would answer his mother's calls. This new Sami would pray. He reached for his prayer rug and unrolled it onto the floor. The rug looked brand new, with a plush black Kaaba in the center and cream-colored fringe so pristine it hadn't yet lost its polyester sheen. Without thinking, he knelt eastward and touched his head to the rug. The thing was so unused that it still smelled vaguely chemical, like the factory in Mahalla that it came from— Cleopatra Textiles, Misr Weaving, something like that. For some reason he thought immediately of Ayat al-Kursi, and as he whispered the verse he felt the soft, untouched threads of the rug on his lips moving with the words. *In the name of God, the Beneficent, the Merciful.* It was the same verse Suad had sworn by when she gave him the rug years ago, back when he was a kid who thought he was a man and had no idea, back when his troubles were laughably minute. Back when—if he could go back—he'd slap himself for being so stupid.

From his spot on the floor, he drew a line out the window and across the river, realizing that he faced not only Mecca but Ras Shaitan, where just days ago he sat on the water, and even worse, he faced Ramses too, doing the very thing wanted to avoid—looking it straight in the eye. It was like looking at her. He pressed his forehead to the rug, but he couldn't crush his thoughts. He wondered if she had risen yet and whether she was looking for him. Would she wake with a bad feeling, the way he had every day for the past few weeks, and turn in bed to see an empty spot beside her? Maybe she wouldn't think anything of it and sleep in a bit longer, like she always did, until the sun's brightness pried her eyes open, at which point she'd realize there was no sound of footsteps creaking on hallway floors and there was no smoke seeping out from the crack under the door. She'd get up and go to the bathroom, alone, and go to the kitchen alone, make coffee alone and sit on that balcony alone, looking out at a city interrupted by revolt, which had somehow swallowed up her only companions—first Jamila, and now Sami.

He heard birds chirping outside, their tweets incessant like the drip of a leaking tap. He tried to block the sound but couldn't. With all his strength he picked himself up off the floor and went to shut the window. He stood for a while with his hands on the sill, too lethargic to make a move just yet. The morning was unusually beautiful. The air was filled with the fragrance of jasmine blooms spilling over the walls lining the street. The sun was brighter than it had been in weeks, casting shadows under branches like the latticework windows of Khan El Khalili. It was a vicious beauty, violent in its disregard for all that had happened.

Stories down, a guard snoozed with arms crossed inside a security post. Sami imagined that if he fell, his body would hit the post with a thud and wake him up. It seemed like an inconspicuous way to die, unlike setting yourself on fire. He thought of the man in room 251B and whether he still wore a body cast or had healed and gone home to Imbaba. Other than that *Egypt Today* article announcing the arrest of the baker, there hadn't been a peep of news since that day he met the president. He'd been a hero then, all eyes on him, and any religious aversion to suicide faded to awe over this man who lit a match to his own skin to die slowly, one cell at a time, until only plaster could hold him together. There was nothing braver.

And if the man in the body cast was a hero, then Sami was a coward—that's what the world would think of him if he let go, right then, and let gravity do the trick. People were out there setting themselves on fire and here was this soft boy *falling* to death, like an accident. Reporters, if they even bothered to cover his death, would dig for details in his life that led to the fall—his grades, the amount of hashish in his bloodstream, his family history. It was only a matter of time until they'd find out about his girlfriend and the unborn baby she'd wanted to name Nadim. At best, they'd simply call it a mistake rather than suicide. Then Sami would forever be known as a bumbling idiot who fumbled his way to death. *See*, they'd say—*that's what happens to a fool like that.* There would be none of the heroism of even stillborn martyrdom, like the man in room 251B. But maybe he was OK with that.

With sleep far-off, jumping overruled, and too much cowardice for self-immolation, there was only one thing left to do. He shut the window, zipped up his hoodie, and descended upon the road to Tahrir.

*****

Night was falling by the time Sami reached the square, where he found a massive street party, the mood brightening in opposition to the sky. Above the crowd, three stripes of red, white, and black cloth snaked over the heads of protesters like a paper dragon. Cooler moms than his own handed out sweets from fanny packs as street children darted throughout, carrying bundles of sesame candy in their ratty pockets. Fireworks made *pops* in the air like celebratory gunshots, and yet the president still hadn't budged.

Overnight, the army had erected cinderblock walls across the main artery rods leading to Tahrir. If Rose was there, he'd ask her why and she'd know the answer. *They're containing the protest. They're boxing you in. They're rounding you all up like lambs for slaughter.* He would have shaken his head, told her she was crazy and didn't know what she was talking about, not ever letting on that for the first time, he wasn't so sure.

A wall caught his eye at the edge of the square. *Enjoy the revolution,* it read in pastel paint. It was written in English, as if it was meant for Rose and her people and not Sami and his. No wonder Rose knew it all. Everything was *created* for her. Even the revolution itself was becoming a spectacle for the whole world to see, broadcast by foreign camera crews across hemispheres, death and struggle turned into entertainment. *Enjoy the revolution,* as if the revolution were a holiday. The way Zane might greet honeymooners in the Sinai. Something fleeting, a treat to be savored. It seemed nonsensical until he remembered that first Friday of the revolution, the swelling tide of Ramses Street, the heavenly clang of crowbars on concrete. He *had* enjoyed it. Now that moment was over—a blissful blip in time like the year he spent with Rose, a last hurrah before returning to the good Mahalla boy he should've been all along. It was a shame the pain wasn't so momentary. Maybe it would fade gradually, like the burn of tear gas weakened to mere stinging, then dissipating completely.

Come to think of it, Sami hadn't felt tear gas for days. Now there was only festivity in the square, and nobody seemed to be fighting back. Even the tanks dotting the perimeter seemed celebratory, draped in flowers—fucking flowers—and trailed by demonstrators queuing up to kiss the cheeks of confused-looking soldiers.

A commotion drew his eyes overhead, where he spotted something dangling from a lamppost. He walked closer until he stopped with a jolt. Was that … a body? Yes, it was a body hanging from a rope. Perhaps he'd spoken too soon about all this celebration. He stared in horror at the cheering crowd. What had become of them all? He'd expected the revolution to devolve at some point but he didn't think they'd be hanging people in the street just yet. In his mind he could hear Suad's voice, see her shaking her head with a *tsk tsk. See? See what happened to your revolution?*

It was only when Sami reached the noose that he realized it was a stuffed replica of the president. There was no mistaking him—the effigy wore a black suit like the one he wore to meet the self-immolator du jour in a hospital room at Qasr El Aini, live on TV. Despite everything Sami had seen until now, he was still in awe at all before him, at all that had happened in the eighteen days since National Police Day, when the only hint of what was to come was the revolutionary silence of Ramses Street. He imagined the failed martyr watching through the holes in his body cast as the man he'd shaken hands with in consolation was suspended in the air. Now the latter was the helpless one—at the mercy of the crowd, who goaded him to fall.

*The people demand the fall of the regime*, thought Sami as he watched a boy burst forth from the crowd. The people cheered as he leapt onto the lamppost and wriggled to the top. When he reached the effigy, he took off his beanie and bowed, then pulled a knife from his pocket and started cutting at the rope. It wasn't easy—not quite the single, dramatic hack he'd probably wanted—but the crowd wasn't put off. In fact, their cheers grew even louder as he sawed away, severing one thread at a time until at last, the dummy fell. The crowds seized upon it like shark chum, shreds of twine and burlap flying, and in minutes there was nothing left but a crumpled black suit on the asphalt.

Gripping the lamppost between his legs, the boy bowed again before falling backward into outstretched arms below. There was a brief tussle and then he reappeared, rope in hand, and marched toward the wall with the crowd trailing. He tied the rope around a single cinderblock and pulled it taut.

Sami did what seemed necessary and took out the Meikorlens. As he shot photos from afar, he wondered whether this scrappy, nameless boy had always been a people's hero or whether it was something brought on by revolution. There was a jaunt to his step, a spring in his knobby-kneed stride that seemed fresh, unpracticed. Sami could tell from the boy's wiry limbs and shriveled, sunbaked skin that he was a worker, perhaps ironically a bricklayer, and here he was leading this corner of Tahrir like a general on the front lines. His battalion was made up of an assortment of different characters—Sami counted youth in hoodies, old men in galabias, street kids and those of the diaspora, marked by the volume of their muddled Arabic. Mismatched, they assembled along the length of the rope and waited impatiently until finally, it was time to pull.

When the cinderblock wouldn't budge, the boy leapt over the wall and pushed from the opposite direction. Together, they all pushed and pulled until the block came loose, inch by inch, before finally, it tipped over and crashed to pieces on the ground. By the time Sami decided he should probably join, it was too late. The other blocks fell before he could even make it to the rope, and within minutes he was swallowed by trilling and clapping hands.

*****

First came the car horns. They bleated a celebratory tune similar to that of weddings—beep, beep, beep-beep-beep. Sami bopped along, searching for a sheath of white gown as a million hands clapped in time to the beat. There was shouting, loud above the horns, and a great roar spread through the square like the deafening crush of a tidal wave. His fingers trembled around the Meikorlens as he looked up to the sky, beyond the waving flags and signs, and saw fireworks exploding in the distance. This was some wedding, he thought, until two words cut him off—

"He left!"

"He left, he left, the president left!"

A man beside him held up his phone for the crowd. MisrTV was playing from its tiny screen. Sami stood on tiptoes to catch a glimpse as people swayed and bounced around him. He saw fatigues first, a drab green like tanks. "The general," shouted the man with the phone, translating the broadcast for those who couldn't see. Sami had never seen him before but apparently he was the leader of the army, SCAF—the same SCAF that had hounded his phone like his mother for the past few weeks, piling text after text in his inbox saying things like "PROTECT EGYPT" and "BEWARE OF CRIMINALS." The same SCAF that had posted tanks on every corner, more each day, full of sons who were eldest and not only. The same SCAF that had declared its neutrality in the uprising, saving them all from a bloodbath in Tahrir Square. If it wasn't for SCAF they would all be dead, the square cleared, and the president would still be in place. But the president was gone, said the general on TV, and God was in the crowd, swirling on the ecstatic tongues around him.

"God bless him."

"God be with him."

"God is great."

"Shhhh, let us hear!"

The general, however, didn't meet the crowd's enthusiasm. His face was drawn and serious, eyelids sagging from age and exhaustion as he read from a script in his hands. *In the name of God, the Beneficent, the Merciful.* His tone grew more somber as he continued his speech, and for the life of him Sami couldn't figure out why, because Tahrir was so joyous it seemed they'd just won the African Cup—no, the World Cup—no, even more than that. The president was gone.

Much of the speech was drowned out by cheering, but Sami strained to make out whatever details he could. The president had said he would leave in September, when the time came for elections—but those plans had changed. He was stepping down *now*, ceding power to the army to lead in the interim period. The army? Sami tried not to dwell on the details. This moment was too big for any hiccups. Like the bombing of Tasseo and the split second that demon had appeared on the mountain before him—moments designed for him alone, too neat in their absurdity to belong to anybody else. He stood in a sea of millions and yet felt like the only person in all of Tahrir. It was sort of like the moment he met Rose, when the whole world dimmed around her and it seemed nobody else had ever existed.

*May God help us all.*

And the gloom of those final words was forgotten in the euphoria that erupted from the center of Tahrir to its outer rim, from the banks of the Nile and up highways named for revolutions past. 6 October, 26 July, 15 May. In the future there would be a road named 25 January. Sami was sure of it. One day he would drive down it and remember.

Wide eyed, he watched a man collapse in shock as strangers rushed toward him. They lay hands on his chest and checked his pulse and breathed air into his lungs, all through tears of joy. This was no emergency. Who wouldn't want to die right there, martyred on the ground that had become sacred in the last eighteen days? Sami envied him. All this time he'd thought of dying to escape—now he wanted death so he could live on. His portrait would be framed and hung above his mother's door, a hero to take the place of the president who'd fallen in the worst kind of way—disgraced, shamed by nameless masses to give up thirty years of rule. *Leave.* All of Sami's mistakes would be trampled under the feet of crowds too joyous to care for details. Details like Rose. Was that what she would become?

He wondered where in the city she was and whether she was somewhere in that same square, and he stood on tiptoes to scan the crowd for her face. He saw everybody—the Jamilas and the Zanes and the Abu Alis, the doormen from this side of the Nile and the other, and all the taxi drivers who'd ever dispatched their political views for the price of a few guinea. But there was no Rose, whose warm breath he'd felt on the back of his shoulder just hours before. Now there was no breath.

He exhaled long and hard, as if willing that breath into existence. She used to sigh like that. It was the only thing Rose had in common with his mother—dramatic sighs. Sighs that said something. Sighs that meant you were in trouble. He did it again just to feel the warm air before him, conjuring that same breath he needed so badly to escape, and for a second he felt like running back to Ramses. Then he remembered it was impossible. Like yearning for the dead.

Just then—as the cheering blurred to white noise, the lights faded to black, and the whoosh and the warmth were just right, right before him—a dark mass came at him from the corner of his eye. It hit him with the force of a mad bull. No, this time it wasn't the memories, but an actual punch. He realized it was a regime goon as he hit the ground, a split second followed by a flash of white and then, black.

*****

Tahrir turned into the Alexandrian corniche. It was spearfishing season, and the water ran red along the shoreline. He was explaining the wintertime migration of deep-sea fish to Rose but she wasn't paying any attention. When he asked what was on her mind, she turned and spat words like bullets. *I. Am. Pregnant.* He had to ask her to repeat herself two or three times over. *How do you know? I took a test. Why didn't you tell me? I'm telling you now. What are we going to do? I don't know.* They sat without speaking for a good hour, watching the frothing sea as Umm Kalthoum crackled from the radio. *I only just started to love my life.*

Sami could name a few fateful moments—the passport Ayah found in his backpack, the pregnancy tests from Abu Ali's pharmacy, the pregnancy to begin with—but that was when it really ended. He knew it then too. It was written in the angry waves as they rushed the corniche, threatening to sweep them away, and in his secret wish that they would. Like Tahrir, he would have liked to die by the sea. Cold saltwater to wash his wounds. Waves to carry him far away. How fitting to die in Alexandria like the revolution's first martyr, Khaled Said.

But Khaled had died in the springtime—during those perfect clear-skied days Sami remembered from childhood trips to the coast, with his mother and father in each hand. It was *that* long ago. The whole landscape was neon, bright sand and electric water, and all the windows of the city were open, clothes hanging on wires to dry. Candy-colored dinghies lay beached in rows, belly-up, and children's heads, slick with seawater, bobbed in the calm tide. He couldn't wait to get in the water, to clutch his father's left arm, Ayah on the other, and swim out to where the big fish swam until Suad called them back for lunch. As a kid he'd dreamed of being the age he was now, at the crest between youth and adulthood. He'd drive fast through the desert, perhaps marry a girl like the curly-haired beauty his mother used to be in those old Polaroids she'd hidden away.

Did Khaled have the same dreams? Was he thinking of quitting hash, taking care of his mother, settling down? Of course, it would complicate things if he ever had a girlfriend like Rose, but that was impossible—martyrs didn't sin, remember? That's why the sea was sparkling, heavenly on the day Khaled died, while for Sami it frothed like a rabid beast coming to take him. Not a martyr, but simply *dead*. Gone. Disappeared. Vanished like the body of Yusuf. To be forgotten and not remembered. An accident—a terrible mistake.

No, Sami could never be a martyr.

A what? A martyr, mar-*tyr* ...

*****

"Martyr!"

When he opened his eyes, a circle of faces stared at him from above. A man was yelling *martyr, martyr*. At first Sami thought he was dying, and he submitted. If he was going to die then it might as well be in Tahrir. It smelled of burnt rubber, charred metal. And the soles of a million feet.

"Martyr!"

*Yes*, thought Sami, *call me a martyr. Take me, let me expire, stub me out and forget all my sins.* Dying took longer than he expected. As he waited, he noticed that his arm was draped elegantly across his chest, as if pleading. *Absolve me.* It didn't get any better than this. And as the man crowed on above him, *martyr*, a woman's voice emerged, sounding just like Suad.

"Shut up, you donkey. He's alive."

The woman helped him to his feet, and as the earth steadied beneath him, he saw the Meikorlens smashed to bits on the asphalt. He dove toward it and gathered all the pieces—the flash, the lens, the logo he had traced with his finger ages ago in that stall in Khan El Khalili. All that was missing was the film. On hands and knees, he looked frantically for the plastic strip, but it was gone. A goon had come for him like the other night, with eyes on that film, no doubt. Through gritted teeth, Sami imagined the strip crunching under his grubby hands as he stuffed it in his pockets and ran into the night.

When Sami stood up the woman was gone. He felt more lightheaded than before. All the flags and signs and lights blurred around him to create one dizzying mass. The man who yelled *martyr* hovered about with a dumb expression, a gap between his front teeth giving him the look of a child. He seemed guilty as he made eye contact—guilty that Sami had lived to hear him literally dance on his deathbed. Now he diverted the crowd with arms held wide, shoulders shimmying to the beat of clapping hands.

Sami thought he was dreaming again when he heard a familiar, droning rhythm. The incessant lyrics. *My beautiful country, my beautiful country.* Somehow, for *some* reason, that fucking song was still bleating from every phone and driver's window on the corniche. *Turn it off,* he wanted to scream, as if anyone would hear him, as if anyone would listen. That song had outlasted everything—Rose and the revolution, the president himself, the Meikorlens, Tasseo and the little bird pinned to the wall. *My beautiful country, my beautiful country.* Except it wasn't her country. Like Rose, she was a foreigner. Perhaps she, too, was so thoroughly steeped in Nile water that it somehow transformed her to a native. He never told Rose about her, which hurt to realize—as if it was an important message he needed to relay, as if it would make any difference to their fate. He wondered if she was listening to the same song at that very moment, sitting on the banks of that same river she'd unwittingly drank from, the river that just might bring her back one day, if all the superstitions he'd once scoffed at proved true. But it would make no difference.

As the song played on, the crowd cried out in triumph around him. Ecstatic protesters—though they were protesters no more—leapt and danced and flashed V signs with parted fingers into every microphone and camera lens, *we won*. Sami mimicked the gesture with shaky fingers.

V for victory. Is that what it was? He heard an *inshallah*, and another, and a third, as if he stood in an echo chamber invoking God's will. Elections, stability, democracy, *inshallah*. Bread, dignity, social justice, *inshallah*. Revolution. *Inshallah*. Steadily, the roar grew louder and became so massive and infinite that it reminded him of the Alexandrian sea that one day, weeks ago, when the waves swelled and howled as if in warning.

Sami walked to the river and leaned over the edge, watching the technicolor lights of feluccas drift across the water once more. In the distance, he could see the silhouettes of Zamalek's villas, the tree-lined streets leading to the dorm he'd return to that night, and the billboard of the soldier with the baby, strewn with bouquets and imprinted with the kisses of adoring crowds.

He reached into his pocket and took out his phone for the first time in God only knew how long. It still had just enough battery to power up. And with a tear in his eye—the last tingle of tear gas, of Rose—he called his mother.

THE END

# ACKNOWLEDGMENTS

Thank you to my agent, Kristy Hunter, who believed in this manuscript before anyone else, back when it probably didn't deserve it. Thank you to my editor, Jennifer Pooley, for helping me hone the story and language, all the way down to every overused colon and em dash. Thanks to the whole team at Blackstone—Haila Williams for taking a chance on this book, Sean Thomas for designing the beautiful cover, as well as Greg Boguslawski, Ciera Cox, Mandy Earles, Lauren Maturo, Megan Wahrenbrock, Josie Woodbridge, and Jeffrey Yamaguchi. Thanks to my earliest readers and gut-checkers: Kacie Scaccia, Lucia Abramovich, Heba Qutami, and Alice Gissinger. Thanks to my talented and supportive workshoppers: Jennie Egerdie, Stephanie Jimenez, and Katherine Sacco. Thanks to everybody who gave me a platform at Guerilla Lit and Inner Loop. And thank you to Cairo for not so much inspiring me as infecting me—for seeping into my blood and making me a native at heart.

Finally, thanks above all to my grandfather, Nasser Jahanbani, who filled my head with stories of revolution long before the Arab Spring and who didn't live long enough to see this book in print but will live on through the page as long as I'm writing.